That Old Scoundrel Death

ALSO BY BILL CRIDER

SHERIFF DAN RHODES MYSTERIES

Dead, to Begin With
Survivors Will Be Shot Again
Between the Living and the Dead
Half in Love with Artful Death
Compound Murder
Murder of a Beauty Shop Queen
The Wild Hog Murders
Murder in the Air
Murder in Four Parts
Of All Sad Words
Murder Among the O.W.L.S.
A Mammoth Murder
A Red, White, and Blue Murder
A Romantic Way to Die
A Ghost of a Chance
Death by Accident
Winning Can Be Murder
Murder Most Fowl
Booked for a Hanging
Evil at the Root
Death on the Move
Cursed to Death
Shotgun Saturday Night
Too Late to Die

PROFESSOR SALLY GOOD MYSTERIES

A Bond with Death
Murder Is an Art
A Knife in the Back

PROFESSOR CARL BURNS MYSTERIES

. . . A Dangerous Thing
Dying Voices
One Dead Dean

THAT OLD SCOUNDREL DEATH

A SHERIFF DAN RHODES MYSTERY

BILL CRIDER

MINOTAUR BOOKS
A THOMAS DUNNE BOOK
NEW YORK

This is a work of fiction. All of the characters, organizations, and events portrayed in this novel are either products of the author's imagination or are used fictitiously.

A THOMAS DUNNE BOOK FOR MINOTAUR BOOKS
An imprint of St. Martin's Press

Printed in the United States of America. For information, address St. Martin's Press, 175 Fifth Avenue, New York, N.Y. 10010.

www.thomasdunnebooks.com
www.minotaurbooks.com

Library of Congress Cataloging-in-Publication Data is available upon request.

ISBN 978-1-250-16562-6 (hardcover)
ISBN 978-1-250-16563-3 (ebook)

Our books may be purchased in bulk for promotional, educational, or business use. Please contact your local bookseller or the Macmillan Corporate and Premium Sales Department at 1-800-221-7945, extension 5442, or by e-mail at MacmillanSpecialMarkets@macmillan.com.

First Edition: February 2019

10 9 8 7 6 5 4 3 2 1

This final book in the Sheriff Dan Rhodes series is dedicated to all the Dan Rhodes book fans who have read, supported, and believed in this series. Whether you have followed the small-town yet bigger-than-life career of Sheriff Rhodes since the beginning in 1986, or have only recently discovered the series, I know my father, Bill Crider, who left this world on February 12, 2018, appreciated each and every one of you. My father was overwhelmed and awed by the support and friendship he received from you, the readers, over the years and the collaboration he had with you, be it through email, social media, or in person at conventions and book signings. You lifted him up and allowed him to bring to life his Texas-sized imagination and the characters we have all grown to love.

—ANGELA CRIDER NEARY

I've looked that old scoundrel death in the eye many times but this time I think he has me on the ropes.

—GENERAL DOUGLAS MACARTHUR

That Old Scoundrel Death

Chapter 1

Sheriff Dan Rhodes looked at the man who was pointing the pistol at him.

Aside from the tattoo of the snake coiling around his neck, the man wasn't impressive. He was around thirty, about five-ten, skinny, dirty blond hair sticking out all over his head, scraggly goatee, bad teeth. He wore a thin white T-shirt with "Don't Taze Me, Bro" printed on it in faded red letters. The shirt was streaked with dirt, and the faded jeans were even dirtier and ripped at both knees. Rhodes didn't think the rips were a fashion statement. The man's brown eyes bugged out a bit because he was a little high, probably on meth even this early in the day. Meth, breakfast of champions.

The pistol wasn't any more impressive than the man. It was a cheap knockoff of a 9mm Glock, most likely picked up at a flea market for a hundred dollars or so, and a rip-off even at that price.

The problem with an unimpressive man tweaking on meth and holding an unimpressive pistol was the combination of all those things, especially when the man was sweating and his hand had a slight shake. You never could tell what might happen.

Rhodes was sweating, too, but not because he was nervous. The blue August sky held only a couple of high, wispy clouds, and the temperature was well over ninety, probably closer to a hundred. Rhodes had a feeling that the spot on the back of his head where the hair was getting thin was going to blister. He really should start wearing a hat or a cap, but having something on his head bothered him.

"Are you planning to shoot me with that thing?" Rhodes asked the man with the pistol.

The man glanced down at the pistol as if he wasn't quite sure he was still holding it, then looked back at Rhodes.

"Might," he said. His voice was high and whiney, no more impressive than the rest of him.

His answer wasn't exactly the one Rhodes had been hoping for, but it was better than a more positive one would have been.

"What about him?" Rhodes asked, looking over at the heavyset young man sitting down and leaning back against the front fender of a gray Toyota Camry parked on the side of the road.

The man wore a vacant expression, and had his eyes closed. Beyond his car, the grass in the ditch and in the field was sparse and brown. It hadn't rained for quite a while.

"He needs shootin', all right," the man with the pistol said. "Cut me off back there on the highway, nearly made me go in the ditch." A rusted-out old Chevy pickup sat in front of the Toyota. "I chased him down and gave him a little scare. Taught him a lesson."

"We aren't on the highway," Rhodes said.

"Nope, we're not. He thought he'd get away from me by takin' this dirt road, but he 'uz wrong about that. After I got him stopped, he 'uz gonna get tough with me, got out of the car and called me a bad name. I showed him the gun, and he changed his tune quick, got pretty dang polite. Got scared, too. I think he's fainted."

Rhodes wondered just how little the scare had been. "Guns can do that to people. Make them faint, I mean."

"Not me," the man said. "Don't seem to bother you, either."

The pistol twitched in his hand, but Rhodes didn't say anything. He was embarrassed about the situation, which had resulted from a mistake on his part. He'd been on the way back to Clearview, the county seat of Blacklin County, from looking into an early-morning dispute between two neighbors near Thurston in the south part of the county. They'd had a little tiff about the ownership of a couple of roosters that had wandered over into the rooster-free pen of the neighbor who didn't want his hens to be laying any fertile eggs. The dispute had become heated, with a lot of shouting and even a scuffle, and one of the wives had called the sheriff's department.

Things had settled down soon enough, however, and the men had reached a peaceful accommodation before Rhodes got there. The accommodation apparently involved one of the roosters becoming Sunday dinner for the man whose pen had been invaded, but Rhodes didn't delve into that.

On his way back to Clearview, Rhodes had seen the two cars parked beside the county road, just a little way off the highway. Thinking that the man slumped by the Toyota was in some kind of distress and that the other was helping him, Rhodes had turned the green-and-white county Tahoe around, pulled off on the country road, and gotten out to help.

Now, having read the situation incorrectly, he was in trouble, and it was his own fault. He didn't like the feeling. He'd called in to Hack Jensen, the dispatcher, and told him that he was stopping to help someone, but he hadn't sounded any alarms. Hack wouldn't worry about him or send any backup. Even worse, when he got back to the jail, Rhodes would have to explain to Hack what had happened.

That is, he'd have to explain if he got back to the jail. Right now he wasn't so sure he'd make it. He could hear a scratchy voice on the radio in the Tahoe. He wondered if he should try to answer it. Probably not.

"Your name's Elroy, right?" Rhodes said to the man with the pistol.

He knew the man's name wasn't Elroy, but he wanted to start a conversation that didn't involve the pistol.

"Hell, no, my name's not Elroy. I don't even know anybody named Elroy. What kind of name is that? I'm Kenny."

"Kenny what?" Rhodes asked.

"Kenny Lambert."

"Right. Kenny Lambert. Well, Kenny, I'm Sheriff Dan Rhodes, but maybe you knew that already."

"I knew it. I guess you don't remember me if you think I was this Elroy fella you called me, but I spent some time in that jail of yours."

"I thought I recognized the tattoo," Rhodes said, although it wasn't true. "Nice work," he added, although that wasn't true, either.

"Had it done at Mink's Ink. You know Mink?"

"I haven't had the pleasure."

"Got a nice touch with the needle. Anyway, that jail of yours is a pretty crappy place, you ask me."

Rhodes hadn't asked. He said, "It's not my jail. It's the county's jail."

"Whatever, it's still crappy. I don't think I wanna go back."

"Not much of a way to avoid it," Rhodes said, "considering you're holding a gun on me, and no telling what you've done to your friend there."

"He's not my friend."

"Even if he isn't, I'll have to arrest you for pulling a pistol on him."

"Not if I shoot you."

"Kenny, Kenny, Kenny. You're not going to shoot me."

Kenny looked puzzled. Rhodes had a feeling it wasn't a new feeling for him. "I'm not?"

"Nope. If you shoot the sheriff the lawmen never give up on you. You know how it is. You've seen it on TV, right? You can run, but you can't hide. They hunt you down no matter where you are."

"They won't find me," Kenny said. "I got friends in Houston."

Kenny wasn't the sharpest blade on the knife, and Rhodes was willing to bet his friends in Houston weren't much better. They'd probably post something on Facebook as soon as Kenny showed up at their place, assuming he could find his way there.

"Houston, Mexico, Canada, doesn't matter," Rhodes said. "The law will get you, and then you'll have to go to worse places than the jail in Clearview. State prison, for one."

"I won't kill you, then," Kenny said. "Just wound you a little."

"Not going to happen, Kenny."

"I think I peed on myself," the man leaning against the Camry said.

Kenny turned his head at the sound of the man's voice, and the distraction was enough for Rhodes to move forward and close the distance between him and the pistol. With his left hand Rhodes grabbed the barrel of the pistol and with his right he grabbed Kenny's wrist. A quick twist, and Rhodes was holding the pistol in his left hand, while Kenny's trigger finger was either broken or badly sprained.

Kenny yelled and turned back to Rhodes, who gave a turn, still holding Kenny's wrist, and swept Kenny's legs out from under him.

Kenny fell down and writhed a little in the dirt near the man who'd peed himself.

"You broke my damn finger," Kenny said.

"I don't think so," Rhodes said, putting a knee in Kenny's back to hold him on the ground, "but we'll get it looked at when we get you to the jail."

Rhodes ejected the magazine from the pistol and slipped the pistol into a back pocket of his pants. He put the magazine into the other, from which he pulled out some zip-tie cuffs. He cuffed Kenny, and said, "I'm arresting you for assault on an officer. You have the right to remain silent . . ."

"I know my rights," Kenny said.

"I have to tell you what they are, anyway," Rhodes said, and he did. "Do you understand what I've told you?"

"Sure," Kenny said. "I'm not stupid."

It was a judgment that Rhodes questioned, although he didn't say so.

"Anyway," Kenny continued, "I didn't assault anybody."

"You need to read more about the law," Rhodes said. He stood up, and got a good look at the man beside the Camry for the first time. The man was somewhere between twenty-five and thirty, wearing a pair of dark slacks and a blue short-sleeved shirt that looked like it might've come from Walmart, like most of the clothing bought in Blacklin County.

"Thanks for speaking up," Rhodes said.

"This is kind of disgusting," the man said. He had a round face and short black hair. He stood up and leaned on the Camry. He was short, his head not much higher than the car's roof. "Fainting and peeing myself. It's embarrassing." He looked down at himself and then at Rhodes. "Thanks for saving me from that crazy guy. He said he was going to shoot me and gut me out like a deer. It scared me pretty bad."

"I don't think Kenny would've done that."

"You didn't see the look in his eyes. He meant it, all right."

Rhodes looked down at Kenny, who looked harmless enough at the moment. The look in his eyes was mainly the meth, not meanness, although the threat was certainly bloody enough, along with the pistol, to bother somebody unused to dealing with that kind of thing.

Kenny didn't comment on the threat. He said, "You just gonna make me lie here? I think I landed in some sticker burrs, and my finger's broke. And grasshoppers are jumping on me."

The dry weather had brought out the grasshoppers, and when Rhodes looked down, he saw one land on Kenny's head.

"Grasshoppers won't hurt you," Rhodes said, taking Kenny's arm and pulling him to his feet.

When Kenny was standing, Rhodes patted him down and took a wallet from the back pocket of his jeans. He checked the driver's license and saw that Kenny's last name was indeed Lambert and that his address was on a county road outside of Thurston.

"I didn't say any of that stuff he told you," Kenny said when Rhodes replaced his wallet. "I didn't say I'd gut him out."

"He said it, all right," the man by the Camry said. "I'm Cal Stinson, by the way. Thanks for saving my life."

Rhodes didn't know Stinson, but there were a lot of people in the county he didn't know, mostly the younger ones, which was a depressing thought.

"You live in Clearview?" Rhodes asked.

"Yessir, I do. I was headed down to Thurston to look at the old school building before they tear it down. You know about that, I guess."

Rhodes knew. There had been some controversy about it, as there always was when a historic building was to be demolished. The town had been using it for a community center, but the place was about to fall down. Some people didn't want to go inside because they were afraid the place might collapse on them. A new metal building was to be constructed to replace it.

"My grandma went to school in the old building," Cal said. "Lots of people's ancestors from that part of the county went there. It's a shame it has to be destroyed."

Rhodes didn't want to get into that. Neither did Kenny.

"My finger's broke," Kenny said, "and all you can talk about is some old building. I need a doctor."

Cal ignored him. "I can't go anywhere looking like this. I'll have to go back home and change my pants."

"Oughta wear Depends if you're gonna cut people off on the highway," Kenny said.

"Tell me what happened," Rhodes said to Cal.

"Son of a bitch cut me off," Kenny said.

"I didn't ask you," Rhodes said.

"I didn't cut you off," Cal said.

"You sure did," Kenny said, and Rhodes gave him a little shake.

"I've already heard your side of the story," Rhodes said. "Now I want to hear his."

"He'll prob'ly lie."

"He'd better not," Rhodes said. "What happened, Cal?"

"I was just driving along, obeying the speed limit, and this moron came roaring up behind me, hit me in the back bumper. You can look and see. I'm sure it's dented. Scared me pretty bad, so I pulled off onto this side road to let him get well away from me. But he turned back and jumped out of his truck and threatened to kill me."

"That ain't the way it happened," Kenny said, "and I ain't a moron."

"You can come to the jail," Rhodes told Cal. "You can swear out a complaint against Kenny here for making terroristic threats and for assault. We might think of a few other things, too."

"I didn't do none of that stuff," Kenny said.

"He sure did," Cal said. "Can I leave now? These pants are uncomfortable."

"Go ahead," Rhodes said, "but don't forget to come by the jail later this afternoon. Do it before you go to Thurston."

"I'll be there," Cal said.

He got in his car, drove a little way down the road until he found a place to turn around, and headed back toward Clearview. Rhodes bundled Kenny into the Tahoe and was tagging and bagging Kenny's pistol when he saw a county car coming down the highway. He stood beside the Tahoe and waited.

The car stopped behind the Tahoe, and Ruth Grady, one of the deputies, got out.

"What's going on?" she asked.

Rhodes explained as briefly as he could, with Kenny protesting occasionally from inside the Tahoe that he hadn't done any of that stuff.

"I wasn't expecting any backup," Rhodes said when he'd finished telling Ruth what had happened. "You missed all the excitement."

"I'm not backup. Hack said you weren't answering your radio, and since I was close, he sent me out to see what was going on. He's been trying to get in touch with you about a problem."

"I've been busy," Rhodes said. "What kind of problem?"

"Hack didn't say."

Rhodes wasn't surprised. It often took Hack a long time to get to the point of anything he had to tell, and the police radio wasn't the place for that kind of talking.

"Did he give you a hint?"

"He just said that you need to get to the mayor's office as soon as you can."

"But he didn't say why?"

Ruth grinned. "He just said you were in trouble. Big trouble."

"As usual."

"That's right," Ruth said. "As usual."

"I guess I'd better go, then," Rhodes said.

Ruth nodded. "Probably be a good idea. Let's get the prisoner out of your vehicle and into mine."

"Let's do that," Rhodes said. "You can have Hack call a wrecker to pick up Kenny's truck and haul it to the impound lot."

"Sure," Ruth said. "Come on, Kenny."

Kenny wasn't cooperative, but they got him moved without too much trouble. When he was stowed in Ruth's county car, Rhodes gave Ruth the pistol and told her to put it in the evidence locker when she got to the jail.

"Will do," Ruth said.

"You think you can handle the prisoner?"

Ruth gave Kenny a disdainful look. "You have to ask?"

"Not really," Rhodes said.

Chapter 2

Clearview was building a new City Hall, but Calvin Clement had told everyone that he was going to keep his office in the old place. He said he liked it there, that people knew where to find him, and it was quiet.

Rhodes walked down the cool, dim hallway toward the office. He could understand the mayor's feelings, but he wasn't sure that Clement would stay. It didn't matter to Rhodes whether he did or not. Clement would summon him from wherever he was.

Clement's administrative assistant was Helen King. She'd been in high school with Rhodes, and she'd been the head cheerleader when Rhodes had starred on the football team for one game. After that he was out with an injury for the rest of the season, but he'd earned a nickname and had sat on the bench with the team at every game.

From the bench he'd had the opportunity to watch Helen in action. She'd been the very embodiment of cheerleading, leaping and prancing and yelling on every play, her long black hair bouncing as she ran up and down the sideline under the Friday-night lights, rousing the crowd to a fine pitch of enthusiasm for the generally lackluster Clearview Catamounts.

The amazing thing to Rhodes was that Helen had remained just as enthusiastic and perky from that day to this, so he was a little taken aback when he went into the mayor's outer office and saw her sitting somber and quiet behind her desk, looking at her computer screen.

"What's up?" Rhodes asked as he entered.

Helen's head jerked up. Her hair was still black, just as it had been in high school. Rhodes figured she had a little help with that.

"Oh," she said. "Hello, Sheriff. You surprised me."

Rhodes nodded. "Sorry about that. I didn't mean to. I thought you were expecting me."

"I was. We are. I mean . . ." Helen looked back at the computer.

"Is everything okay?" Rhodes asked, not knowing what else to say.

Helen looked away from the computer toward the closed door to Clement's inner office, then back at Rhodes.

"Not really," she said.

For a long time now, the feeling had been growing on Rhodes that nobody was ever going to tell him anything straightforwardly again. It seemed to him that he spent far too much of his time trying to drag information from them. Holding back was something that came naturally to Hack, the dispatcher, and Lawton, the jailer, but surely not to everyone else. Maybe there was something in the Clearview water that caused the problem.

"You want to tell me what it is?" he said.

"It's Mayor Clement."

"I know. He called and asked me to come by."

"Yes. It's just that . . . I've never seen him like this before."

Rhodes figured he'd gotten all he was going to get from Helen. "Maybe I'd better just go in and see what he wants."

"Yes. That might be a good idea. But be careful. He's in a real bad mood."

"I'd kind of guessed that," Rhodes said.

"You don't have to knock," Helen said. "He's been waiting for you."

"What if I hadn't showed up?"

"I don't even want to think about it," Helen said.

Rhodes shrugged and opened the door into Clement's office. Being mayor of Clearview was in some ways a mostly honorary position. Clement was paid only a dollar a year, and for that salary he presided over a sometimes rambunctious city council, tried to keep as many citizens as possible satisfied and happy with their city services, and made at least some attempts to improve the town and to make it a better place to live. He didn't make everybody happy all the time, but nobody could do that, and Rhodes thought that he did a good job for the most part, even though he did seem to think that he was Rhodes's boss, which wasn't the case. The county commissioners were responsible for the Sheriff's Department, and the city of Clearview had a contract with the county for law enforcement services. There were times, however, when Clement thought that Rhodes was responsible directly to him, and this was one of those times.

"It's about time you showed up," Clement said as Rhodes stepped through the door. "I'm glad you could find a spot in your busy schedule for me."

Clement's full-time job was as a financial adviser, and he dressed the part, in a dark navy blue suit, white shirt, and navy blue tie. He was bald on top and his gray hair was cut short on the sides. His gray beard was neatly trimmed. None of this went with his face at the moment because it was a dark red, almost purple. He looked like a man whose blood pressure had just peaked around 250/150.

"I got here as soon as I could," Rhodes said.

Clement hadn't looked at Rhodes since he'd entered, and he didn't do so now. He was staring almost bug-eyed at the computer monitor on his desk.

"What's the problem?" Rhodes asked, taking a chair in front of the desk without an invitation to do so.

"This," Clement said, and he turned the computer monitor around so Rhodes could see the web page Clement had been looking at.

Rhodes was familiar with it. It was called *Digging that Blacklin County Dirt*, and it was devoted to gossip about the county in general and the Clearview city government in particular.

"The other thing was bad enough," Clement said, "and now we have this."

Rhodes assumed that "the other thing" was a blog called *A Clear View for Clearview.* It was produced by Jennifer Loam, who had been a reporter for the local paper until it downsized and she lost her job. Instead of leaving town, she'd started a news blog that had in a short time gained many more readers than the paper had, and which sold enough advertising to bring in more money than she'd been making as a reporter. She had a generally positive attitude toward the town and the county, but she did sensationalize some things, including a lot of Rhodes's own exploits. He wished she wouldn't do that, but she'd told him that his doings were by far the most popular feature of the blog. Clement seemed to Rhodes to be a bit jealous of that fact, and what Rhodes saw on the computer monitor wasn't likely to make Clement feel any better. In fact, Rhodes now understood the reason for Clement's barely contained fury.

The headline read "Clearview's Nincompoop Mayor." Rhodes couldn't read the rest without fumbling out his reading glasses, and he didn't want to do that.

"Seems uncomplimentary," he said.

"Uncomplimentary! It's libel, that's what it is. Libel!"

Rhodes was tempted to say something about sticks and stones, but he restrained himself. He didn't know a lot about the defamation laws in Texas because libel wasn't something that came up often, but he did know that name-calling wasn't included.

"What does the article say?" he asked.

"It says I'm a nincompoop!"

"I can see that much." Rhodes kept his voice level. "I meant do they offer any proof?"

Clement glared at him. His eyes bugged out. "Proof? What proof could they possibly have of something like that?"

Rhodes sighed, dug around in his shirt pocket for his reading glasses, and put them on. He leaned forward a little until he could read what was on the screen. When he was through, he folded the glasses and stuck them back in his pocket.

"That's not really so bad," he said as he leaned back in his chair.

"Not bad?" Clement was incredulous. "Not bad? They called me a nincompoop."

"It's just a word," Rhodes said. "There's nothing bad about you in the article."

Clements wasn't mollified. "Other than that I'm a nincompoop, you mean. Who uses words like that anymore, anyway?"

"For that matter," Rhodes said, "who are 'they'?"

"Anonymous cowards, that's who," Clement said, "hiding behind fake names. Thomas Paine and Patrick Henry, my foot. I want you to find out who they are and put a stop to this."

Rhodes wasn't ready to launch into a defense of freedom of the press, if blogs were the press. He was sure that Jennifer Loam's site was real journalism, but he wasn't quite so certain about *Digging that Blacklin County Dirt.* Still, there was the issue of freedom of speech and the First Amendment. Clement would most likely think of those things himself when he calmed down.

"There's really nothing to the article," Rhodes said. "It's just kind of a joke about your not wanting to move into plush new accommodations when the new City Hall is finished. The writer thinks you're a nincompoop for not doing it."

Clement's face looked a little better now. "Let the next mayor make the move. I'm not." He looked around his office. "I like this old place. Sure, it just has one small window. Sure, there's a water stain on the wall there by the filing cabinet. Sure, it's small and old-fashioned. I like small and old-fashioned. People know how to find me here, and I don't want to go anywhere else. So that's that. Besides, whoever writes this stuff has said things about me before."

"I wouldn't know," Rhodes said. "I don't generally read things on the internet."

"Good for you." Clement pointed to the stain on the wall. "They blamed me for that water leak."

Rhodes could see how that might be a sore point. The leak had been an annoyance during heavy rains. It had affected other offices in the old building, and Clement had asked the council to have an expensive study done to see how to fix it. As it turned out, the problem had been nothing more than a stopped-up drain from the roof.

Luckily someone on the council had suggested that the drains be checked before the study was done. Clement had looked a bit like a nincompoop that time for sure, but the city had saved a lot of money. Things could have been worse.

"This whole blog thing's a smear job on the city and the county," Clement went on, "and it's run by hypocrites. How can they call me a nincompoop about not wanting to move into the new City Hall when they wrote for days about how it was a waste of taxpayer money to build it in the first place?"

The new building was causing trouble, in a small way, like the new community center in Thurston, except that nobody had proposed tearing down the old Clearview City Hall when the new one was built. At least not yet.

Rhodes had forgotten about that. The rogue website had done some solid investigative work into the costs and benefits of a new City Hall. There was real journalism going on there, all right. Maybe not all the time, but some of it.

"Hypocrites or jokers, it doesn't matter," Rhodes said. "They have a right to free speech, and the law's not going to shut them down."

Clement nodded. "Okay, that's probably true, but they need to be held accountable instead of hiding behind fake names. I want to know who's doing this stuff. If people are going to say I'm a nincompoop, I want to know who they are."

"Finding that out isn't my job," Rhodes said.

Clement brushed his beard with his right hand. "You're right, now that I think about it. I was upset, so maybe I got a little excited and went overboard. I realize that now. I'm not going to ask you to find out who these people are." He brushed a hand over his beard. "There are other ways I can find out."

Rhodes didn't like the sound of that. He started to say so, but Clement cut him off.

"I can hire a private detective. We've never had one of those in Clearview before, but someone's just opened an office. I can give him a call."

Rhodes sighed. This was turning out to be worse than he'd thought it would.

"Seepy Benton," he said.

"So you've heard about it," Clement said. He turned the computer monitor around, made a few clicks with his mouse, and turned the monitor back to Rhodes.

Rhodes looked at the screen. He'd seen the website before. The banner across the top announced that the viewer had reached the site of C. P. Benton, Confidential Investigator.

"I believe this Benton has helped you out on a few cases," Clement said. "Isn't that right?"

"In a way," Rhodes said.

"And you can vouch for him?"

Rhodes had to think about that. C. P. Benton, or Seepy as Rhodes thought of him, had come to Clearview to teach in a community college branch that had been established there by a school from a neighboring county. Rhodes had the impression that Seepy had left his former job at a college somewhere down on the Gulf Coast because of an unrequited love affair, but Rhodes had never asked for details. He didn't think it was any of his business. After arriving in Clearview, Benton had sat in the Citizen's Sheriff's Academy and started thinking of himself as an official member of the department. More than once he'd provided Rhodes with some valuable assistance and had even helped solve a case or two.

Those accomplishments weren't enough for Seepy, however. As

he would have been the first to tell anyone who'd listen, he had a big brain, and he wasn't afraid to use it. He'd not only devoted some of his spare time to helping Rhodes, but he'd opened his own ghost-busting business, which had led to some interesting times for Rhodes, among others. For a brief time Seepy had even done some reporting for Jennifer Loam's *A Clear View for Clearview,* and now, having grown bored with busting ghosts and writing clickbait headlines, he was a private detective.

Rhodes couldn't help thinking that it was partly his own fault. Seepy had asked for help in meeting the requirements to become an investigator, and Rhodes had done him the favor he needed. The requirement that Seepy had to meet was three years of private investigation experience, and Rhodes had vouched for him as an investigator for the sheriff's department. It involved a bit of fudging, but not enough to bother Rhodes's conscience. Benton had done good work, as much as Rhodes sometimes hated to admit it.

"Well?" Clement said. "Can you vouch for him or not?"

"Yes," Rhodes said. "I can vouch for him."

"Does he know computers like it says on his website?"

"He knows computers."

"So he can help me find out who those dirt diggers are?"

"Maybe," Rhodes said.

"Good," Clement said. "I'll give him a call."

"You're not going to harass the bloggers if you do find out who they are, I hope."

"I'm not that dumb. I'll be satisfied if I can just put a face on my accusers."

Rhodes hoped that's all there was to it. Even though he'd calmed down a good bit, Clement had looked angry enough to twist someone's head off earlier.

"I'll give this Benton a call," Clement said. "I'll tell him you recommended him."

Rhodes stood up to leave. "I'd rather you didn't. I like to remain anonymous when it comes to private eyes."

"If you say so," Clement said.

"I do," Rhodes said.

"Then I won't mention you."

"Good," Rhodes said.

Chapter 3

When Rhodes left the mayor's office, he gave Helen a thumbs-up, and she gave him a smile.

"Did you solve his problem?" she asked.

"He solved it himself," Rhodes said, which might've been an exaggeration. There was no guarantee that Seepy could do what Clement wanted, but it was better to be optimistic about it than to depress Helen.

"You probably helped," Helen said.

"Maybe a little," Rhodes admitted.

Rhodes left and drove to the Blacklin County jail, where he'd have to face up to the mistake that he'd made with Kenny Lambert. As it turned out, however, Hack wasn't interested in talking about Kenny. When Rhodes asked if Ruth had brought in the prisoner, Hack got that out of the way fast, which was unusual if not unheard of.

"Yeah," Hack said. "We got snake-boy all booked and printed and settled in a nice, clean cell. You better write up an arrest report quick, else his lawyer'll get him before a judge, get a bail set, and have him outta here before you get the report done. He's whinin' about his finger bein' broke, but it's just swollen a little. That lawyer won't bother to make anything of it. He'll just get him loose."

Lawton, the jailer, came through the door before Hack had finished talking and said, "Happens ever' time. Right back out on the streets. And speakin' of snakes—"

"Now just a dang minute," Hack said. "I'm the one talkin' here."

Rhodes sat at his desk and readied himself as best he could for what he knew was coming. Something had happened, and both Hack and Lawton knew what it was. Instead of telling him straight out, however, they'd try to make him drag the story out of them. They always did when they had the opportunity and time wasn't pressing. Rhodes sometimes thought they believed they were a reincarnation of the old comedy team, Abbott and Costello, and in fact, they resembled them in a small physical way. Hack was lanky and had a thin mustache, and Lawton was a bit chubby. That was as far as the physical resemblance went, and where Rhodes was concerned, the humor resemblance had never materialized. Or if it had, he couldn't detect it. Hack and Lawton seemed to get a big kick out of tormenting him, but then so did everybody else in the county.

Rhodes wondered for a second if he was getting paranoid but decided he wasn't. He was just sticking to the facts.

"I got a right to talk, too," Lawton said.

"You ain't got a right to interrupt me, though," Hack said.

"I thought you was finished."

"Well, I wasn't. I was goin' to say that real snakes've been sneakin' around. The sheriff needs to know stuff like that."

"What real snakes?" Rhodes asked.

"Giant ones," Lawton said, and Hack glared at him.

"We have giant snakes in Blacklin County?"

"That's what George Gore said when he called," Hack told him. "Said it was a giant snake at his house and he needed some help identifyin' it."

Rhodes was glad he hadn't been called on for that job. He wasn't fond of snakes. "Did you send Alton?"

Alton Boyd was the county's animal control officer and fully qualified to take care of all snake calls as far as Rhodes was concerned.

"Yeah, I sent him."

"Wasn't so giant when he got there," Lawton said.

"Who's tellin' this?" Hack asked, half rising from his chair.

"I guess you are, but you're tellin' it wrong. See, what George wanted to know was what kind of snake he was dealin' with, it bein' a giant an' all. Not ever' day a man sees a giant snake in his yard."

Hack came all the way out of his chair. "I'm telling this."

"All right," Lawton said. "Tell it then."

Rhodes knew better than to say anything. He didn't want to encourage them, so he just sat there, waiting for whatever was to come.

"Overreacted is what Alton said George did," Hack said, sitting back down. "Made it hard for Alton to help him out with what he wanted to know."

Rhodes had lost track of the conversation. "What did he want to know?"

"What kind of snake it was," Lawton said. He made a clucking noise with his tongue. "I said that already." He gave Rhodes a pitying look. "They say memory's the first thing to go when a fella starts to get old."

"I thought it was the second thing to go," Hack said.

"What's the first thing? If you can remember."

"I can remember, all right," Hack said. "Better'n some I could name. Anyway, it's hair. That goes first."

It wasn't easy for Rhodes to resist reaching up to touch the top of his head, which he was sure was a little blistered.

"First or second," Lawton said. "Hair or memory. Don't have anything to do with snakes, I guess."

"'Course not," Hack said. "So why'd you bring it up?"

"'Cause the sheriff couldn't remember, and I thought that was a bad sign. A lawman's gotta have a good memory. I got a mind like a steel trap, myself."

"A worn-out rusty one," Hack said. "Anyway, when he got to George's house, Alton thought he could identify the kind of snake, but he wasn't sure."

"The giant snake," Rhodes said. "What about the giant part?"

"That was kinda hard to tell by the time Alton got there," Hack said. "Like I told you, Alton said George got kinda carried away."

"Claimed it was ten feet long, at least, though," Lawton said, drawing another glare from Hack. "More long than giant, maybe, but it'd be a world's record if it was that long, I bet."

"Alton said it was a coachwhip," Hack said. "You know how they are. Long, but not very big around."

"Ten feet long?" Rhodes said. "I never heard of one that long."

"A giant snake," Hack said. "I told you that. 'Cept we won't really know for sure."

Rhodes didn't want to ask, but he couldn't help himself. "Why not?"

"George got carried away," Lawton said. "Remember? We told you that. He must not like snakes."

"Had himself a sharp garden hoe," Hack said, ignoring Lawton for a change. "Went after that snake and chopped that sucker up into so many pieces, Alton said they couldn't put it back together to tell how long it was to start with. Besides that, George has a couple of sorry old dogs, and they got hold of some of the pieces and carried them off somewhere, so that'd make it come out short, no matter how good a job they did puttin' it back together."

"Not that they tried that," Lawton said. "Anyway George got what he wanted. Alton told him it was a coachwhip. Harmless. Mostly just eats the kind of pests that people want to get rid of. George shoulda left it alone. Mighta had a world's record, he'd left it alone."

Rhodes was a little ashamed to admit it even to himself, but he was pretty much on George's side. Even harmless snakes weren't pleasant companions. Still, they didn't deserve to be chopped up.

"Harmless?" Hack said. "You know how that kind of a snake got its name?"

"Never thought about it," Lawton said.

"Got it because they used to wrap people up in their coils and whip 'em to death with their tails, that's how."

Lawton looked skeptical. "I know they're supposed to chase people, but I kinda have my doubts about that whippin' stuff."

"You prob'ly don't believe in Bigfoot, either."

Lawton laughed. "I wouldn't say that, but a snake whippin' somebody to death with its tail? You gotta admit that's kinda stretchin' it."

"Guess we'll never know for sure," Hack said. "Speakin' of snakes, what kinda snake you think that is tattooed on our new guest's neck?"

"Rattler," Lawton said. "Or water moccasin. Some kind of pit viper, anyway. Saw the head, but I didn't look to see if there was rattles on the tail."

Rhodes wanted to get off the subject of snakes, so he asked if Cal Stinson had been in to file a complaint against Kenny Lambert.

"Nobody's been in to file any complaints 'gainst anybody," Hack said. "What kinda name is Stinson, anyhow? I never heard of any Stinsons from around here."

"New people comin' to town all the time," Lawton said, "not that most of them hang around for long."

Rhodes was thinking that he'd made another mistake. He should've asked Stinson for some identification, but it hadn't seemed necessary. Stinson was the victim, not the perpetrator, and it wasn't as if they needed Stinson's complaint since Rhodes had plenty of charges he could press against Kenny if he wanted to. Still, it would be better to have the citizen file the complaint and get the whole story of what had happened on the books.

"Look around on that computer of yours," Rhodes told Hack. "See if you can locate him. Said his name was Cal, but that might be short for Calvin. He should be easy to find if his last name's unusual."

"I'll see what I can find," Hack said. "Might not be easy if he's new in town."

"He said he was headed for Thurston to look at the old school building before they tear it down, so he must have some connections here."

"I'll do what I can," Hack said, and Rhodes left him to it. He had to write up his report on Kenny's arrest, so he did that while Hack got busy.

About half an hour later, Hack said, "Ain't no such person."

Rhodes looked away from his own computer, which he used mainly for writing reports. He wasn't good about anything else related to it.

"How can that be?" he asked.

"I don't know how it can be," Hack said. "I'm just givin' you the facts. Ain't no such person. Not in Texas, anyhow. Used to be one by that name, but he's over sixty-five years old, and he's moved to Missouri."

"You found out all that?"

"It's easy if you know how and can get to some of the databases that we can. Might be good for you to learn stuff like that."

"One day when I have time," Rhodes said. "You're sure about this?"

"Sure as I can be. Fella lied to you. Don't ask me why. Computer won't tell me that."

Rhodes wondered why Stinson, or whatever his name was, would lie about something like that. Maybe he was wanted for some crime or other under his real name and had just pulled one out of the air.

"Prob'ly won't matter," Hack said. "Fella like that, one that lies to a sheriff, he always turns up again one way or the other."

Hack turned out to be right about that. The man who'd called himself Cal Stinson turned up again the very next day. Only this time he was dead.

Chapter 4

Rhodes was sitting on the back steps of his house watching his two dogs, Speedo, a black and white border collie, and Yancey, a Pomeranian who looked like a mobile dust mop, get their morning exercise. Yancey, though much the smaller of the two, never seemed to notice the difference in size, and he was tussling with Speedo over a new squeaky toy that Rhodes had bought for them a few days before. It had looked sort of like a raccoon when Rhodes bought it, but it was rapidly getting chewed into an unrecognizable shape.

Speedo had hold of the head, and Yancey had the tail. Speedo was silent, but Yancey was growling as he tried to shake the toy away from the bigger dog while Speedo backed up slowly, dragging Yancey across the yard a little at a time.

"I hate to break up the fun," Rhodes's wife, Ivy, said, opening the screen door, "but Hack is on the phone. He says it's an emergency."

Rhodes stood up. "We seem to be having a lot of those lately. Did he say what the emergency was?"

"He didn't tell me. You go on in, and I'll watch the dogs."

Rhodes held the screen door open, and Ivy came out onto the steps. She was about six inches shorter than Rhodes, and her short hair had a good bit of gray in it. Rhodes bent down and gave her a kiss on the cheek, then went inside. He glanced back to see if Speedo had taken full possession of the squeaky toy yet. He hadn't, and Yancey wasn't giving up. Nothing new there. He never did.

Rhodes went to the phone, probably one of the few landlines left in Blacklin County. Rhodes liked having it because all you could do with it was make phone calls. He had a cell phone, of course, but he wasn't fond of it. He wasn't sure the world had been much improved by a device people used to escape having to engage with things and people around them.

Rhodes picked up the landline phone and said, "What's the emergency?"

When it came to emergencies, Hack was all business. "Got a dead man down in Thurston at the schoolhouse. Woman named Wanda Wilkins just called it in. You better get down there."

"She's sure he's dead?"

"She says he's not moving or breathing and doesn't have a pulse. That sounds dead to me. I told her not to touch anything and to hold off calling for an ambulance, that you'd take care of that after you looked at the crime scene."

"Who's on duty down that way this morning?"

"Andy Shelby."

"Get him to go on and secure the scene. I'll meet him there."

"I'm way ahead of you," Hack said. "Already done that. You leavin' now?"

"I'm halfway there already," Rhodes said, and hung up the phone.

He went out through the back door and told Ivy where he was going and why. The dogs were still tussling over the new toy.

"Don't let Speedo hurt Yancey," Rhodes said.

Ivy laughed. "No chance of that. He has too much fun tormenting him to hurt him."

"He's not tormenting him," Rhodes said. "Just playing."

"Right," Ivy said. "You be careful today."

"I always am," Rhodes said, and Ivy was still laughing when he turned the corner of the house and got into the Tahoe.

Rhodes didn't break the land speed record getting to Thurston, but he made good time. The small town had only one main street, the highway that went right through the middle of it. The old schoolhouse was two blocks off the highway, and Andy Shelby was already there. Rhodes stopped the Tahoe in the parking area beside Andy's county car and got out. He didn't see any other cars and wondered where Wanda Wilkins had parked.

The schoolhouse was a two-story building of redbrick, built so long ago that it had never been air-conditioned. It sat right in the middle of one square block of land that was covered in dead grass, dirt, and sticker burrs. High windows lined the facade on either side of the arched entrance, and from the front the building didn't look as if it might fall down at any minute. The inside was probably different.

Rhodes hadn't thought to ask where the dead man was, but he didn't think he'd have any trouble finding him. He went to the tall double door and pulled it open. It was cooler inside, but only a little. The floors were clean, but there was a musty, moldy smell, along with a whiff of pine-scented cleaner. The lights were on, and Rhodes walked past a couple of offices to his left and right, went up a couple of steps, and entered the main hallway. In front of him was the auditorium, and to the left and right were classrooms.

"Down here, Sheriff," Andy Shelby called from Rhodes's left.

Rhodes turned and walked down the hallway. Someone had recently mopped the floor, and the smell of pine-scented cleaner was stronger. On his left was a classroom, and he went inside. The dead man lay facedown on the floor in the front of the classroom. Not far away lay a piece of chalk. Above him there was an old blackboard, washed clean except for one ragged chalk mark that started a couple of feet above the chalk tray and descended from that point like the falling line on a stock report.

The blackboard was the only sign that the room had been used for classes. There were no desks for students. Instead of a teacher's desk there was a small table with two chairs. In the back of the room were several long folding tables leaning against the wall, with folding chairs leaning against them.

Andy Shelby sat in one of the two chairs at the small table in front. In the other was a woman Rhodes didn't know, though he assumed she was Wanda Wilkins.

Andy stood up when Rhodes came into the room. He was a compact young man with an athletic build that Rhodes envied. Andy had been a bit inclined to rashness when he first came on the job, but he'd settled down and was a good lawman. The only thing that worried Rhodes about him was that he was dating Jennifer Loam. Rhodes wasn't sure it was a good idea for a deputy to be dating a reporter, but so far there hadn't been any problems.

"This is Wanda Wilkins," Andy said, indicating the woman who was still seated at the table. "She found the body. Ms. Wilkins, this is Sheriff Rhodes."

Wanda stood up. Rhodes couldn't guess her age, other than that she was old, somewhere between sixty and a hundred. Her thin face was lined, but her blue eyes were bright. She wore what appeared to be a man's blue shirt and a pair of faded baggy jeans. White hair stuck out from the camouflage baseball cap on her head. When she spoke, her voice was as strong and firm as a youngster's.

"Pleased to meet you, Sheriff," she said. She stuck out a hand, and Rhodes shook it. She had a firm grip. She looked at the body. Some people might have been uncomfortable with a dead man in the room, but it didn't seem to bother her at all. "What are you going to do about this?"

Rhodes looked at the dead man, too. He didn't see any blood on the floor, but there was some blood behind his right ear. He'd take a closer look after he'd talked to Wanda.

"I'm not sure what we'll do," Rhodes said. "We'll have to investigate and find out how he died, and more besides. How did you happen to find the body?"

Wanda's laugh had a sort of cackle in it. She seemed very calm in the presence of a corpse. "I watch a good bit of TV, Sheriff, so I can tell you're suspicious of me because I was the first one on the scene. I didn't kill him, though."

"I never thought you did," Rhodes said, although he reserved the right to reconsider. "I just wondered how you found him."

"I live right across the street," Wanda said.

Rhodes had noticed the little frame house when he got out of the Tahoe.

"I went to this school when I was a girl," Wanda said. "That was a while ago. I always win the prize for being the oldest graduate at the homecoming every year. We had homecoming back in June, and the classes all meet in the auditorium. It's kind of dangerous because it's not kept up as well as this little room. This is the only one that's really taken care of." She paused. "Where was I going with this, anyway?"

Rhodes looked over at Andy, who shrugged.

"You were going to tell us how you found the body," Rhodes said.

Wanda nodded. "Oh, yes, of course. I live across the street. Did I mention that?"

"Yes," Rhodes said. "You did."

"Good. It's a nice house, kind of small, but big enough for me. I like a small house. Not so much work as a big one, or a place like this school. I used to do some cleaning over here, but I haven't done any for the last few years except for this room and the hallway. It's just too much for me. Here at the school, I mean. I can take care of my house just fine." She glanced at Andy, who hadn't said a word. "Don't you look at me like that, young man. I'll tell this my own way. I'll get to the body in just a minute. Where was I?"

"It was too much for you," Rhodes said. "Cleaning this building, I mean."

"Yes, it was, but I thought I could do one other thing, at least. I could keep an eye on the place since I have windows that face over this way. During the day when I think about it, I look out and see if anything's going on, like some kids trying to get in and tear things up. What would most likely happen is that they'd just get hurt, and then their parents would sue, and that would be the end of the building, for sure. You did know that the city has plans to tear it down?"

"I did," Rhodes said, resigned to hearing a lot more than he wanted to before Wanda got to the point. He wondered if she were related to Hack or Lawton.

"I don't know how the city got the building, but it did, so it's really the city's problem to take care of it. The money's just not there, though. It's cheaper to build something new than to fix this old place up. Some of us would like to keep this building, though. It's a historic place. Did you know that Patrick Gibson went to school here?"

Gibson had been the state representative from the district for years and had then served in the senate. Without distinction, as Rhodes remembered. He'd left politics when he was in his eighties and died soon afterward, years ago.

"I'd heard he was from here," Rhodes said.

"Some other famous people went here, too," Wanda said. "I can't think right now who they were, but this is a historic place and ought to be saved. That's what the dead man thought, too."

"How do you know that?" Rhodes asked.

"Because he told me."

"When would that have been?"

"Yesterday, when I saw him snooping around over here. I told you that I look over here now and then, and late in the afternoon, around five, I saw him poking around outside. I thought he might be up to something, so I came right over and had a talk with him."

"Did he tell you what his name was?"

"Yes. He said he was Bruce Wayne and—"

Rhodes looked at Andy, who grinned.

"Are you sure?" Rhodes asked.

"I might be old, but I can still hear," Wanda said. "I can remember pretty good, too. Bruce Wayne, that's what he said."

Rhodes let it go. "What else did he tell you?"

"That he was interested in the history of the school. Said his grandmother went to school here and that he'd like to look around for a while. I have a key to the building, so I let him in. I never saw him come out, but when I came over here late yesterday evening to lock up and check on him, his car was gone." She pointed to the dead man. "But when I came back today, there he was."

"I didn't see a car," Rhodes said.

"It was here yesterday," Wanda said. "I don't know what happened to it. I might've been watching TV when he left."

"What kind of car was it?"

"I don't know anything about cars. They all look alike to me and have since the sixties. It was gray, and that's all I know about it. Just about all cars are that color now. I can remember when there were two-tone cars and even three-tone cars. I had one myself, a nineteen fifty-nine Ford that I bought secondhand. It was baby blue on the bottom and had a white top."

Rhodes thought he'd gotten all the information he was going to get from Wanda, so he said, "I appreciate your help with this. You can go on back home now and let us work the crime scene. I might have to talk to you again about things, and if you think of anything else that would help, call the sheriff's department."

"I'll do that," Wanda said. "I need to lock up when you leave, so stop by and let me know."

Rhodes told her he would, and when she was gone, Andy said, "She's a talker."

"But not a very helpful one," Rhodes said. "Bruce Wayne?"

Andy shook his head. "I've already taken photos and emailed them to the jail. We'd better have a look at him. He might be wearing a Batman suit under his clothes."

Rhodes pulled a pair of nitrile gloves from his back pocket. He had a box of them in the Tahoe and had brought a pair for Andy, but the deputy had his own. Rhodes went to the body and examined the bloody spot behind the right ear.

"Shot," he said. "Small caliber. Won't be an exit wound. The bullet will still be in there. Must have scrambled his brain."

"No brass," Andy said. "I looked around already. Revolver, or somebody who was careful."

Rhodes nodded and turned the body over. A tingle ran up his spine when he saw the man's face.

"His name wasn't Bruce Wayne," Rhodes said.

"You know him?" Andy said.

"We met yesterday. He said his name was Cal Stinson, but I'm not sure that's true any more than Bruce Wayne was. Hack couldn't find any record of him."

Rhodes felt diminished by any man's death, even if it was someone he didn't know. The feeling was magnified in this case because he'd just talked to the man the day before. Feelings didn't matter now, however, because Rhodes had a job to do. He began to look through the dead man's pockets. He found nothing, no wallet, no cell phone, no car keys.

"You think he was robbed and his car stolen?" Andy asked.

"Could be," Rhodes said, but he didn't really believe it. That didn't fit with the chalk mark.

He wondered where Kenny Lambert had been the previous evening. He hadn't been in jail more than a few hours before he'd bonded out and gotten his truck off the impound lot. He could easily have been in Thurston that evening.

"If it wasn't that, what else could it have been?" Andy asked.

Rhodes said he didn't know and added, "It's always better not to form any opinions before you investigate, and speaking of that, I'll let you work this scene while I look around the building."

"There's not much of a scene," Andy said.

"I know. Just do what you can. Call Hack and have him send the Justice of the Peace to declare this man dead, and get the EMTs here after you've done your job."

Andy looked at the body. "I don't think I'll find anything."

"Remember, don't form opinions too soon," Rhodes said.

"Okay, but it looks to me like he started to write on the blackboard and somebody stepped up behind him and shot him."

Rhodes thought the same thing, and said so. "But," he added, "I'm keeping my options open."

Andy nodded. "Right. It's getting hot in here. Would it be all right if I opened the windows?"

"I don't see why not," Rhodes said. "Just be careful not to mess up any clues."

Andy nodded. "I'll be careful."

"So will I," Rhodes said, and headed for the door.

Chapter 5

Rhodes wondered what Cal Stinson or Bruce Wayne or whatever his name really was could have been looking for in the old school building. Maybe Andy was right and Stinson had been killed for his money and his car, but if that were true, who'd done it? Someone who'd wandered into the building and seen Stinson as a target of opportunity? Or someone who was living or hiding in the building? Rhodes had a little experience with people living in abandoned buildings, but he thought that if anyone had been living here, Wanda Wilkins would've spotted him. She claimed she didn't spend all her time watching the building, but she'd have known if someone were staying inside. Rhodes didn't quite believe she watched so much TV that she wouldn't know if someone went into the building, either. He wondered why she hadn't seen whoever had killed Stinson and taken the car. It was possible the killer had waited until after dark to take the car, which might explain that part of the riddle, but Rhodes was still suspicious.

And what about Kenny Lambert? He lived in the area. Could he have seen Stinson's car and stopped for a little talk and a bit of revenge? Rhodes had kept Kenny's pistol, which was now safely stowed at the jail, but Kenny could have gotten another weapon with no trouble. He might even have had one at home.

Finding out who Stinson was had become more important than ever. Blacklin County was small, and while everyone seemed to know everyone else, that wasn't the case. People drifted in and out all the time. Even the ones that stayed didn't always become known, even to their neighbors. It was the people who'd lived there all their lives who knew each other, along with the people who came in and made themselves a part of the community. Otherwise it was easy enough to lead an anonymous life, keeping a distance from everybody, shopping in the crowds at Walmart, and staying out of trouble. Cal Stinson must have been like that, but where had he come from, and what was he doing in Blacklin County? Rhodes needed to know.

He hoped he might find an answer in the school building, so he started at the front, looking in the two offices on either side of the entrance. Both rooms were divided into inner and outer offices. The outer offices were for the gatekeepers, and the inner ones for the principal and the superintendent. Rhodes knew this because faded signs over the doorways told him that a principal named Burkett and a superintendent named Martin had once occupied those offices. That had been a long time ago, and the offices showed no signs of their presence now, or anybody's presence. Bare walls and dusty floors were all Rhodes saw.

After looking in the empty offices, Rhodes went down both hallways and looked in the classrooms, which were all bare. The plaster on the walls was stained brown in spots by water leaks, and the wall in one room was badly cracked in the corner. Rhodes took a look at the crack and saw that it went all the way through the wall.

The next room he looked into had been a chemistry lab. The lab counters were still there, with sinks and gas outlets that Rhodes was sure hadn't worked in generations. The counters were covered in dust that hadn't been disturbed for years.

Rhodes checked out the auditorium next. The theater seats had been removed, and the stage curtain was gone as well. Rhodes saw no sign that anyone had been inside the place recently. Dark gray spiderwebs drooped from the light fixtures high above the floor.

On a hallway behind the auditorium on a lower level about halfway underground was the old cafeteria. There were no tables, but the serving counter was still there, now rusty and useless. Rhodes remembered just how a cafeteria had smelled when he was in school, but there was no odor of burgers or corn dogs or Friday tuna in this one, just the smells of mold and age.

Rhodes left the cafeteria and looked into the restrooms on either side of it. The urinal in the men's room was on the floor, and the stall doors were missing. So were the toilets. In the women's room, the toilets were also gone, and so were the stall walls.

The boiler room was between the men's room and the cafeteria. The huge boiler was still there, rusty and inoperable. Rhodes wondered when it had last been put to use, but he couldn't remember when the school had closed.

Rhodes left the boiler room and went up to the second floor. Along the front hallway were two large rooms, one of which had been the library. Parts of the old bookshelves still lined the walls, but there was nothing else there.

The other room might have been a study hall, and at the far end of it a few wooden desks from another era were stacked up against the wall. Rhodes took a look at the desks, which were so old that they came from a time when boys must still have been allowed to carry pocketknives to school. The tops of the desks that he could see were decorated with carved graffiti. A lopsided heart had A.J. + F.R. inside it, and Rhodes wondered what had happened to the two people with those initials. They might still be alive. Were they married, and if so were they married to each other? He didn't have a clue about that, and the desks had no clues to anything else for him.

The other classrooms on the floor were empty, and while Rhodes didn't find any more cracks that looked on the outdoors, many of the walls had large cracks that ran from the ceiling almost to the floor. It was no wonder that some people believed the building needed to be replaced. It would cost a lot of money to repair it, if it could even be repaired, and money wasn't in large supply in a small town like Thurston, which had a population of around five hundred.

And yet Rhodes could understand why some people wanted to save the building. It was easy to develop a sentimental attachment to something that had meant something to you in the past or that had been an important part of the community, like the old City Hall in Clearview. Mayor Clement didn't want to move out of his office, and he didn't want the building to be torn down. His reasons might not have made sense to everybody, but they seemed sound enough to Rhodes.

The floors of the hallway were dusty, and Rhodes saw what might have been evidence of someone's passing there. Not footprints, more like scuffings in the dust, as if someone might be trying to disguise footprints. Rhodes couldn't be sure.

There was one more room that he needed to look into. It was above the cafeteria, and he entered it from the landing of the staircase leading to the second floor. At one time it had served as the school's gym, and although it was much smaller than a regulation basketball court, it had a hardwood floor and rusty metal basket rims hung from wooden backboards at either end. No traces of the nets remained.

In Rhodes's high school the gym had smelled like sweat and dirty socks, with a tinge of disinfectant thrown into the mix. This one smelled like the rest of the building, moldy, except that the smell was even stronger here. The heat in the room was stifling, and that might have added power to the smell. Narrow windows high along the only outside wall let in light but no air.

To Rhodes's left was the shower room, and as he stood looking around, he heard something from that direction. He didn't think the sound was made by anything human, given that there were no tracks in the dust that covered the gym floor, but he had to check it out. And because he was the cautious sort, he took his Kel-Tec PF9 from his ankle holster. He'd been criticized for carrying his pistol in such a hard-to-reach place, but he didn't like to wear it openly. He'd also been criticized because it was a small, lightweight weapon, but it held seven 9mm cartridges, and Rhodes believed that if he ever met anybody he couldn't handle with that kind of firepower, he probably couldn't do any better even with a .44 Magnum.

The shower area had no door, and Rhodes stopped at one side of it to take a quick look inside. He saw nothing other than a barrier wall placed to conceal the showers. The noises were louder.

Rhodes went to the barrier, walked to the end, and took another quick look. Light came from windows like those in the gym proper and allowed Rhodes to see what was making the noise. Rats, big ones, the size of small kittens. Four of them. They skittered around on the concrete floor, chattering and squealing as if looking for something. Rhodes wondered if they'd come up through the decrepit plumbing or if they'd gotten in some other way. Not that it mattered. If they were looking for a way out or some water to drink, he couldn't blame them. It was so hot in the gym that he felt as if he were being baked like a biscuit. At any rate, he wasn't interested in the rats, and they weren't interested in him. He backed out of the shower area and into the gym, where he stopped and put the pistol back in the ankle holster.

The rats, their stomachs dragging, could have moved the dust in the hallway around, and it was quite possible they'd been out there. Rhodes hoped they didn't make their way down to the body on the first floor before the ambulance came. He didn't think it was likely.

Having looked into all the rooms and found nothing, Rhodes had one more thing to check out. He left the gym and went back up to the second floor, where at the end of the hall a tall window led to the fire escape. He saw a locking mechanism, but it wasn't engaged, so he put his hand on the horizontal rail on top of the lower sash and pushed up. The window went up easily, without a squeak or any sound at all, leaving an opening about four feet high.

Rhodes looked at the windowsill. The dust on it hadn't been disturbed, but someone could step through without touching it. He had to stoop to get through, but he didn't touch the dust, and he stepped outside with no trouble. He stood on the landing of the fire escape and looked around. As hot as the day was, it wasn't as hot as the inside of the building. Rhodes's damp shirt clung to his back, but the faintest of breezes came around the corner and cooled it a bit.

A chinaberry tree grew over part of the landing and up to the top of the building. Rhodes had seen a lot of those trees in his youth, but now they were regarded as an invasive species and no one wanted them around.

The fire escape was rusty with age but still solid. Rhodes pulled the window down until it closed, and started down the iron steps. There were no counterweights, so the steps went right down to a cracked concrete landing that was littered with fallen chinaberries. It would be quite easy for someone to get into the building by way of the fire escape and to get out the same way.

Rhodes searched around the bottom of the fire escape but found nothing but chinaberries, some of which were crushed as if they might have been stepped on. He looked up from the chinaberries and across the lot behind the school and peeled off the nitrile gloves. His hands had never been sweatier. He stuck the gloves in his back pocket.

The lot in back of the school was overgrown with dead weeds, and beyond it were open fields. Rhodes walked around both sides of the building, but he found nothing more of interest. The closest houses on either side were a couple of blocks away. He went back to the front, where he saw an ambulance and a black Ford. The EMTs and the JP had arrived.

Inside the room where the body was, the EMTs, a man and woman that Rhodes didn't know, sat at the table near the front. A gurney stood by the table.

The JP for the precinct and Andy were looking at the body. Rhodes knew the JP, a woman named Kelly Randolph. Once upon a time Rhodes's wife had run for JP, but her being a woman had doomed her chances. Times had changed.

Kelly was tall and slim with short black hair and a narrow face. She turned to look at Rhodes with brown eyes that didn't miss much.

"He's dead, Jim," she said.

Rhodes had never seen *Star Trek*, but he understood the reference.

"You don't know who he is?" Kelly asked.

"Not yet. He called himself Cal Stinson when I met him yesterday, and he told the woman who lives across the street that he was Bruce Wayne. I have a feeling both names are fake."

"Fake, maybe, but imaginative."

"I guess you could say that."

"I did say that, and now my work here is done. It's hot in here, and I'm leaving. I'll certify the death of an unidentified person if you think that's best."

"For now it is," Rhodes said.

Kelly nodded. "Then that's what I'll do. See you later, Sheriff." She looked at Andy. "You, too, deputy."

"Sure," Andy said, but she was already out the door by the time he got it out.

"Find anything?" Rhodes asked him.

"Nothing. If there was anybody in here with him, he didn't leave a trace."

"We can let the EMTs have the body, then," Rhodes said, and motioned for them.

They got up and pushed the gurney forward. Rhodes watched them lift the body and lay it on the gurney.

"Take it to Ballinger's," Rhodes said.

Ballinger's Funeral Home was where the autopsy would be done since Blacklin County was lucky enough to have a retired doctor who was qualified to perform them.

"Will do," the male EMT said as they wheeled the body from the room.

"This just isn't right," Andy said when he and Rhodes were alone. "I learned in the academy that the perp always brings something into the scene and always takes something away. There's just nothing here at all that was brought in, not that I could find. Maybe those

CSI people on TV could find out who he is from that piece of chalk, what with all the tech they have."

"What we can do is check the window leading to the fire escape for fingerprints," Rhodes said. "We have the tech to do that. Check the fire escape, too."

"If that's all we can do, I'll do it," Andy said.

"I might be able to persuade the commissioners to buy us a magnifying glass," Rhodes said.

Andy laughed. "I didn't mean to sound whiny. I'm a little frustrated."

"So am I," Rhodes said, "but we'll find out who killed Bruce Wayne even without any high-tech equipment."

"You don't think he was really named Bruce Wayne, do you?"

"No, but we'll find his real name, too."

"You sound pretty sure."

"You have to believe," Rhodes said.

"You think that helps?" Andy asked.

"Sure," Rhodes said. "Don't you?"

Andy shrugged. "If you say it does, I believe it. Where do we start with this, then?"

"You start by going on patrol," Rhodes said. "I'll start by going back to Clearview and seeing if Hack's dug anything up on Bruce Wayne. Or Cal Stinson, as he called himself yesterday."

"And if that doesn't work?"

"Do I detect disbelief?" Rhodes asked. "That's why you fail."

Rhodes had seen *The Empire Strikes Back* on TV. He preferred older and less well-made movies, like the Italian-made Hercules movies from the fifties. He did, however, make the occasional exception.

"Sorry," Andy said. "I'll try to be more positive."

"Do. Or do not," Rhodes said. "There is no try."

Andy laughed. "I get it. You don't look much like Yoda, though."

"More like Harrison Ford?"

Andy laughed again. "Well, I wouldn't say that, either."

Rhodes didn't ask him what he *would* say. It was time to get back to Clearview and get busy finding out about Cal Stinson.

Chapter 6

Rhodes remembered the number of the county road and the address he'd seen on Kenny Lambert's driver's license, so he thought it might be a good idea to pay Kenny a visit and talk to him about his whereabouts on the previous night. His route took him past Thurston's Methodist church, a few houses, and on out of town as the road turned from blacktop to gravel to dirt. The pastures and fields he passed were uniformly brown, and the few cattle he saw looked hungry and thirsty, although he knew that was just his imagination. Cows looked like cows.

The Lambert house was set back about fifty yards from the road. It was surrounded by elm and hackberry trees, and a little woods stretched out behind it. A barbed-wire fence ran across the front of the property, but there was an opening for vehicles to pass through. Rhodes drove up to the house on a rutted dirt lane and parked the Tahoe on the dead grass of the yard.

The house itself was old and rickety, set up on wooden blocks. It looked as if the Big Bad Wolf could blow it down with only a little bit of huffing and puffing. Puffing alone might have done it if the wolf didn't feel like huffing.

A detached garage sat off to the back on one side of the house. It was, if anything, in worse shape than the house. About half the roof was missing. A rusty old Chevrolet sat inside, and about half the roof appeared to have fallen in on the car. Neither the house nor the garage had seen a paintbrush in decades.

A room air conditioner hung out of a window on the side of the house. It was as rusty as the car and vibrating slightly. Rhodes saw water drip from one corner of it.

Rhodes hadn't asked Hack if Kenny had reclaimed his pickup from the impound lot, but it was nowhere in sight. Maybe Kenny had picked up some other transportation, like a Camry formerly owned by Cal Stinson.

The place looked deserted, but somebody was there or the air conditioner wouldn't be running. Nobody would waste electricity on an empty house.

Rhodes parked and stepped out of the Tahoe. As soon as he did a dog rushed out from under the house. It didn't bark, which Rhodes took to be a bad sign. A barking dog was issuing a warning. One that didn't make a sound was planning an attack. Rhodes should've been expecting the dog. A lot of people who lived in the country had a dog for protection, for companionship, or both, and this wasn't the first encounter of this kind that Rhodes had experienced. Rhodes got back into the Tahoe and shut the door.

The dog was spotted like a leopard dog, but there was something else in the mix, maybe two or three something elses, Doberman or Rottweiler, maybe, and the dog's disposition was decidedly unpleasant. It threw itself against the Tahoe's door, jumping up high enough to slap its head into the window and bare its teeth at Rhodes. The incisors were sharp and looked like thick ivory needles.

A man came out on the porch. He was whippet thin and looked to be somewhere between forty-five and fifty. He had long, unkempt hair, and he held a silver chain with a fabric choke collar dangling from the end.

"Come 'ere, Betsy," the man said.

Betsy either didn't hear him or didn't intend to come there. She jumped against the Tahoe again. Rhodes wouldn't be surprised if she dented the door.

"Betsy!" the man said.

Betsy ignored him. He stepped down from the porch and walked toward the Tahoe. Betsy didn't even look at him. Instead, she leaped up and bared her teeth at Rhodes again.

When she dropped to the ground, the man dropped beside her and slipped the choke collar on as Rhodes watched through the window. The man stood up and pulled the collar tight.

"She's not a bad dog," he said. "Just don't care for strangers coming for an unannounced visit." He looked at the Blacklin County Sheriff's Department logo on the Tahoe door. "She can't read, so she don't know you're the law. I'll get her chained up, and you can get out."

He walked to the porch, and Rhodes saw that there was an iron ring attached to one of the porch's support posts. The man hooked the chain to the ring and turned back around.

"You'll be okay now," he said. "Betsy will behave herself."

Rhodes wasn't convinced, but it wouldn't do for the county sheriff to show fear. He got out of the Tahoe and went to the porch. Betsy waited until he was nearly there before leaping toward him, but the chain caught her short before she reached him. Rhodes was surprised she hadn't pulled the support from underneath the porch roof and brought the whole house down. She stood straining against the chain and baring her teeth.

"Well," the man said, "she usually behaves herself after I get the chain on 'er. She must not like you even a little bit."

"I got that impression," Rhodes said.

"Maybe she just doesn't like lawmen."

"That might take some training," Rhodes said.

The man looked at Betsy. "She ain't had no training of any kind a'tall. She's a good guard dog, and that's what I got her for." The man walked over and sat on the edge of the porch on the opposite side of the steps from where Betsy was chained. "Why're you here, anyhow? I ain't done nothing wrong. Just staying in my house and minding my own business."

"I'm looking for Kenny Lambert," Rhodes said. "Any relation?"

"I'm Curtis Lambert, Kenny's old man. What's he done now?"

"He was arrested yesterday. He tell you about that?"

"You mean that fella that ran him off the road?"

"That's not exactly the whole story," Rhodes said.

Curtis shifted his position on the porch and didn't say anything. Rhodes listened to the air conditioner chugging away on the side of the house. After a few seconds, Curtis dug a package of cigarettes out of the pocket of his faded green shirt. He shook out a cigarette and lit it with a paper match from a folding book that he kept stuck between the cellophane and the pack itself. After he'd taken a puff, he said, "Maybe Kenny didn't tell me the truth. Sometimes he's like that. You want a smoke?"

"No, thanks," Rhodes said.

"I didn't figure you would, just being polite." Curtis stuck the cigarette pack back in his pocket. "You gonna stand out there in the yard, or you want to sit down?"

Rhodes moved over to the side of the porch well away from Betsy and sat down. The porch slanted a bit toward the yard, and Rhodes braced his feet on the ground so he wouldn't slide off.

Curtis blew a smoke ring and said, "Tell me the whole story about Kenny. I'd like to hear your side of it."

Rhodes told him. When he was finished, Curtis said, "Well, that sounds like Kenny, all right. He was prob'ly tweaking. He can handle meth better than most people, but it does tend to make him a little feisty and mouthy when he uses it. He don't do it often."

"He ever do anything worse than get mouthy?" Rhodes asked.

"You mean like gutting somebody out like a deer?" 'Course not. Kenny's not like that even when he's not high."

"Where is Kenny, anyway? I'd like to talk to him."

Curtis took a last drag on his cigarette and crushed it out on the porch before tossing the butt into the yard. Betsy strained to get at it, but the chain was too short.

"What you want to talk to Kenny about?" Curtis asked.

"About the man he ran off the road."

"He pressed any charges?"

"Not yet," Rhodes said, but he didn't add anything about the man's current situation. "There are enough charges against Kenny without him. Is Kenny here?"

"Nope. He went off with some friend of his, Noble Truelove. Ain't that a name for you?"

Rhodes was familiar with the name. If Noble Truelove's parents had hoped his name would give him high ideals, they'd been wrong. Noble had been in and out of the county jail a number of times, never on anything to keep him there very long, but things that showed what kind of person he was, things like petty theft, assault, and DUI.

"A good name, all right," Rhodes said. "I don't see a car. How did Noble Truelove get here?"

"I didn't say he was here. Kenny went off in his truck to get him."

So Kenny had gotten the truck from the impound lot. "When will Kenny be back?"

Curtis laughed. "How the hell would I know? Kenny's a grown man. He comes and goes as he pleases."

"You happen to know where he was last night?"

"He was here for a while. Then him and Noble went off somewhere or other in that old pickup of Kenny's. They don't tell me their plans, and I don't ask. None of my business."

Rhodes thought about that. It was probably true. Curtis didn't seem to care much about his son or what he did. The thought of Noble and Kenny together and at loose ends made Rhodes wonder if they'd driven by the school and seen Stinson's car. They could've parked in back, gone inside by way of the fire escape, and killed him. It was something to think about. Rhodes wasn't sure about Kenny, but he thought Noble was up to the job, and Kenny would be the kind to go along.

"When Kenny comes back," Rhodes said, "have him give me a call."

"I'll do that, Sheriff," Curtis said. "I surely will."

Rhodes knew he didn't mean a word of it, but there was no use to start an argument about it. He slid off the porch and said, "I appreciate you talking to me, Mr. Lambert. Tell Betsy I was pleased to meet her."

"You can tell her yourself," Curtis said.

The dog was lying down now, but she still had her eyes on Rhodes.

"I don't want to upset her," Rhodes said. "I'll just be on my way. Don't forget to have Kenny give me a call."

"I'll remember," Curtis said, but Rhodes knew he'd never get a call. That was all right, though. He'd pay Kenny another visit soon. For now he'd go on back to the jail and see what else was going on in the county.

When he got back to the jail, Rhodes wasn't entirely surprised to see Seepy Benton making himself at home in the chair beside Rhodes's desk.

"Don't bother to get up," Rhodes said to Seepy, who'd started to stand.

"He might need to get up," Hack said. "He's been sittin' in that chair for an hour. I told him you might not be back for a while, but he said he didn't care."

Seepy lowered himself back into the chair and shifted around a bit. When he'd settled himself, he said, "Hack and I have been discussing some famous private investigator cases. The ones from books and movies. I haven't had any famous cases yet."

Rhodes sat at his desk. "Only a matter of time. You'll be like Philip Marlowe."

"Seepy don't look like Bogart," Hack said.

That was true. Seepy looked more like Elisha Cook, Jr., but older and with less hair.

"I'm thinking of buying a trench coat," Seepy said. "Maybe a new fedora."

Seepy's current fedora rested on Rhodes's desk. It was old and well worn, with a couple of unidentifiable grayish stains on the sides.

"That might be a good idea," Rhodes said. "You want to look professional if you're planning to get any clients."

"I already have one," Seepy said. "A good one."

Rhodes had a feeling he knew who the client was.

"That's why I came by," Seepy said. "To thank you for recommending me to the mayor. I'm not teaching summer school, and I can devote all my time to his case, not that it's going to take me that long."

Rhodes thought about telling Seepy that he didn't exactly recommend him, but he thought he might as well not disillusion him.

"Of course it looks tricky," Seepy said, "but I have a big brain—"

"—and you're not afraid to use it," Rhodes said. "I know."

"I may have told you that before."

"Several times," Rhodes said.

"Well, that doesn't make it any less true. You know what the mayor wants me to do, don't you?"

"He wants you to find out who's running *Digging that Blacklin County Dirt*. It doesn't seem like a very hard job for a computer whiz like you. You just trace the internet address of the blog to its owner."

"That would be easy, all right," Seepy said. "If they were using their internet address. I took a look. They're going through a VPN."

Rhodes decided he wouldn't ask what a VPN was. He said, "By 'they' you mean Patrick Henry and Thomas Paine."

"Not their real names," Seepy said, "but you must have guessed that."

"I have a big brain," Rhodes said, "and I'm not afraid to use it."

Seepy laughed. "Good. Now let's talk about VPNs and what they do."

Rhodes took a wild guess. "They hide your internet address."

"I'll be danged," Hack said. "I'd've bet you didn't know that."

"I have a big brain," Rhodes said, not showing his own surprise, "and—"

"Never mind that stuff," Hack said. "It's gettin' old already."

"It's not quite that simple," Seepy said, "but by going through a VPN, somebody in Texas can appear to be working on the internet in Turkey or Turkmenistan or anywhere else in the world. Very hard to trace."

"You can do it, though," Rhodes said. "Mayor Clement is counting on you."

Seepy picked up his fedora. "I might be able to do it if Tom and Patrick are using a cheap VPN. If they're paying for a more expensive one, it's going to be tough."

"I heard about those private eyes who like to drag out a case to get more money," Hack said. "Philip Marlowe would never do that."

"I wouldn't, either," Seepy said. He settled his hat on his head, covering up the bald part. "I have a code of ethics. All us private eyes have a code of ethics. My code is my own, and I never talk about it. If you talk about it too much, you lose it."

Rhodes wasn't sure that made any sense, but he wasn't going to argue the point.

"Besides," Seepy said, "I'm giving the mayor my bargain rate. All us private eyes have a bargain rate for certain clients."

"I'll remember that if I ever need a peeper," Hack said.

"Shamus is better," Seepy said. "Peeper is derogatory."

"I'll keep that in mind," Hack said. "I don't want to hurt your feelings."

Seepy stood up. "I have to get to work, but I did want to come by and thank you for the recommendation. I'll break the case as soon as I can, and the mayor will be happy with both of us."

"He won't be happy with Tom and Patrick," Rhodes said. "You'll be invading their privacy."

"That's if he can find 'em," Hack said.

"I can find them," Seepy said.

"I've heard of private eyes who'd hold that over them for blackmail," Hack said.

"It's blackmail only if I ask them for money or something else," Seepy said. "My code won't let me do that."

"You ever been tested yet?" Hack asked.

Seepy shook his head. "This is my first big case, but my code is solid."

"Hack's just messing with you," Rhodes said. "Don't let him bother you."

"I wouldn't mess with anybody," Hack said, a blatant lie, as Rhodes knew all too well.

"I'm not easy to bother," Seepy said. "See you later."

He went out of the jail, and Rhodes turned to his desk.

"Well?" Hack said.

"Well, what?" Rhodes asked.

"You gonna tell me or not?"

"Tell you what?"

"You know what."

Rhodes did know, but it was his turn to mess with somebody now. It wasn't an opportunity that came around often.

"No," he said. "I don't know what. You'd better tell me."

Hack shot him an accusing look. "You do too know."

"Nope," Rhodes said. "Don't know. You'll have to tell me what you want to know."

Hack grumbled under his breath, but he finally said, "Who the heck was the dead man in Thurston?"

Rhodes grinned. "Bruce Wayne," he said.

Chapter 7

Hack's face got a bit red when he heard Rhodes's answer. "No call for you to be a smart aleck with me."

"I'm not being a smart aleck," Rhodes told him. "That's the name he gave Wanda Wilkins. She's the one who found the body."

"I know who found the body," Hack said. "I'm the one who took the call. She didn't tell me anything about some character named Bruce Wayne."

Lawton walked in from the cellblock at that point and said, "Bruce Wayne's the Batman."

"I know that," Hack said. "Don't you think I know who the Batman is?"

"Bet you don't know what Robin's name was," Lawton said.

"Burt Ward."

"Nope, that was just the guy who played him on TV."

"Robin was Bruce Wayne's ward, right?" Hack said.

"Yeah."

"So you're telling me that the ward was played by a Ward?"

"I guess I am."

"So I was right," Hack said.

"Nope. Bruce Wayne's ward was Dick Grayson."

"So the ward wasn't really Ward?"

Rhodes had sat in on a few surreal conversations between Hack and Lawton, but this one was reaching new heights. Before long they'd be asking who was on first base.

"Yeah," Lawton said. "Ward was really the ward, but only on TV. In real life—"

"There ain't no Batman in real life," Hack said.

Lawton frowned. "What I meant was—"

Luckily for all concerned, Lawton was interrupted at that point in the conversation when Jennifer Loam walked in. She was short, blond, and about as smart as anyone in the county. Seepy Benton would put himself at the top of the list, but Rhodes thought that even Seepy would have to put Jennifer at number two.

"I hope I'm not breaking up anything important," she said.

"It was an intellectual discussion," Rhodes said.

"What was it about?"

"Never mind," Rhodes said. He didn't want to get Hack and Lawton started again. "I was just about to tell these two about the dead man down in Thurston."

"Then I'll sit down and listen if you don't mind," Jennifer said. "That's what I came here to find out about."

"He wasn't really gonna tell us," Hack said. "He was messing with me."

Jennifer sat in the chair near Rhodes's desk. "I can't imagine the sheriff doing a thing like that. You must be mistaken."

"Hah," Hack said.

“Do you want to hear about it or not?” Rhodes asked.

“Go ahead,” Hack said.

Rhodes went through the story, and when he was finished, Jennifer said, “So the dead man gave you two different names, and you think neither one was correct?”

“That’s right,” Rhodes said. “He’ll be fingerprinted before the autopsy, and we’ll run the prints through the usual databases. Maybe that will help us.”

“Not if he ain’t in the database,” Hack said. “I’m guessin’ he won’t be.”

Hack was probably right, but they had to try everything.

“And you think he was in Thurston to look at the old school building?”

“That’s what he said, anyway,” Rhodes told her. “His story was that his grandmother went to school there and he wanted to look the old place over.”

“There’s a lot of controversy about the demolition of that building,” Jennifer said. “I’ve written about it several times.”

Rhodes knew she had, and he’d even glanced at her articles, but he didn’t remember much about them.

“I saw the building,” he said. “It’s a mess. The repairs would cost more money than the town has available.”

“Some people think the money could be raised if people made the effort.”

“Who thinks that?”

“The Hunleys, to start with,” Jennifer said. “I’m sure you know the Hunleys.”

“Not well,” Rhodes said, “but everybody knows about the Hunleys.”

The Hunleys were a military family, going back a long way, to the Civil War at least, or so Rhodes had heard. Asa Hunley had been a soldier in WWII and had won a number of medals. Asa's son, Con, had won his medals in Vietnam, and Con's son, Pete, had distinguished himself in the first Gulf War. Pete didn't have any children. Asa and Con had both attended school in Thurston, but after that the school had consolidated with Clearview, which is where Pete had graduated.

"They're about as famous as anybody who graduated from Thurston High School," Hack said. "The three of 'em earned enough medals to sink a ship."

"Maybe their name recognition would be good enough to get a finance campaign going," Rhodes said, "but they'd still need a lot of help. People with money."

"The Falkners live down that way," Lawton said. "Leslie and Faye. They got money."

Rhodes knew that was true, although nobody was really sure how the family had gotten rich. One somewhat plausible rumor had it that some obscure relative had started a successful fast-food chain in California and sold out for a fortune. When he died, he left all his money to the Thurston branch of the family because he had no other relatives.

"The Falkners won't be helping the Hunleys," Jennifer said. "They want the school torn down and a new community center in its place. Various other families are lined up on one side or the other, but those two are the leaders."

Rhodes had a few more questions to ask about the school controversy, but the phone rang and Hack listened to some excited caller for a minute before hanging up and turning to Rhodes.

"Somebody says shots're being fired out on the way to Milsby, County Road 164. Take a left off the main road about half a mile. You better get out there, and I'll send Ruth for backup."

"I'm on my way," Rhodes said.

• • •

Rhodes was out of the jail, into the Tahoe, and on the road quickly, but Jennifer Loam was almost as quick. Rhodes saw her little car in his rearview mirror, and he supposed that she was actually quicker than he was but was just being polite by not zipping out ahead of him. He'd thought about telling her not to come, but he knew that wouldn't have worked. She'd have started in lecturing him about the freedom of the press and taking valuable time. So he'd kept his mouth shut, knowing that she'd be right there with her phone camera, getting all the shots she could. He might have considered telling her to be careful, but that would have been just more wasted breath, and it would've insulted her besides. Rhodes might not have learned much over his lifetime, but he did know that many times it paid for him to keep his mouth shut.

Milsby had once been a town but there was hardly any sign of it left, only the ruins of an old school building and a few deserted houses. People still lived all around along the country roads, but there was no town and hadn't been for years. County Road 164 was white gravel and dirt, and when Rhodes turned onto it the Tahoe's wheels threw up a cloud of dust. He hadn't driven more than a hundred yards when he heard a couple of gunshots.

He drove on for about half a mile, and when he crested a small hill he saw immediately what the situation was. An old unpainted house sat back among some trees, and parked about thirty yards in front of it was a rusted out Chevy pickup that looked familiar to Rhodes. Two men crouched down beside the pickup, using it for cover. Rhodes thought he knew where Noble Truelove and Kenny Lambert had gone.

Rhodes pulled onto the rutted path leading to the house and drove forward just far enough to block the exit. He unlocked the shotgun from the rack beside him. It was loaded with alternating shotgun shells and rifled slugs, which had considerably more range than the shotgun shells. Rhodes could hit a target at a hundred yards with one of the slugs.

He got out of the Tahoe, went around to the rear, opened the tailgate and got out his bulletproof vest. By the time he got the vest on, Jennifer Loam was parked behind him.

Rhodes didn't say a word to her. Telling her to stay in her car wouldn't make a bit of difference. She'd do what she wanted to do. Rhodes shut the tailgate and jogged up the road as a couple of bullets from the house slammed into the Chevy pickup.

Noble and Kenny saw him coming, but they didn't wave in greeting. They just sat there with their backs to the pickup as if they were innocent bystanders who'd just happened onto the scene. Rhodes reached the pickup and dropped down beside them.

"Hey, Sheriff," Kenny said. "You come to save us?"

"Maybe," Rhodes said. "What would I be saving you from?"

"The bad guys," Kenny said. "Ain't that right, Noble."

"Sure is," Noble said. He was shorter than Kenny but wider, with close-set eyes. "We were just driving along, looking at the country the way a fella likes to do now and then, and those guys opened up on us."

"How do you know they're guys?"

"Just guessing," Noble said.

"Anyway, we naturally had to defend ourselves as best we could," Kenny said. "You can see that."

Kenny held a .25 automatic that looked even cheaper and less impressive than his imitation Glock. As far as Rhodes could tell, Kenny's trigger finger was no longer swollen.

Noble had what looked like Kenny's pistol's twin. Two Saturday Night Specials if Rhodes had ever seen them, practically useless for the current situation. Not that either Noble or Kenny seemed bothered by that.

"This is a funny place to be sightseeing," Rhodes said.

"Yeah," Noble agreed, "but we saw that old house and thought we'd look it over. Sometimes you can find good stuff in old deserted houses."

Rhodes had to give Noble credit for an explanation that sounded almost plausible. Almost.

"You'd better give me those pistols," he said.

"We got permits," Kenny said. "We got a right to defend ourselves."

"I'm in charge of the defense now," Rhodes said. "Hand them over."

Kenny looked disgusted, but he handed his pistol to Rhodes, who slipped it in his back pocket.

"You, too, Noble," Rhodes said.

Noble looked at Kenny, who shrugged. Noble handed Rhodes the pistol, and Rhodes stuck it in his belt at the back of his pants.

"When you decided to look in the house," Rhodes said, "you had no idea anybody was inside?"

"That's right," Kenny said. "We just got outta my truck and they started shooting."

Rhodes saw Ruth Grady's squad car pull off the road into the drainage ditch. She got out after arming herself. She got her Kevlar vest from the trunk and put it on before running past Jennifer and up the road to join Rhodes and his new best friends.

Nobody had shot at Rhodes, and nobody shot at Ruth. Whoever was in the house didn't want to get any deeper in trouble than they already were, or so Rhodes thought.

"What's going on?" Ruth asked.

"These two were just sightseeing," Rhodes said, "and the people in the house started shooting at them."

Ruth shook her head. "My, my. People shooting at innocent sightseers. What's the world coming to?"

"Sad, ain't it?" Kenny said.

"You bet it is," Noble said.

Rhodes stood partway up so that only his head showed over the side of the pickup.

"Hello, the house!" he yelled. When he got no response, he said, "This is Sheriff Dan Rhodes. I'm going to come up there and have a little talk with you. My deputy will stay here and make sure nobody does any shooting."

Still no response, which seemed a bit suspicious. Rhodes stood all the way up, and sure enough he heard a car start in back of the house.

"Stay with these two," Rhodes told Ruth, "cuff them."

He ran down to the Tahoe, got in, secured the shotgun, and took off, hoping that he wasn't too far behind whoever had been doing the shooting from the house.

He reached the house and saw a black pickup bouncing across the field behind it. Rhodes went right after it, the Tahoe rocking from side to side like a carnival ride. Rhodes hung on to the wheel and hoped he didn't run into a hole in the ground, or at least not a deep one.

The pickup turned left, and Rhodes followed. It appeared to be headed for a little woods, but Rhodes thought it would have to make another turn. The trees were too big and too thick for the pickup to get through them safely.

He was right. At the edge of the woods, the pickup turned left again and headed toward the road. There was no way out of the field except through a barbed-wire fence and across the drainage ditch that ran along the road. The pickup could break through the fence, but Rhodes didn't think it could jump the ditch, which Rhodes figured was about twenty feet wide. Maybe one chance in a hundred, if that.

The pickup driver didn't seem to care, or maybe he wasn't thinking straight. Desperation might have entered into it. People who were desperate to escape the law didn't always think clearly.

The pickup gained speed, and maybe it could've jumped the ditch, after all, if only the wire had parted quickly. Being old and rusty, maybe it should have, but it didn't. Only one strand did, and the other three held, which resulted in staples popping from old fence posts, some of which cracked and broke with sounds almost like gunshots. The wire finally gave way, but the truck had slowed, and it didn't clear the ditch.

The front bumper hit the side of the ditch near the road, and the rear of the truck raised up into the air like the hind legs of a bucking bronco. The rear of the truck end hit the near side of the ditch with the rear wheels still spinning, and the air bags went off.

Rhodes stopped the Tahoe and watched as the rear wheels spun. Nobody moved in the pickup, so he unlatched the shotgun and got out. As he did, two people jumped from the pickup and started running down the road in the direction away from the house. Rhodes recognized both of them. They were Ben and Glen, the black-sheep sons of the Whiteside family. Their parents were teachers, and they had an older sister who was a dean at a community college on the Gulf Coast. Their older brother was a CPA with a firm in Dallas. Ben and Glen had decided, however, that their talents lay in not conforming to society's demands about jobs and family, so they'd become modern-day outlaws, a step or two above Kenny and Noble.

They were always in trouble, about to get in trouble, or just getting out of trouble.

Rhodes aimed over their heads and fired the shotgun. The first shell was double-ought buck, and Ben and Glen were already too far away for it to bother them even if it hit them, but he wanted to let them know he was back there. He figured they'd stop and wait for him.

They did. They'd tangled with Rhodes so many times that they knew when to give up, which was most of the time. They stood at the side of the road, and when Rhodes was within ten yards of them he said, "Time to take a little ride to town and visit your second home."

The two men, both in their early twenties, were dusted with fine white powder from the pickup's air bags. They didn't look much like brothers. Ben was at least a couple of inches taller than Glen, and Glen was heavyset, whereas Ben was almost scrawny. Both had the same gray eyes and thick black hair, though, with thin-lipped mouths that never smiled. Ben wore a T-shirt that said "Vote for Pedro" on the front. Glen's black T-shirt had no slogan. The arms of both men were heavily tattooed. Rhodes wondered if they'd had the work done at Mink's Ink, but he didn't ask.

"We ain't got no first home," Ben said.

That was true. Their parents had given up on them years ago and kicked them out. The two lived wherever they could, in cheap rentals when they had the money and in the woods or abandoned houses when they didn't.

"You been living out here?" Rhodes asked.

Neither man had an answer for him, but Rhodes didn't mind. He said, "We'll be going now. You two can just walk on past me. We'll stop at your pickup and turn it off, and I'll have a look at it just to see what I can see."

Ben and Glen had nothing to say to that, either. They didn't like talking to the law, and Rhodes understood why. As many times as they'd been in trouble, keeping their mouths shut was their best course of action. So Rhodes cuffed them and they walked silently down the road.

Chapter 8

The pickup engine had died by the time they got to the spot where the truck nearly spanned the ditch, so Rhodes didn't have to turn it off. He decided to ask the two prisoners a few questions.

"What happened with Kenny and Noble? They told me they were sightseeing and you started shooting at them."

Glen decided to answer. He said, "Sightseeing? That's a good one. They came driving up to the house and pulled those little worthless guns on us. Started shooting, so we shot back."

"You chased them away?"

"Not far," Ben said. "They got nerve. That's all they got, though. Those are sorry little guns they have. I bet both of 'em are jammed."

"Let's walk on down there and see," Rhodes said. "You have guns in the pickup?"

"In the cab," Ben said.

"Good to know," Rhodes said. "Let's move along now."

When they got back to where Ruth was holding Kenny and

Noble, Jennifer Loam was gone. Rhodes thought that was just fine, but he worried about what she might post on *A Clear View for Clearview.* It would be positive, of course, but it might be *too* positive.

Rhodes decided not to worry about it. He said to Ruth, "You keep an eye on these two while I call Hack."

"My pleasure," Ruth said. "You gentlemen have a seat on the ground here. Not too close to Kenny and Noble, though. I don't want any pushing and shoving or anybody saying 'he's touching me.'"

Ben and Glen did as she said, sitting with their backs to the pickup as far from Kenny and Noble as they could get.

"No talking, either," Ruth said. "I like peace and quiet."

Nobody said a word.

Rhodes got Hack on the radio and asked him where Buddy was patrolling.

"Out east. You need him?"

"Yeah. Tell him to get out here as soon as he can."

"You know how he is," Hack said. "He'll speed."

Rhodes grinned. "I wouldn't be surprised."

Buddy arrived about fifteen minutes later, siren wailing, driving much too fast on the unpaved road. He would've been driving too fast even if he'd been on a paved road. He stopped the Charger behind Ruth's car and jumped out, eager for action. He carried a .357 revolver that was nearly as big as he was, not quite Dirty Harry's weapon, but close. It was his lifelong dream to ask some punk if he felt lucky. So far, however, he'd never shot anyone or even come close to it.

"What's the deal here, Sheriff," Buddy asked. He looked at the four men sitting on the ground. "Looks like you've rounded up the usual suspects. Want me to interrogate 'em?"

"Nope," Rhodes said. "I want you to take a couple of them to the jail, advise them of their rights, and get them booked. I think Ben and Noble would be the ones to ride with you. Ruth can take Glen and Kenny. That way there won't be any unnecessary discussion."

"Okay," Buddy said. "Ben, you and Noble stand up now and come with me. Don't make me have to come get you."

The two men struggled to their feet, and Buddy led them to his county car. After he'd settled them in the backseat, he said to Rhodes, "You want me to go back on patrol when they're booked? I could stay around and give 'em the third degree if you want me to."

"I'll take care of that myself," Rhodes said, and Buddy left.

Ruth loaded up Glen and Kenny and followed him, and Rhodes stayed around to look over the house and the pickups. He didn't find anything of interest in Kenny's pickup, although maybe he'd been hoping to find the keys to a Toyota or something else to connect Kenny and Noble to the death of the man in the schoolhouse. He could easily imagine them driving aimlessly around, spotting the car, and going into the building with their cheap small-caliber automatics. It was harder for him to imagine them killing anyone, but he'd learned enough about human nature to know that something like that was entirely possible.

The inside of the house was just about what he'd expected. The heat radiated downward from the rusty tin roof, and he felt as if he were baking in an oven. The place had the peculiar odor of old houses, overlaid with the smell of fast food. Ben and Glen had been living there for a while, sleeping on an old mattress on the floor. Greasy fast-food wrappers and Styrofoam containers were strewn all around. Housekeeping wasn't one of Ben and Glen's virtues. In fact, Rhodes wasn't sure they had any virtues worth mentioning.

It took him a while to find what he thought he might. It was hidden under the floor, and he had to move the mattress to discover the prised up floorboard and the black garbage bag stashed under the floor. Ben and Glen had been selling a little marijuana, it seemed. Rhodes figured that Kenny and Noble either wanted free weed or planned on taking it all and setting up their own operation. That was about how their thinking would go.

Rhodes knew that Ben and Glen would say they had no idea that the marijuana was there, that it most certainly wasn't theirs, and that they'd never seen it before. If there were fingerprints on the bags, he could prove them wrong, but they might've been smart enough to wear gloves when handling things.

Rhodes marked the bags as evidence, put them in the Tahoe, and went on to search Ben and Glen's pickup. As they'd told him, there were guns in the cab, a .30-.30 rifle and a genuine Glock niner. Kenny and Noble, whether they'd known it or not, had been severely outgunned. They were lucky Rhodes had come along before they got themselves shot up. Ben and Glen were lucky, too, because they might have killed the other two or at least wounded them badly, and even if they'd done it by accident, it would've gone hard with them.

Rhodes put the guns into the Tahoe and called Hack to tell him to get the trucks towed and put in the county impound lot.

"Won't be there long," Hack said. "Those fellas Ruth and Buddy brought in will be out of here before you know it."

"Not before I have a little talk with them," Rhodes said.

"Wanna bet?" Hack asked.

Rhodes didn't want to bet. "I'll be back in twenty minutes."

"Might not be quick enough."

"We'll see," Rhodes said.

Rhodes should've bet. The prisoners were still there, as their lawyer wasn't available at the moment. Rhodes wasn't sure anybody would talk to him without a lawyer present, but it turned out that Kenny would.

The interview room wasn't a pleasant place, just an old scarred table and a couple of chairs, one on each side of the table. Rhodes sat in one and Kenny in the other.

Things went about as Rhodes had thought they would. Kenny didn't know a thing about the school building in Thurston. He and Noble had gone out for "a few beers" the previous night but hadn't been in Thurston at all. Rhodes wasn't sure he believed that, but he let it pass.

Kenny also repeated the story that he and Noble had just been out sightseeing when the Whitesides began firing on them.

"I tell you, Sheriff," Kenny said, "it was bad. Here me and Noble are, just taking it easy, driving along a country road like people do, and somebody starts shooting at us. We had to defend ourselves. You can see that, can't you?"

"I have a feeling that Ben and Glen didn't see it that way," Rhodes said.

Kenny gave his head a shake. "Yeah, maybe not, but you know those two. They're liars and the truth's not in 'em."

"Unlike you and Noble."

"You got it. The two of us don't like to lie, 'specially to the law."

Rhodes nodded, admiring Kenny's ability at tale telling. If he'd gone into politics before he went bad, he'd probably be at least a state senator by now. Not that it was too late for a dramatic reformation and reinvention of himself. It would never happen, though. Kenny didn't have the drive for it.

"If you're so worried about that old schoolhouse," Kenny said, interrupting Rhodes's thoughts, "you oughta talk to the people who care about an old dump like that. And that don't include me or Noble. They can tear that place right down to the ground and drive a 'dozer over it, and it won't bother us even a little bit."

He had a point there, not so much about himself and Noble but about other people living in Thurston who were taking sides in the fate of the schoolhouse. Rhodes would have to go back to Thurston and start poking around there. He wasn't going to get anywhere with Kenny, Noble, Ben, and Glen when it came to the murder, and the murder was what really mattered. He sent Kenny back to his cell to wait for his lawyer and went out to do his paperwork, although it wasn't really on paper anymore.

Rhodes had just gotten settled at the computer when Seepy Benton came in.

"Case closed," Seepy said, sitting in the chair beside Rhodes's desk.

"Already?" Rhodes said. "That was quick. I thought it would be harder to trace a VPN."

"I didn't have to trace it," Seepy said. Removing his fedora, he crossed his legs and set the hat on his knee.

Rhodes waited, but Seepy didn't say anything else. It was like talking to Hack or Lawton or just about anybody else in the county. Everybody seemed to get pleasure out of making Rhodes drag information out of them.

"So what did you do?" Rhodes asked after a couple of seconds.

"Advertising," Seepy said.

"You advertised for the culprits to give themselves up?"

Seepy laughed. "I didn't think of that. I thought about the advertising on the site. Not a lot of people want to advertise on a site like that, but it has a few ads from local people. So who solicits the ads?"

"I'm getting old and slow," Rhodes said. "I didn't think of that."

Seepy gave him a pitying look. "You can't think of everything. Anyway, I checked with a couple of the advertisers, pretending that I might like an ad on the site for my new business. I found out that they didn't initiate the contact. They were all solicited by email. The ones who decided to risk an ad were told to send payment to an online payment collection service."

"You're not going to tell me you hacked the payment service."

"No, I'm not going to tell you that, but to do business that way, you have to use an email address. Maybe I can't track down somebody using a VPN, not very quickly, anyway, but I can track down an email user. Want me to tell you how?"

Rhodes shook his head. "Even if you did, I wouldn't understand it, would I?"

Seepy didn't bother to hide the slightly condescending tone in his voice. "Probably not. It doesn't matter, though. What I'd like to do is verify that the person with that email address is the one who's running the website the mayor's worried about. You want to go with me?"

Rhodes wasn't sure what Seepy was trying to get him into. "I'm not involved in this mess. It's between you and the mayor. Besides, I don't want to intimidate anybody into thinking he might have to stop doing a blog."

"It wouldn't be like that."

"Yes it would."

"Let me put it another way," Seepy said. "I'm a little worried about doing this. What if I get myself into a situation that I can't get out of? You'd feel guilty if anything happened to me."

Rhodes sat silently.

After a few seconds Seepy said, "Well?"

"I'm thinking it over."

"It would be a big favor to me."

Rhodes thought some more, then said, "All right, I'll do it, but you'll have to do most of the talking."

Seepy smiled and picked up his hat. He set it on his head and said, "I'm good at that."

Rhodes drove the Tahoe and followed Seepy to one of Clearview's older residential areas. In some places in town, the older houses had been allowed to age ungracefully, but in the part where Seepy led Rhodes, most of the houses had been repaired and freshened over the years. The asphalt of the street was cracked, and the lawns were all dead because of the dry, hot summer with dirt showing through in places, but the houses themselves gleamed with neat siding or clean bricks. Colorful swing sets stood beside wading pools, although no children were in evidence. It was too hot for them, or for anybody, to be outside.

Seepy parked his car at the curb in front of a house on a corner. The house was surrounded by a chain-link fence and was hard to see because of several very old trees that hid most of it from the street. Rhodes stopped the Tahoe behind Seepy's car, got out, and was immediately wrapped in the oppressive heat. The air was so still that not a leaf moved on any of the trees.

"This is the place," Seepy said.

"I'm a trained cop," Rhodes said. "I figured it out for myself."

Seepy went to the gate in the fence. It opened easily with just a little squeak.

"Did you ever think there might be a dog in there?" Rhodes asked.

Seepy closed the gate. "I don't see a 'Beware of the Dog' sign."

"That doesn't mean much," Rhodes said.

"You go first, then," Seepy said.

Rhodes didn't mind. He didn't think there was a dog. He'd just wanted to give Seepy a little jolt.

From the gate a cracked sidewalk led to the front door of the house. Rhodes had to bend down to avoid tree branches that overhung the walk.

"Are you back there?" he asked Seepy without turning around.

"I'm here," Seepy said. "Any sign of a dog?"

Rhodes saw a carport to the right of the house. A gray Chevy Cruze several years old sat inside it, but Rhodes didn't see any dogs.

"No dogs," he said, walking up to the front door of the house. The sidewalk led directly to the door. There was no porch.

Rhodes figured that since he was in the lead, he might as well knock. He tapped the door frame a couple of times and waited. He heard a noise in the house and noticed that there was a peephole in the door. It was always possible that whoever was inside would take a look and keep the door closed. It wouldn't be an unreasonable thing to do.

To Rhodes's surprise, however, the door opened almost at once. A young man looked at Rhodes and said, "Sheriff, I'm glad you're here. Come on in. I need to talk to you."

Chapter 9

Rhodes got over his surprise and went inside the house. The interior was dark and cool after the oppressive heat of the early afternoon. He followed the man along a narrow hallway and into an old-fashioned living room, filled with what looked like furniture from the nineteen fifties, an upholstered couch, a couple of squarish low-backed chairs, and a low coffee table, above which a ceiling fan turned slowly. A writing desk sat up against one wall. A floor lamp stood beside the desk.

The man stopped near the coffee table and said, "Have a seat, Sheriff. Your deputy, too."

Rhodes looked around. Seepy had followed right along, and he'd respectfully removed his fedora.

"He's not exactly my deputy," Rhodes said.

"Well, that's okay, whoever he is. Please. Sit down. Can I get you something to drink? I have some Diet Dr Pepper."

Rhodes didn't drink diet drinks, although a genuine Dr Pepper would have tasted just fine.

"No, thanks. What about you, Seepy?"

"No, thanks. Water would be good, though."

"I'd take some of that," Rhodes said.

"Great," the man said. "I'll be right back."

As he left the room, Seepy sat in one of the chairs and put his fedora on the floor beside him. Rhodes sat in the other chair. It wasn't what he'd call comfortable.

"Who is that man?" Seepy asked. "And why is he so glad to see us?"

"It's me he's glad to see," Rhodes pointed out.

"Okay, I grant you that. Why is he so glad to see you?"

"I have no idea," Rhodes said.

They sat quietly until the man came back into the room. He carried a glass tray with a pitcher of ice water and three glasses on it. He set the tray on the coffee table and poured a glass of water.

"Don't get up," he said, handing the glass to Rhodes, who took it and drank. The cold water felt good as it slid down his throat.

Seepy took his glass, and then the man poured a glass for himself before sitting on the couch. Rhodes looked the man over. He was fairly young, under forty, and had black hair that he wore in a buzz cut. In spite of the dark hair, he was clean-shaven with no trace of a shadow on his cheeks. He wore a short-sleeved white shirt, jeans, and a pair of some kind of running shoes. Rhodes wasn't good on brand recognition.

"I'm Roger Prentiss," the man said after taking a sip of his water. "I know you're Sheriff Rhodes, but I don't know your . . . associate."

"That's Dr. C. P. Benton," Rhodes said. "He teaches math at the community college. He's helped me out a time or two."

If Seepy wanted to mention his private-eyeness, that was up to him. Rhodes wasn't going to bring it up.

"Pleased to meet you, Dr. Benton," Roger said.

"I'm glad to meet you, too," Seepy said.

"Are you any relation to Howard Prentiss?" Rhodes asked Roger.

Roger smiled. "I'm not surprised that you remember him. He was everybody's friend, never met a stranger, and I'm related to him, all right. He was my dad. I grew up here when he was working at the Ford dealership. We moved away not long after I went to college, and I never came back here until a couple of years ago when I bought this house and moved in. I was living in Dallas, and the big city didn't suit me. I always liked it here in Clearview, though. The small-town life was what I wanted, and I can live anywhere, doing the kind of work I do."

"So you came back to dig the old Blacklin County dirt?" Seepy said.

Roger set his glass back on the tray with a click and looked at Seepy. Seepy looked back. Rhodes stood up and took his own glass over to the tray and set it down, then went back to his chair. Seepy did the same. Roger just watched them.

"Well?" Seepy said after a few more seconds had passed.

"How did you find out about me?" Roger asked.

"I'm a private detective," Seepy said. "I have a big brain—"

"And he's not afraid to use it," Rhodes said, "but that's not why I'm here."

"It's not?" Roger said.

"That's why *I'm* here," Seepy said. "I just wanted to confirm that the blog was yours. I guess I've done that."

"It's not mine, exactly," Roger said. "If you're not here about the blog, Sheriff, what are you here for?"

"Why don't you tell me why you wanted to see me," Rhodes said. "Then we'll talk about why I'm here."

"It has to do with the blog in a way," Roger said. "I think."

Here we go again, Rhodes thought. "Just tell us, and then we'll see."

"It's my friend," Roger said. "Lawrence Gates. Not Larry. He hated that nickname. He was always Lawrence."

"I don't know him," Rhodes said.

"He's not from here," Roger said. "He was my college roommate, and I lost touch with him over the years. Then we connected on Facebook a couple of years ago, and one thing led to another."

"What things are we talking about?" Rhodes asked.

"The blog," Roger told him. "It wasn't my idea. It was Lawrence's."

"What would be his interest?" Seepy asked. "You said he wasn't from around here, after all."

"He just seemed to think it would be fun, or that's what he said. We'd gotten along well in college, and he said we'd be good housemates. I didn't argue with him. I have a little inheritance, and I make a little money doing freelance writing for some websites, but I thought having some help with the mortgage payment wouldn't hurt. So Lawrence moved in and started the blog. It's not the only thing he does. He writes for internet sites, too. Military history. He knows more about things like the Roman wars with Persia or the Battle for The Hague than just about anybody."

"You said he wasn't from around here," Rhodes said. "Nobody who wasn't from here could find out some of the local things he wrote about."

"We just read the local paper and that other Clearview blog. You know the one?"

"*A Clear View for Clearview*," Rhodes said.

Roger nodded. "That's it. We'd start there, and sometimes we'd come up with original stories. Lawrence would go out and talk to people casually and get information. Nobody knew who he was, but they'd talk to him for some reason. That's the kind of guy he is, like my dad. Never met a stranger. Anyway, we picked up on things that seemed controversial, or Lawrence did, mostly, and we ran with them. I looked at it as sort of a public service. We were gadflies, maybe a little annoying but doing something good by calling attention to things that didn't get any attention elsewhere."

"Calling the mayor a nincompoop is being a gadfly?" Seepy said.

Roger laughed. "Okay, sometimes we might've gone a little too far, but that was just clickbait stuff. We never meant to hurt anybody. At least I didn't. Lately I haven't been too sure about Lawrence."

Rhodes had wondered if Roger would ever get to the point. Now he seemed to be approaching it.

"You mean he's gotten more vitriolic?" Seepy said.

"Not so much that," Roger said. "It's more like he's obsessed with a certain issue, and won't let go of it."

"What issue is that?" Rhodes asked.

"The Thurston school. You said you didn't know Lawrence, but you did meet him, just yesterday. He was going to Thurston to do some looking around, and he had a run-in with some crazy road rager who threatened to kill him. Then you came along."

Rhodes felt a chill on the back of his neck. "I just happened to be passing by."

"Lucky for Lawrence that you were. He was really embarrassed about having to come home and change clothes before he could go back to Thurston. Lawrence has been talking about that place a lot and not anything else. It's nearly all he talks about. We haven't had a really new story in a good while because I've been busy with my own writing. I got the feeling that there was more to the school story than Lawrence was telling me. It's just an old building, after all."

"Not to some people," Rhodes said.

"Maybe not," Roger agreed, "but that's not the real problem I needed to see you about."

Rhodes had a sad feeling he knew what the real problem was, but he asked anyway.

"Lawrence has disappeared," Roger said. "He was going to Thurston yesterday, he said. You know about that. The thing is, he never came back. That's why I wanted to see you. I thought maybe you were here to tell me something about Lawrence. I was afraid that redneck he had the confrontation with might have done something to him."

Rhodes said, "What kind of car did Lawrence drive?"

Roger stiffened. "He has a gray Camry. Has he been in an accident?"

"No," Rhodes said. "Not an accident. Describe him for me."

Roger described someone who looked a lot like Bruce Wayne or Cal Stinson.

"Did Lawrence ever use aliases?" Rhodes asked.

"All the time," Roger said, relaxing with a grin. "It was a joke with him. When he was out talking to people, he didn't want them to know who he was. He used all kinds of names if anybody asked him for one. He used to laugh about it when he told me about it. He said he used one with you, which I guess is why you didn't know you'd met him."

"He used an alias, all right," Rhodes said. "I think I can tell you why he hasn't come back."

Roger leaned forward. "You didn't arrest him and put him in jail for using an alias, did you?"

"I didn't check his ID. I should have."

"So he's not in jail?"

"He's not in jail. I didn't arrest him."

"Is he okay?"

"No," Rhodes said. "He's not okay."

"What's the matter, then?"

There was no easy way for Rhodes to put it. There never was, not in this kind of situation. He said, "Lawrence is dead."

Chapter 10

It had been Rhodes's experience that he could never predict how someone would react to the news of a death, whether of a friend, a family member, or an acquaintance. Some people became emotional and wept, some were too surprised at first to react in any way at all, and some were just numbed. In this case, even Seepy was a little surprised.

"Dead?" Seepy said. "How do you know?"

"I've seen the body," Rhodes said. "There's been no formal identification, but I'm sure it's Lawrence."

Roger's voice shook a little. "What happened?"

Explaining that someone has died in an accident or of natural causes was one thing. Explaining that someone has been murdered is something else. Again, there was no easy way.

"Someone shot him," Rhodes said.

"That redneck?"

"I don't know," Rhodes said. "It's something I'm investigating."

"I want to see him."

"I can take you to Ballinger's," Rhodes said. "You can make the formal identification if that's all right with you."

He was careful not to say that Roger could see the body.

"Yes," Roger said. His voice was steadier now. "I can do that. Just give me a minute."

He stood, picked up the tray with its pitcher and glasses, and left the room.

"That couldn't have been easy," Seepy said. "Telling him, I mean."

Rhodes nodded but said nothing.

"This is a lot different thing from just some blog post that insulted the mayor," Seepy said. "I never thought my first case would involve a murder."

"This isn't your case," Rhodes said. "It's not even related to your case."

"You never can tell," Seepy said. "There could be a connection."

Rhodes didn't think so. "What are you going to tell Mayor Clement?"

Seepy looked thoughtful for a second or two, then said, "Nothing much. I'll tell him I found the man who's writing the blog. Or one of the men. That I talked to him and no harm was meant. The mayor might not be satisfied with that, but I'm not going to give him a name or go any further with it. You can tell him the rest if you want him to know."

"You go ahead and tell him the whole story," Rhodes said. "Or as much as you think he needs to know. It might be good for him to hear it from you. Don't do any speculating about why Lawrence was killed. Just give the mayor the facts and let him make his own decisions about what he's going to do. If anything."

Considering the murder angle, Rhodes thought it would be best if the mayor did nothing at all and said even less. He hoped Clement would see it that way, but he wouldn't want to hear that from Rhodes. He'd take it better from someone he'd paid to get the information, like his private eye.

"Are you hinting that you'd like for me to go talk to the mayor now?" Seepy asked.

"More or less," Rhodes said. "There's nothing left for you to do here."

"You're right." Seepy stood up and put on his fedora. "You can tell our host that I had to leave in a hurry."

"I'll be glad to," Rhodes said.

Roger came back into the living room shortly after Seepy left. He now wore a blue blazer, white shirt, and a tie, although he still had on the jeans and running shoes.

"I'm ready," Roger said. He didn't ask about Seepy. "You don't have to take me. I can go in my car."

"All right," Rhodes said. "I'll meet you in front of Ballinger's."

"That's fine," Roger said. He led Rhodes to the front door. "I'll go out the back way. I appreciate your helping me deal with this, Sheriff."

"I should tell you that the identification isn't going to be anything like what you might've seen on TV or in the movies," Rhodes said. "It's entirely different."

"That could be a good thing," Roger said.

"It is," Rhodes said, and Roger thanked him again for his help.

Rhodes didn't think he'd been of any help, but he said he was glad to do what he could. He went out to the Tahoe, and as soon as he'd gotten into the driver's seat, he turned on the engine and started the air conditioner. Then he got on his cell phone and called Clyde Ballinger, the owner of Ballinger's and the funeral director, to let him know that he was on the way there with someone to identify the body that had been brought in earlier that day.

"Has Dr. White performed the autopsy yet?" Rhodes asked.

"No," Ballinger said. "He hasn't been here. He'll do that this evening. I'll have things ready when you get here. Just come right to the viewing room."

Rhodes thanked him and ended the call.

Ballinger's Funeral Home was housed in what had once been the finest mansion in Clearview, built during the oil boom years. The family who built and owned it had eventually left town for Houston, where there were more oil millionaires to associate with, and the mansion had sat vacant for a few years until Clyde Ballinger had bought it and converted it to its current use. Rhodes sometimes wondered what the original owners would have thought about that, but he realized it didn't matter. It was just a building, after all, although it was a particularly fine one, with its white columns two stories high from its front porch, its well-cared-for lawn, still green thanks to an in-ground sprinkler system, its clean-swept walks, its immaculate brick facade. The people who wanted the school preserved in Thurston must have envied Ballinger's building and its excellent condition.

Roger's Cruze was parked in the shade of the elm trees that overhung the street, and Rhodes parked behind him. When Rhodes got out of the Tahoe, Roger stepped out of the Cruze and joined Rhodes on the sidewalk. They walked together up to the wide concrete porch and went through the door into the funeral home.

Rhodes led the way to the viewing room where Clyde Ballinger was waiting.

Outside his professional capacity, Clyde was an outgoing sort, the kind of man that Roger's father had been. He never met a stranger. He liked a good joke, and he knew a lot of them. He liked to read old paperback books and had collected them for years. He enjoyed telling Rhodes about them when they talked. In his work at the funeral home, however, he was different, quiet, assured, and a complete professional. He stood at the door of the viewing room, dressed in a dark blue suit, white shirt, and dark blue tie, with an expression both solemn and concerned as Rhodes introduced Roger Prentiss.

"Let's just step inside here," Clyde said, his voice low but clear.

Rhodes and Roger went inside, and Clyde followed. The room held a big glass-topped desk with nothing on its smooth surface other than a clipboard. Two chairs covered in red leather faced the desk. The clipboard held what appeared to be a blank sheet of paper.

"Have a seat," Clyde said, and Rhodes and Roger sat in the chairs while Clyde went behind the desk. When they were settled, Clyde said, "Mr. Prentiss, has Sheriff Rhodes told you anything about the identification process?"

Roger shifted in his chair. "He just said that it wouldn't be like it is on TV."

"It's not." Clyde touched the clipboard. "We won't be leaving this room. The identification is done by way of a photograph." He pushed the clipboard across the smooth glass top of the desk toward Roger. "The photograph is on the clipboard. It's facedown. You can take all the time you need to turn it over, and then take as much more time as you need to look at it. The Sheriff and I will be here for you no matter how long that might be."

Roger reached out and took the clipboard from the desk. It

seemed to Rhodes that he was a bit hesitant about unclipping the photograph and turning it over, but after a few seconds he did it. Rhodes could see the picture from where he sat. It showed only Lawrence's face with a blue sheet bunched up around it. Roger stared at it in silence for several seconds. Then he said, "That's Lawrence. Lawrence Gates." His voice had only the slightest tremor in it.

"You're certain?" Rhodes asked.

"I'm certain. I need to let his family know."

"I can do that for you," Rhodes said.

"No, I'd rather do it myself. It would be better coming from someone they know, even if they don't know me very well. I'm sure they'll want the body sent home for burial."

"All they have to do is call me," Clyde said. "I can make all the arrangements."

"They'll want to know what happened," Roger said, looking at Rhodes.

"He was shot by an unknown assailant," Rhodes said.

"I don't understand why anyone would shoot Lawrence."

"I'm going to find that out," Rhodes said.

"His parents will want to know why," Roger said.

"So would I," Rhodes told him. "You can let them know that I'll find out who did it and why. It might take a while, but it will get done."

Roger didn't look convinced.

"You can believe what he's telling you," Clyde said. "Sheriff Rhodes always gets the job done."

"He does if you can believe *A Clear View for Clearview*," Roger said.

"Things you read there are often exaggerated," Rhodes said, "a little like *Digging that Blacklin County Dirt*, but in a different way."

"Point taken," Roger said with a glance at Clyde, who looked a bit puzzled at the byplay. "I'll do whatever I can to help."

"You could tell me all about what Lawrence was working on, and you can let us look at his room and his computer."

"No problem. Come tomorrow and look at anything you want." Roger looked at the photograph again. "I can't quite believe he's dead."

That was a familiar reaction to Rhodes. It sometimes took a while for the reality to sink in.

Roger clipped the photograph back on the clipboard and put the clipboard on the desk. "Is there anything else you need from me?"

"Just one thing," Rhodes said. "I need Lawrence's cell phone number."

"Of course. I tried calling Lawrence several times, but I got no answer."

Roger told Rhodes the number, and Rhodes thanked him.

"Is there anything else?" Roger asked.

"Not right now," Rhodes said. "I'll talk to you tomorrow."

Roger stood up. "I'll be going, then. Thank both of you for making this as easy as possible."

Clyde and Rhodes also stood up and Clyde said, "I'll show you out."

Rhodes sat back down and while they were gone, he tried the number Roger had given him. It was out of service, which probably meant that the phone had been destroyed. Rhodes wasn't surprised.

Clyde returned to the room, went behind the desk, and sat down. He took the clipboard and put it in the middle desk drawer.

"Well?" Clyde said when the clipboard was stowed.

"Well, what?" Rhodes asked.

"Is he a suspect?" Clyde asked.

"Everybody's a suspect," Rhodes said, "just like in those books you read."

"I haven't read a good one in a while," Clyde said. "I don't seem to enjoy them so much now that I can't find them at garage sales and in thrift stores. Getting them on the internet for an eReader is too easy. I miss the old days."

"Don't we all," Rhodes said.

"You ever think about it?" Clyde asked, a professional tone back in his voice.

"About what?" Rhodes asked.

Clyde looked around the room. "About how one of these days you might turn out to be one of my clients."

"That's a cheerful thought," Rhodes said.

"Just something to think about. Maybe it's because of my profession, but I think about what's going to happen to me eventually."

"You have a plan?"

"I'm thinking about taking in a partner. Somebody a lot younger than I am. That way I'll have somebody to do the job right."

"I don't think it will matter to you," Rhodes said.

"I know it won't," Clyde said, "but it matters to me now. I want to think that my end will be handled the way I'd like it to be handled. It would be a comfort to me to know that. But not you?"

"I don't think about it a lot," Rhodes said. "Hardly at all, in fact."

"Well, you ought to. I could set you up with a prepaid plan that would guarantee you just what you wanted at a discount price."

"You've never given me a sales pitch before."

"I know," Clyde said, "but today I got to thinking about it. You don't have to do anything with me, but you need to let Ivy know what your wishes are. Just in case."

Rhodes grinned. "I don't think I'll need your services. I think I prefer cremation. Maybe get my ashes scattered somewhere out in the country."

"You know the law about that?"

"I'm the sheriff," Rhodes said. "I know the law. It says that you can scatter ashes over land that's not inhabited and over private property with the owner's permission."

"You can even leave the container if it's biodegradable," Clyde said.

"I know that, too," Rhodes told him, "but it's not something I'm planning on for a while."

"I can't handle the cremation," Clyde said, "but I can send you off to the right place for it."

"That's a real comfort."

"I knew you'd think so," Clyde said.

Chapter 11

Rhodes had missed lunch, which was not unusual. He thought he might as well stop at the Dairy Queen and get something, maybe just a Heath Bar Blizzard, which might not be healthy but would cheer him up.

They knew him well in the Dairy Queen, where a Heath Bar Blizzard was known as "the usual" when Rhodes came in. He didn't even have to ask. A woman named Julia was behind the counter, and when she saw Rhodes come in, she said, "Heath Bar Blizzard, coming right up."

Rhodes paid and sat down to wait. When the Blizzard was ready, Julia came out with it, stood by the table, and turned it upside down.

"No freebie for you, Sheriff," she said, righting the treat and setting it on the table.

"Maybe next time," Rhodes said.

"Not if I'm here," Julia said. "I never forget to turn 'em upside down."

"I'll wait for a trainee," Rhodes said.

Julia laughed. "Good luck, and enjoy your Blizzard."

"I plan to," Rhodes said, and went outside.

As he sat in the DQ parking lot eating the Blizzard, Rhodes thought about Lawrence Gates. He had been secretive about his identity with all his aliases, and for some reason he'd been interested in the Thurston schoolhouse controversy. That seemed odd for someone who wasn't from Blacklin County, but maybe he was just looking for a big story for the blog, something that would pull a lot of page views.

Rhodes wondered about Mayor Clement and how he'd taken the news about who'd been writing the blog and about what had happened to Lawrence. It was barely possible that Clement had somehow learned who was doing the blog even before Seepy had, and that would make him a suspect. It was hardly worth considering but not something Rhodes could disregard completely.

Thinking about what might have happened, Rhodes thought that Lawrence must have known whoever shot him. They were together in the schoolroom, and Lawrence had allowed someone to get close to him as he was about to write something on the blackboard. It was too bad that Lawrence hadn't been able to leave a dying message the way some victims did in mystery novels and movies.

As Rhodes reconstructed the crime, someone had come into the building through the second-floor window, met Lawrence, killed him, taken his car keys and other personal items, and driven away in Lawrence's car. It would have been easy to do, and anyone seeing the car leaving the school would assume that it was being driven by the owner. If Rhodes could find the car, he might get a step closer to the killer, but the car could be anywhere by now, sold in Houston or even sent across the border into Mexico. The killing had resulted from something more than just a car theft, however. Rhodes was sure of that.

Could the destruction of the school building have led someone to kill? Maybe, but were people really that upset? He'd start by talking to Wanda Wilkins again. She might have thought of something she hadn't told him, or she might have remembered something else Lawrence had said. Or something she'd seen.

And as he'd told Clyde, even Roger Prentiss was a suspect. He could've gone to the school with Lawrence, even though Wanda Wilkins hadn't seen him. He could have killed Lawrence and driven the car home, disposing of it or hiding it later.

Rhodes scraped the last of the Blizzard from the cup and ate it, crunching the bits of the Heath Bar that remained. He'd gotten the smallest-size Blizzard, so he thought of himself as being somewhat virtuous. He got out of the Tahoe and put the empty cup in the trash, then got back in and headed for Thurston.

Wanda Wilkins came to the door when Rhodes knocked. She was wearing the same camouflage baseball cap. She also wore jeans, but this time her shirt was green.

"Good afternoon, Sheriff," she said. "You come for supper?"

"Is it suppertime?" Rhodes asked.

"It is for me. I like to eat early. I go to bed early, too. Sometimes I like to have breakfast for supper, and that's what I'm having tonight. Scrambled eggs, sausage patties, toast, and grits. Sound good?"

Rhodes was tempted, and he felt a bit guilty because he'd had the Blizzard, even though it was a small one. He knew that Ivy would fix something healthy for their supper, possibly something involving kale. Sausage patties were preferable to kale. Most things were preferable to kale, but Rhodes summoned up some inner strength and said, "Sounds fine, but I'm not here for supper."

"What're you here for, then?"

"To talk."

"I like talking almost as much as I like early supper. Come on in."

The door opened directly into a small living room, which contained furniture that Rhodes thought might be as old as he was. It didn't look excessively worn, just old. A blue-and-pink-floral-print couch sat against one wall, and two matching chairs stood nearby. They looked a little like those in Roger Prentiss's living room, except less comfortable. The coffee table in front of the couch had claw feet, and it had a glass top that could be lifted off with the handles on each end. The only modern thing in the room was the flat-screen TV set that sat on a stand against the wall opposite the couch.

"Have a seat, Sheriff," Wanda said. "I don't get a lot of visitors since I'm so old. Nobody but old people like to visit old people, and there aren't many people in town as old as I am except for the ones in the cemetery, and they don't get out much." She laughed at her own joke. "The couch's more comfortable than the chairs. I'd sit there if I were you."

Rhodes sat on the couch, and Wanda took one of the chairs. She sat up very straight, and as soon as she was seated, she said, "What do you want to talk about?"

"The schoolhouse," Rhodes said. "Who wants to keep it and who wants it to go."

Wanda didn't appear interested in that topic. She said, "You ever find out who that dead man was?"

"I did. His name wasn't Bruce Wayne. It was Lawrence Gates.

He lived in Clearview, and he was down here to find out about the schoolhouse."

"I told him about it."

"He must have wanted to know more. Somebody met him there and killed him. I want to find out who."

Wanda smiled. "I already told you I didn't do it."

"I remember," Rhodes said. "I wondered if you'd had time to think things over and maybe make a suggestion or two about who might've done it."

Wanda pushed up the brim of her cap and gave Rhodes a piercing look. "I don't rat people out."

"So you know who did it?"

"That's not it," Wanda said. "I might not have told you that I'm the president of the Thurston Ex-students Association. A lot of people who live here are members, and if I went around talking about them, they'd feel like I was a gossip, which I'm not. That Lucy Perkins who lives over on the other side of town, now, she's a gossip. She can't help you, though. She didn't go to school here. Moved here with her husband when he retired about ten years ago and thinks she knows it all because they come from the big city. Her husband didn't go to school here, either. They just wanted to move to a little town for some peace and quiet."

Rhodes overlooked the digression. He said, "All I want to know is who's most interested in saving the schoolhouse and who's most interested in having it torn down. That wouldn't be gossip. It's information I need in an investigation." He paused. "I could always go talk to Lucy Perkins, though, if you don't want to help me out."

Wanda sat up even straighter. "You wouldn't get anything you could trust from Lucy Perkins. She's not from here, and she doesn't know the people in this town like I do."

"I'm sure that's true," Rhodes said. "That's why I came to you. I need to get the facts, and I knew you were the one who could give them to me."

"Well," Wanda said after a few seconds' consideration, "I guess I could help you a little bit, but you can't spread around where you got the information."

"I'd never do that," Rhodes assured her. "Everything you tell me is strictly confidential."

"All right, then. You need to look at the Hunleys and the Falkners first, but the Reeses are worth a look, too."

"Charlie Reese?" Rhodes asked.

Reese was a rancher who'd once owned property all over the county and in other counties, too. He'd started buying land years ago when it was cheap, and while he'd held on to a few choice acres, he'd sold most of his property as the prices went up. He'd done quite well for himself, and he might have been as rich as the Falkners. The Hunleys weren't rich, but they had such a good reputation in the county that they were sometimes thought of as rich.

"That's right, Charlie Reese. You know he carries a pistol out in the open?"

The Texas open carry law hadn't proved to be much of a problem in Blacklin County. Most people who carried a weapon preferred to keep it concealed, but Charlie Reese was different. He liked to dress in cowboy garb, and wearing a revolver in a holster was part of the rig.

"I know," Rhodes said, "but he's never been in trouble."

"He's a bully," Wanda said. "He doesn't have to use his gun. He pushes people around without it."

Rhodes had heard a story or two about Charlie's bullying. He was a big, imposing man, a couple of inches over six feet and over two hundred fifty pounds, not much of it fat. If he was doing the pushing, not many people were going to push back, especially with that gun on his hip.

"He's a hunter, too," Wanda said. "Kills things like deer and feral hogs."

"With the hog problem we have around here," Rhodes said, "we could use a few more hog killers."

"I think he does it for fun," Wanda said, "not because he's trying to help control the hog problem."

"I'll talk to him," Rhodes said. "Is he for or against the demolition."

"For it. From what I've heard, he didn't have a very good time of it when he was there. That's just gossip, though, and I don't gossip."

"You told me that," Rhodes said.

"Well, I don't, and you can believe it. And don't forget Charlie's wife."

"What about her?"

"Arlene, that's her name. She's as bad as he is, lording it over people because she has a lot of money, not one penny of which she earned herself. Got it all by marrying Charlie, although I guess that's the same as earning it the hard way. She wants that building down in the worst way. She was never one of the popular girls, and she hates the place because of that. Faye Falkner's no prize, either."

"What about her?" Rhodes asked.

"Anything I had to say would just be gossip, and I don't repeat gossip. Just what I know firsthand."

Rhodes pressed her, but she wouldn't go further, so he said, "I'll talk to everybody you've mentioned and see what I can find out for myself. Anybody else I should talk to?"

"You can ask the Hunleys and the Falkners and Charlie Reese about that. They might know. I don't."

Rhodes knew he'd have to be satisfied with that. "Did you happen to remember seeing anything else over at the schoolhouse last night? Cars? Pickups? Did you see anybody drive away in Lawrence's car?"

"I didn't see any of that." Wanda pointed with a thumb at the TV set behind her. "I was watching TV. That's what I like to do at night. There's a lot of good programs on if you have the satellite, which I do. You can watch the old shows in black-and-white if you want to, or you can watch the new ones. The old ones are better, mostly."

At that point in the conversation, a big orange cat strolled into the room. It walked over to Rhodes and rubbed up against his leg. Rhodes reached down to give its head a pat and asked its name.

"That's Leroy," Wanda said. "He's a mess. Sleeps most of the day and goes out at night for a while." She gave Leroy a thoughtful look. "Come to think of it, I might've seen something when I let him out last evening."

Rhodes was glad Leroy had shown up. "What did you see?"

"Not much, just some old pickup that drove by. Looked like a junker."

"What model?"

"I don't know anything about pickups or cars. Used to be able to tell them all apart when I was a girl. Now they all look alike. Cars, too. Might as well buy one as another if you're going for looks. All just the same."

Leroy jumped up onto Rhodes's lap. Rhodes rubbed his head, and Leroy started to purr. He turned around a couple of times, then settled down and closed his eyes.

"He's a lazy one," Wanda said. "If he's bothering you, just put him on the floor."

"He's not bothering me," Rhodes said. "Now about that pickup you saw. You said this was an old one."

"Not that old. Might've been a Chevy, but I wouldn't swear to it."

That could have been Kenny, Rhodes thought. He said he hadn't been in Thurston, but Kenny was as big a liar as he claimed the Whiteside boys were.

"I didn't get more than a quick look at it," Wanda said. "Soon as Leroy went out the door, I went back to the TV."

"I guess I don't have any more questions, then," Rhodes said.

He set Leroy on the floor and stood up. Rhodes's lap was warm where Leroy had lain. Leroy gave him a resentful look and went off to sleep elsewhere.

"I appreciate you giving me the time," Rhodes told Wanda.

Wanda stood up as well. "I like talking, like I told you. You sure you don't want some early supper? I got my own hens out back, so the eggs are fresh. Had to buy the sausage at the store, but it's not bad."

Rhodes wanted to say yes, but he didn't. "My wife will be expecting me for supper. I don't want to disappoint her."

"She might be glad to have supper by herself for a change."

"She might," Rhodes said, "but then I'd be disappointed."

Wanda laughed. "I like you, Sheriff. Any time you want to come by for a talk, you'll be welcome."

"I'll keep it in mind," Rhodes said.

It was getting late in the afternoon as he drove back to Clearview. He had just about enough time to go by the jail for any updates he needed before going home. Mika Blackstone, the fingerprint tech and just about every other kind of tech the department had, might have come up with something from the prints Andy had collected at the school.

Rhodes didn't think about the fingerprints for long, however.

He thought about sausage patties and scrambled eggs all the way back. He wondered if Leroy got any bites of the sausage as a treat. Probably not. Rhodes wished he had a bite, but that wasn't going to happen. Maybe supper with Ivy wouldn't involve kale. He could always hope.

Chapter 12

When Rhodes arrived at the jail, he could tell that Hack and Lawton were dying to tell him something, or not tell him something and make him drag it out of them, but he waved them off. It wasn't quite five o'clock, so there was a chance he could call the courthouse and find the county judge still there. He wanted to get a warrant for Lawrence Gates's cell phone records.

Sure enough, Judge Casey was there, although he said he'd been on his way out the door when the phone rang. Rhodes asked about getting the warrant for the cell phone records and explained why he needed it.

"Send somebody over in the morning, and I'll have it ready," the judge said. "You know the phone provider will drag its feet, warrant or not."

"I know," Rhodes said, "but the sooner I get started, the better." He thanked the judge and hung up.

Hack started to say something, but Rhodes waved him off again.

"Was Mika able to do anything with the fingerprints Andy got in Thurston?"

"She sent a report to your computer," Hack said. "I been thinkin' about those fingerprints. When's the last time we solved a case by usin' fingerprints?"

Rhodes knew the answer to that, and Hack did, too, but Rhodes went along with him. "Never, but we can't pass up the chance that this will be the first time."

"We got a first time thing for you," Lawton said.

"Let me look at this report first," Rhodes said. He put on his reading glasses and called up the report. It was clear from the start that this wouldn't be the first time they solved a case with fingerprints. There were a lot of prints in the room where Lawrence had been shot, but they were no help at all. None of them showed up in any of the national databases. Andy hadn't gotten any prints from the window on the second floor of the school, just smudges, as if someone might have been wearing gloves.

"You ready to hear about our first time thing?" Hack asked when Rhodes closed the file and looked away from the computer.

Rhodes sighed. "Go ahead."

"Happened last night," Lawton said, "but we just found out about it an hour or so ago."

"Assault case," Hack said. "One man in the hospital."

"Who?" Rhodes asked.

"Bailey Dalton. Lives out east of town. Happened in his backyard."

"Never heard of anything like it before," Lawton said.

"I'm tellin' this," Hack said, giving him a hateful look. "I'm the one took the call."

"Go on and tell it, then," Lawton said. "I was just tryin' to help."

"More of a hindrance than a help," Hack said.

"If you say so."

"I do say so."

"Hold it," Rhodes said, stopping them before they descended to the grade-school level, if they hadn't already. "That's enough of that. Just tell me what happened."

"Bailey was assaulted by an armadillo," Hack said.

"That's not right," Lawton said. "Shot is what he was. That's not assault. That's a different thing."

"Didn't we just say that I was tellin' this?" Hack asked.

"You said it, not me."

"I'm sayin' it again."

"That's enough," Rhodes said again. "Hack, if you're going to tell it, tell it."

"Lawton won't let me," Hack said. "He keeps interruptin'."

"He won't interrupt you again. Right, Lawton?"

"You're the sheriff," Lawton said. "I guess I gotta do what you say or you'll take me in the back room and give me the third degree."

"You need it," Hack said.

"You ain't the sheriff."

"Never mind who's the sheriff," Rhodes said. "Tell it, Hack."

"I'm tryin'." Hack rolled his eyes and resumed his account. "You know how it is with armadillos sometimes when they get on a person's property?"

"I'm not sure what you're talking about."

"They root it all up, just like a wild hog does, except not nearly as bad, what with an armadillo bein' so small. They can root a place up pretty good, though, for somethin' their size. Do it at night so nobody can catch 'em at it."

"I know about that," Rhodes said.

"Okay. Well, Bailey was tired of this armadillo rootin' up his yard, so he decided to stay up one night and catch him at it. Turned out he stayed up until nearly the next mornin' 'bout an hour before daylight."

"I bet he went to sleep some durin' that time," Lawton said. "He's nearly seventy. Old guy like that can't stay up all night."

"You oughta know," Hack said.

"Well, I'm not as old as you are."

"You are, too. Older, even."

"Hack," Rhodes said. "Lawton."

"Anyway," Hack said, as if none of the byplay had happened, "Bailey had him a thirty-eight revolver, and when he heard the armadillo in his yard, he went out to shoot it. He didn't turn on any lights, 'cause that would've scared the armadillo off, but he thought there was enough light from the streetlight to see by. So he shot the armadillo three times."

"The armadillo didn't shoot back but once, though," Lawton said. It was as if he couldn't resist, although Rhodes knew he could if he wanted to.

"The armadillo didn't shoot him, and you know it," Hack said. "That's just crazy talk. What happened was that the bullets ricocheted off the armadillo's shell, and one of them hit Bailey right square in the face. His wife got him to the hospital, and they got his jaw all wired up. He'll be okay, but he might not be as pretty as he was. That is, if he was pretty. I don't know what he looked like. The hospital reported the bullet wound this afternoon and told me all about it. Said they'd never heard of anything like it."

"Armadillo escaped," Lawton said. "Got clean away. Back on the streets to shoot somebody else."

Hack ignored him and said to Rhodes, "Hospital says that Bailey wants you to get down there and get that armadillo. Not arrest him for assault or anything. Kill him, is what Bailey told the hospital to say. He's pretty mad at that armadillo."

"You better get Alton Boyd on the case," Lawton said. "'Cept Alton don't like to kill things. He's a real softie like that."

"We don't kill armadillos," Rhodes said. "Not even if they go around shooting people. We're protectors, not executioners."

"Bailey won't like that," Hack said. "Might not vote for you in the next election."

"I might not even run the next time," Rhodes said. "It might be time for me to step down."

"Don't talk like that," Lawton said. "It'd take me and Hack forever to break in a new sheriff."

Rhodes didn't think anybody else would put up with them.

"You'd miss us," Hack said. "Who'd tell you stories if you weren't the sheriff?"

"I don't know," Rhodes said, "but I'd manage."

"That's what you say now. You'd feel different if you knew you wouldn't be around here. Besides, you got to catch whoever killed that fella down in Thurston."

"I hope that won't take me until the next election," Rhodes said.

"Then you better get busy," Lawton said.

"I'll do that," Rhodes told him.

Sure enough, Ivy was preparing a supper that involved kale. Rhodes thought he'd probably jinxed himself by thinking of it.

"You'll love it," Ivy said. "It's spicy chicken breasts stuffed with corn and kale. Pepper jack cheese is the spicy part."

Rhodes liked pepper jack cheese and corn and even chicken breasts, but he wasn't fond of kale.

"Yancey's excited about it," Ivy said.

They were in the kitchen. Yancey pranced around Rhodes's feet, but then he always pranced around Rhodes's feet when Rhodes came home, kale or no kale.

"The cats aren't excited," Rhodes said.

There were two cats, Sam, black as midnight, and Jerry, who appeared to be wearing a tuxedo. They liked to sleep by the refrigerator, although they were awake now and giving Rhodes suspicious looks.

"What have you been up to?" Ivy asked Rhodes.

"I've had a strange cat sitting in my lap," Rhodes said. "Not odd strange. Just a stranger. His name is Leroy. Our two don't have anything to be jealous of. They're much better-looking than Leroy."

The cats didn't look convinced that he was telling the truth, but they'd always seemed skeptical of him, even though he was the one who'd taken them in.

Rhodes ignored their looks and went on to tell Ivy about the murder and about Wanda Wilkins and Leroy. Yancey must have been bored by the account, since he left the room, probably to go sleep in his doggy bed. Rhodes tactfully left out the invitation to early supper and the sausage and scrambled eggs.

"I know the Falkners a little," Ivy said when he'd finished. "They have insurance with us."

Ivy worked at an insurance firm. She'd started as a secretary, but now she was a full participant in selling policies.

"Tell me about them," Rhodes said.

"First you tell me about your heroic gun battle out at Milsby."

Rhodes sighed. "You've been on the internet again."

"It was a slow day at the office," Ivy said. "I can't resist checking in on *A Clear View for Clearview.* I'm not on Facebook, so I have to go somewhere for the local news. I'm glad you didn't get shot."

"I'm glad, too, but there wasn't much danger of it. See, the cats aren't impressed."

Sam and Jerry had gone back to sleep. They were champion sleepers and could drop off anytime.

"The cats don't know anything about being shot at," Ivy said. "Or about car chases across open fields. Did I mention there was video?"

"No, but I knew there would be." Rhodes didn't want to discuss it. "Can we talk about the Falkners now?"

"Let's sit at the table," Ivy said.

They sat, and Ivy said, "Leslie Falkner seems like a nice enough man, but I wonder sometimes about his wife. Faye's her name."

"What do you wonder about her?" Rhodes asked.

"Whether she's mentally stable."

That was interesting, Rhodes thought, considering what Wanda had told him. "What gives you the idea she might not be stable?"

"She threw a hissy fit in the office one day. She and Leslie had come in to ask about some coverage, and it turned out that they didn't have exactly what she thought they'd been paying for. They were a couple of cubicles down from me, talking to Wendy Solis, but I could hear the yelling from where I was. I talked to Wendy about it later, and she said it was just a minor thing but that Faye went ballistic. Wendy's pretty levelheaded, and she laughed it off, but it was scary when it was happening."

"I'll be talking to her tomorrow," Rhodes said. "I hope she doesn't throw any fits. I don't deal well with fits."

"You deal well with everything. Now why don't you go out in the backyard and give Speedo some exercise while I fix the delicious chicken breasts?"

"Sounds like a good plan to me," Rhodes said. He tried not to think about the kale.

Seepy Benton called around nine-thirty. First the kale, then Seepy Benton. And the worst part was that Seepy called when Rhodes and Ivy were watching *The Brain That Wouldn't Die* on TCM. Rhodes didn't get many chances to see the kind of old bad movies he enjoyed, and when he did, he didn't approve of interruptions. It was a good thing that he could pause the DVR.

"Sorry to bother you," Seepy said, "but I thought you'd like to hear what happened when I talked to Mayor Clement."

Rhodes did want to know, but he was still a bit peeved. "You could've called earlier."

"Nope," Seepy said. "I had a date with your deputy, and we just got through eating barbecue at Max's."

There was no kale at Max's. Rhodes said, "I don't want to hear about that. Just tell me about the mayor."

"He's satisfied just to know who was behind the blog."

"I hope that's true."

"He's had time to calm down, and he doesn't plan to carry it any further. He realizes he shouldn't have pried into this to begin with. Maybe something you said to him helped. The murder has him worried, though. He's afraid it will reflect badly on the town when word gets out."

"It's not going to be on the national news," Rhodes said.

"He's worried that Jennifer Loam will give it a big play when we find the killer. Sometimes the big-city papers pick up a story like that."

"What do you mean *we*?" Rhodes asked.

"I also talked to Roger Prentiss," Seepy said. "He's agreed to hire me as a private investigator to look into what happened to Lawrence."

"You know better than to interfere in a police investigation."

"I'm not going to interfere. I'll be a big help. I have permission to look at Lawrence's computer tomorrow. Roger knows the password. I'll tell you if I find anything."

Rhodes had to admit that would help, as he'd had to use Seepy for computer-related work before. "All right. It's unorthodox, but I'll go along with you. You have to let me know anything you find that's relevant to the case."

"I always did that even before I was a private eye. I'm not going to change."

"I'm not entirely convinced," Rhodes said.

"You're going to hurt my feelings, talking like that," Seepy said.

"I wouldn't want to hurt your feelings. I didn't know you were so delicate."

"It's okay. I know you were only kidding."

"Right," Rhodes said. "Only kidding. You just be sure you call and report what you find."

"You can count on me."

"I hope so," Rhodes said, and hung up.

When he went back to the couch and sat down, Ivy said, "You're not going to be grumpy and spoil the movie, are you?"

"Me?" Rhodes said. "Grumpy?"

Ivy laughed. "We don't have to watch the rest of the movie, you know. There are other things we could do."

"Such as?"

“I think you have a pretty good idea.”

“Ah-ha,” Rhodes said. “I paused the movie, so I can just exit and watch it later.”

“Come along, then,” Ivy said, standing up.

Rhodes stood up, and then he went along.

Chapter 13

The Hunley families lived on a piece of land outside of Thurston that backed up on an old rock pit, now long since abandoned. It had filled up with water years ago, and rumor had it that Con had stocked it with bass and catfish. Supposedly several people had caught lunker bass there, but Rhodes wasn't one of them. He loved fishing, but he hadn't had time for it in much too long.

Past the rock pit was a large wooded area, and the Hunleys' two houses were well shaded by trees, including some tall native pecans. There was nothing fancy about the houses. The larger one, which Rhodes figured was where Con Hunley lived, was an older ranch-style place, wide but probably not deep, with a columned concrete porch and an attached two-car garage. Rhodes saw security cameras at the corners of the house. He didn't know what was in the garage, but a black Chevy Suburban, polished to a high shine, sat in the driveway. The grass in the yard was mostly brown and dead, but even in that condition it didn't look bad, and the soil didn't show through. It had been well cared for before the summer really set in, but Hunley apparently hadn't cared enough about it to water it. Maybe he didn't like mowing. If that was the case, Rhodes didn't blame him. Rhodes didn't like mowing, either.

Next door to the bigger house was another ranch-style one, also with a columned porch but with only four columns instead of five. Rhodes knew that Pete Hunley and his family lived there, and it occurred to him that he knew nothing at all about the wives of either Con or Pete, or any offspring other than Pete. The Hunley men were famous in the county. The wives not so much. He supposed he'd find out more about them before the day was over.

In front of both houses were tall flagpoles with the United States flag on one pole and the Texas flag on the other. The Texas flag was on a shorter pole than the U.S. flag, and both hung limp in the motionless air. That the flags were flown wasn't surprising in Blacklin County, even when military families weren't involved. Most people in Blacklin County still believed in God and country and of course the state of Texas.

Rhodes had driven down in one of the Department's Dodge Chargers instead of the Tahoe, and he parked it behind the Suburban and got out. When he did, Con Hunley came out of the garage. He was tall, though not as tall as Rhodes, and solidly built. He was in his early seventies, but he looked strong and healthy. He had on jungle camouflage pants, shirt, and cap in various shades of green and black. The pants were tucked into a pair of shiny black combat boots. What got Rhodes's attention wasn't the clothing, however. It was the AR-15 cradled in the crook of his arm.

"Glad to see you, Sheriff," Hunley said. His voice was deep and commanding. "I guess you must've heard about what's going on around here and come to check on it."

As he had with Roger Prentiss on the previous day, Rhodes got the feeling that he'd walked into the middle of a situation that he had no clue about. He said, "You mean besides the murder?"

"I heard about that," Hunley said. "Terrible thing. That's not what I was talking about, though."

"Just what were you talking about, then?"

"Mischief," Hunley said. "Lots of mischief going on."

"Let's get back to the murder. You ever meet a man named Lawrence Gates?"

Hunley didn't even think about it. "Never heard of him."

"He was here to talk about the school to someone. He didn't get in touch with you? He might've been using another name. You have any calls from anybody wanting to talk to you?"

"Now that you mention it, there was some fella named Watson who called. John Watson. I told him I wasn't interested in talking to him, though, and he never called back."

That had to have been Gates, Rhodes thought. "You're sure?"

"Sure I'm sure. Now let me tell you about the mischief."

"What kind of mischief would that be?"

"The latest is that last night somebody came slipping around here and threw out a bunch of lighted firecrackers. Did the same at Pete's house, too. Sounded a little like gunfire at first, but only at first. I knew it wasn't gunfire, and so did Pete. It didn't bother me, but it upset Pete. He's not over his war the way I'm over mine. Didn't make our wives any too happy, either." He patted his rifle. "They were gone by the time I got out of the house, not that I'd have shot at them if I'd had the chance."

Rhodes wondered how much truth was in that statement, and as he was thinking it over, a woman came out of the garage. She was dressed almost identically to her husband, including the combat boots. The difference was that she didn't have an AR-15. Her face was wrinkled and tanned, and if she had long hair, it was all tucked up under her camouflage cap.

"Morning, Sheriff," she said. Her voice was almost as deep as her husband's and a bit raspy. "I don't believe we've ever met. I'm Edwina Hunley." She stuck out a hand and Rhodes shook it. "It was those Falkners that threw out those firecrackers if you want to know who did it. They've been harassing us for a good while now. We never called you because it seemed too petty to complain about, but it's getting real bothersome."

"That's what I'm here to talk about," Rhodes said, although that wasn't quite the truth. He figured that the conversation would get around to the schoolhouse controversy soon enough.

"Let's go inside, then," Con said. "It's already too hot to stand out in the yard."

"Lead the way," Rhodes said.

"We'll just go in through the garage," Edwina said, turning and going back through the open door. Con and Rhodes followed.

Inside the garage was another Suburban, just as black and just as highly polished as the one outside. Where that one would have been housed there was an old oak table that someone had refinished. The top gleamed even in the dim light. The garage smelled of varnish and kerosene.

"Bought that table for my son," Con said with a glance at the table. "Just about got it done. Might put one more coat of varnish on the top."

Rhodes thought it was fine as it was and said so.

"Maybe," Con said. "Come on in."

A door from the garage led directly to the kitchen, and Rhodes felt as if he'd stepped back in time, right back into the nineteen seventies or maybe it was the eighties. The cabinets were dark wood; the countertops were avocado green, as were the porcelain sink and the refrigerator. At the far end of the kitchen was a breakfast nook with a table that looked a lot like the one in the garage, with four oak chairs around it. Four avocado green place mats sat on the table in front of the chairs.

"Have a seat at the table," Con said. "Edwina will fix us some coffee. I'll be right back."

Rhodes said, "Sorry, but I'm not a coffee drinker."

Con had left the room, so Edwina said, "I thought all lawmen drank coffee."

"Maybe most do," Rhodes said. "I never had a taste for it."

"I have some orange juice."

"That would be fine," Rhodes said.

Edwina started the coffeepot, and Rhodes thought, as he often had, that if coffee tasted as good to him as it smelled, he'd have drunk a quart every day. It didn't work that way, however.

Edwina got the orange juice out of the refrigerator and poured a big glass of it. She set the glass on the mat in front of Rhodes and said, "Go ahead and get started. The coffee will be ready in a minute."

Rhodes took a drink of the juice, which was cold and sweet, just as Con came back into the room. He'd left the rifle behind, but both he and Edwina kept their caps on.

Con pulled out a chair and sat at the table. Edwina put a cup of coffee in a saucer in front of him, then brought over one for herself and sat down. Neither of them put anything in the coffee.

"Tell me about the mischief," Rhodes said.

"It's the Falkners," Edwina said. "Like I told you. First it was phone calls. Now it's firecrackers."

"Tell me about the calls."

"They must've been made from throwaway phones. We didn't know the numbers that showed on our phone screens. Bad language and threats."

"What kind of threats?"

Edwina took a sip of her coffee. "Let Con tell you."

Rhodes looked at Con, who said, "Things like 'you'll have to leave town before all this is over' and 'everybody in town hates you; time to get out.' I'm not going anywhere, though."

"Tell him about the garden," Edwina said.

"I have a little garden out back," Con said. "One day when we were gone somebody got into it and tore it up. I'd taken a lot of trouble with it, watered it, pampered it. Had green beans, potatoes, squash. After the Falkners got through with it, I didn't have a thing."

"You know for sure they did it?" Rhodes asked.

Hunley shrugged. "Who else could it be?"

"What about your security cameras?" Rhodes asked. "Didn't you get any video of any of this?"

"Sure, but they always park out of range, and all I get are pictures of two people in hoodies. They tear up the garden or throw firecrackers, and they run back to their car. Has to be the Falkners."

Rhodes could think of two more people it could be, but he didn't say so. Instead he asked, "Is this stuff related to the schoolhouse?"

"Sure it is," Con said. He sipped some coffee. "The Falkners want that building down, the sooner, the better. I have other ideas."

"What other ideas?"

"It would take a lot of money to restore the building. I know that, but the money could be raised. The Falkners alone could pay for it, or the Reeses, who also want it razed, but even if they wouldn't help, there are ways to get the money. Razed. I think I have a slogan: Raise the money. Don't raze the building."

Rhodes smiled as best he could. "How would you get the money?"

"Fund-raising sites on the internet. I know of several, and they're all on the up-and-up. We could get contributions from ex-students but from all over the world, too. Plenty of people are interested in preserving historic buildings. We just need somebody to set the thing up."

"Why not you?"

"I can tell you that," Edwina said. "People would say Con's using his service record to raise the money. They'd imply that somehow he was cheapening the medals he won and the things he did. It would be the same if Pete did it. They're heroes, but they don't want to use their reputations to raise the money."

The kitchen door from the garage opened, and a man walked in. He said, "Did somebody just mention my name?"

Pete Hunley looked like a younger version of his father, and he was dressed like his parents in camo clothing, except that his was desert camo, all in different shades of brown. Different clothes for different wars, but the same effect. It was kind of overdoing things, he thought.

"I saw the sheriff's car parked in the driveway," Pete said to his parents, "so I thought I'd better come over to see if I could keep you two out of jail."

Edwina stood up and said, "We're not going to jail. You sit right down and I'll get you some coffee."

Pete pulled out the remaining chair and had a seat. "Glad you're not going to arrest them, Sheriff. Are you here about the firecrackers?"

"Among other things," Rhodes said. "We've been talking about the school building."

Edwina came to the table with Pete's coffee and set it on the mat. He apparently took nothing in it, either. He took a sip of it immediately and didn't seem worried about burning his mouth. He swallowed, set down his cup, and looked at his father. "That old building means a lot to some people."

"A lot less to others," Con said.

"Is anybody upset enough about it to kill somebody?" Rhodes asked.

"You talking about the man they found dead in the schoolhouse?" Pete said.

"That's right," Rhodes said, and he went on to explain that Lawrence Gates had been partially responsible for *Digging that Blacklin County Dirt* and had been at the school to investigate the controversy.

"So you think somebody killed him because he was looking into that?" Edwina asked.

"It's one possibility," Rhodes said. "Maybe somebody just killed him to steal his car, or maybe there was something else involved. I'm just getting started on the investigation."

"Well, we didn't kill him," Edwina said, looking first at Con and then at Pete. "We'd like to see the building saved, but not enough to kill anybody."

"We had enough killing in our wars," Pete said. "All that's over now."

"I'm sure all of you can account for your whereabouts the night before last," Rhodes said.

"That's kind of insulting, Sheriff," Pete said.

"I have to ask."

"Maybe so, but I'm a man who fought and bled for his country. I've looked that old scoundrel death in the eye to protect our freedoms. My word should be good for something."

"It's okay," Con said, breaking in. "Edwina and I were right here all evening. Pete was at home with his wife, Linda. We didn't kill anybody."

"I'll have to ask Linda that question, too," Rhodes said. "The one about whether you were there with her."

Pete bristled. "I don't see why. Dad just told you I was with her."

"He wasn't there to see," Rhodes said.

He already knew what Linda would tell him. Everybody was alibiing everybody else, which wasn't unusual. Often everybody was telling the truth, but it was nevertheless an awkward situation.

"Ask her, then," Pete said. "I don't care, but I'm telling you we didn't do it."

"What about the Falkners?" Rhodes asked. "Con says they're causing you trouble. How violent do you think they'd get?"

"Plenty," Edwina said. "That Faye's crazy."

"Don't say that," Con said. "You're not a psychiatrist."

"I don't need to be. Crazy's not a technical term, and I know crazy when I see it. That woman has a temper like a rattlesnake. I've had a run-in or two with her. You're going to talk to them, aren't you, Sheriff?"

"Them and the Reeses," Rhodes said. "I understand they want the school demolished, too."

"I don't care much for the Reeses," Con said, "but they're better than the Falkners by a good stretch."

Rhodes stood up and said to Pete, "I'll stop by your house before I leave. You want to go with me and introduce me to your wife? I've never met her."

Pete stood. "Sure. Thanks for the coffee, Mom."

"Thanks for the orange juice," Rhodes said.

"You're welcome," Edwina said. "You'll see what I mean about Faye Falkner, Sheriff. She'll probably try to claw your eyes out."

"I'll take that risk," Rhodes said. "You ready, Pete?"

"Let's go," Pete said, and he led the way out the door.

Pete and Linda's kitchen was a bit more up-to-date than that of the elder Hunleys. It was mostly white, from the appliances to the cabinets to the countertops. It had an island that was used as a table with stools, and the breakfast nook was empty. Rhodes assumed that the table Hunley had refinished would go there, although it wasn't white.

Linda Hunley was the only member of the family not dressed in a camouflage outfit. She wore jeans, a blue shirt, and running shoes. She was small, with a round face, blond hair, and blue eyes. Her voice was light and high. She and Rhodes sat at the kitchen island. They weren't drinking anything. Rhodes had had enough orange juice for one day.

"Nobody's really bothered us," Linda told Rhodes, who'd asked Pete to let him talk to Linda alone. "We did get a few of the phone calls, but Pete and I aren't involved in the schoolhouse argument. We don't really care one way or the other what happens to it. We naturally side with Con and Edwina, but that's only because they're Pete's parents."

"The incident with the firecrackers seemed to bother Con a good bit," Rhodes said. "He said it bothered Pete even more."

"That's because of the war. Pete is a hero, you know. His daddy's so proud of him. He won a lot of medals, and he's proud to have served his country."

"That's what I've heard," Rhodes said. There had been a good many articles in the local paper about Pete's service in the first Gulf War and all his exploits and medals. Con was always at his side, and the articles didn't dwell on Con's own heroics nearly as much as they did Pete's.

"He has flashbacks sometimes," Linda said. "He was in a lot of fighting, and those firecrackers brought it all back. He thought for a second he was back in the war and jumped out of bed to get his rifle. He keeps it close by. That's how a hero is. He didn't fire his rifle, but he did run out in the yard. The Falkners were gone when he got there, lucky for them."

Everybody was sure it was the Falkners except Rhodes. "What time was that?" he asked.

"It was a little before three. I looked at the clock."

"Why are you so sure it was the Falkners?"

"That's what Pete told me. I always believe him."

Pete must have been a convincing kind of guy, or maybe Linda was just loyal. Rhodes asked the important question. "Was Pete here all night?"

"Yes. Why?"

"There was a murder last night. Maybe you heard about it."

"I saw it on the internet. A terrible thing, but Pete would never kill anybody. He says he did enough of that in Iraq. Anyway, he was here with me all the time."

"You're sure?"

"Of course I'm sure. We watched TV and then we went to bed."

"A solid alibi," Rhodes said. "I hope you understand that I had to ask."

"I was here, too, you know. So I didn't do it, either."

"Good to know," Rhodes said.

Chapter 14

The Falkners didn't live far from the Hunleys, so Rhodes visited them next. Their house was considerably more elaborate than the two the Hunleys lived in, and a good bit newer. It had four red-brick sections, one behind the other, and each was a bit offset from the one in front of it. The front section had a peaked roof, while the other roofs were flat. A semicircular drive was in front of the house, and there was only one flagpole. It flew two flags, with the U.S. flag on top and the Texas flag beneath it. The back section of the house stuck out quite a distance, and Rhodes figured it was a garage. About fifty yards in back of the house was a big red barn. The doors were closed, so Rhodes couldn't see inside, although he would have liked to.

Rhodes went to the front door of the house and pushed the doorbell. He heard a gong inside and then footsteps. There was a pause, and Rhodes thought someone was looking at him through the peephole in the door. After a couple of seconds he heard the rattle of a chain and the click and slide of a deadbolt.

The door opened, and Leslie Falkner stood there. "Good morning, Sheriff. What brings you down this way?"

Rhodes had met Falkner at a few countywide events, but he didn't know the man well at all. He was tall and thin, with a head that seemed too big for his skinny neck.

"A murder, for one," Rhodes said. "A little mischief for another. Can I come in and talk to you?"

"Sure thing." Leslie stepped aside and pulled the door all the way open. "Faye's around somewhere if you want to talk to her, too."

"I do," Rhodes said, and Leslie led the way down the hall to the den, which Rhodes appreciated. He was tired of kitchens.

The den had two couches in front of low coffee tables, and a giant flat-screen TV set, bigger than any Rhodes had seen, hung on one wall. There were a couple of recliners and some bookshelves on another wall, and a small upright piano sat against another.

"Have a seat on the couch there," Leslie said, pointing. "It's the most comfortable. You want something to drink? We have coffee."

"No thanks," Rhodes said. "I just want to ask a few questions."

Leslie sat on the couch beside Rhodes. "Ask away. Faye should be here in a minute."

"What do you know about the murder here last night?" Rhodes asked.

"Not much. Just that old meddler Wanda Wilkins found someone dead in the schoolhouse. He'd been shot, I believe."

"That's right," Rhodes said. "His name was Lawrence Gates, and he was here to talk to someone about the problems the town's having about the schoolhouse and whether to tear it down or not. Did he ever call you about that?"

"Never heard of him," Leslie said. "I got a call from somebody who said he was a journalist. Can't remember the name he gave me, but it wasn't Gates. I gave him my opinion and hung up on him."

"What did you tell him?"

"That I don't see any problems, myself," Leslie said. "Tear that sucker down and build something that's not leaking and falling apart. Time to move on from the past and start living in the twenty-first century."

"Some people think the history of the town should be preserved."

"By some people you mean the Hunleys? They just think so because they think Con's a big hero and maybe they can get some kind of historical marker on the place if it's still standing. All they can think about are what big heroes Con and Pete were. They don't care about the community, just their own reputations. It's all they can talk about. Bronze star this, silver star that. Their military careers and their medals are all that matter to them. Anyway, they can put up a plaque at the new building if they want to. I don't think anybody would object to that."

"That might work," Rhodes said, although he didn't think the Hunleys would be satisfied with that solution. "Seems as if the Hunleys been having some problems with vandalism lately, too."

Leslie shrugged. "I've heard about it. Mainly from them. You've talked to them, I suppose."

"Just this morning," Rhodes said. "They think you and Faye are responsible."

"Well, they're wrong," Faye Falkner said, walking into the den. She was almost as tall as her husband, but a bit heftier. "They blame everything on us. If there was a tornado, they'd blame us. They don't like us because we don't agree with them about the school, and they don't like us because we have more money than they do. They make me sick," Faye continued, raising her voice. "I wish they'd move away from here. It would improve the town a lot. They don't contribute anything. They just brag on themselves."

"Now, Faye," Leslie said. "Calm down."

"Don't you tell me to calm down," Faye yelled. "I'm perfectly calm."

"I know you are," Leslie said. "Sit down here on the couch and let the sheriff ask his questions."

Faye crossed her arms. "Maybe I don't want to sit down."

"Of course you do. It's much more comfortable than standing."

Faye laughed. "Who cares? I'm going to stand up. I like standing up."

"That's fine if it suits you," Leslie said. "Now you go ahead, Sheriff. Ask those questions."

"Aside from the vandalism, there's that murder," Rhodes said. "I don't know who the victim was planning to meet with, but since he was investigating the school controversy, it would be natural for him to meet with someone involved. So I'd like to know where the two of you were last night."

"I just bet you would," Faye said. "Well, it's none of your business."

"I'm the sheriff," Rhodes said. "That makes it my business."

"I can answer for both of us, Sheriff," Leslie said. "We were right here at home all night, and we had nothing to do with any murder or any firecrackers or anything else."

"That's right," Faye said, still not using her indoor voice. "Right here all night, and you better believe it."

Everybody was giving everybody else an alibi, which didn't surprise Rhodes. It didn't help him any, though.

"If anybody killed anybody," Faye went on, "it was those Hunleys. They all have guns. Rifles, pistols, you name it. Con and Pete were in wars. They've killed before. Once you start killing, what's one more? You ask 'em that, why don't you."

"Don't tell the sheriff how to do his job," Leslie said.

"You going to try to stop me?" Faye said.

Rhodes stood up. "I think I've gotten the answers I need for today. I'll come back if I have any more questions."

"You just do that, Sheriff," Faye said. "You just do that. See if we care."

Leslie took Rhodes's elbow and guided him away from the couch, past Faye, and into the hall. When they got to the door, he went outside with Rhodes.

"Faye's not usually like that," he said. "All this about the schoolhouse has her upset."

"I can see that," Rhodes said, but he thought that there was a lot more to it than that. Faye had a lot of problems.

"You come back any time, Sheriff," Leslie said. "We're always happy to cooperate with the law."

"I'm glad that someone is," Rhodes said, and he went to the Charger and got in.

Rhodes was tired of families, but he had to visit the Reeses. They lived on the other side of Thurston, and to get there Rhodes had to drive back through what was left of the little town. Long ago, like Clearview, it had been a thriving place, with a drugstore, a hardware store, several grocery stores, a variety store, a couple of cotton gins, and a café or two. Hardly anything was left now. Even most of the buildings were gone. A branch of Clyde Ballinger's funeral home was the most prosperous place in the town.

One of the grocery stores was still there, however, and though it was more like a convenience store now, it also had a grill and served hamburgers, which reminded Rhodes that he didn't want to miss lunch again. He'd stop by for a burger after he talked to the Reeses.

The Reeses had a ranch-style house that was about twice the size of the one the Hunleys had. It was spread out over an area the size of a football field, or that's how it seemed to Rhodes. The Reeses had a large barn with a corral nearby, and Rhodes figured that Reese liked to live up to his cowboy image by riding a horse in the corral or maybe around the property, which was extensive.

The driveway beside the house led to a three-car garage, on which one of the doors was open. Rhodes saw a brand-new red Ford-150, the King Ranch edition. It wasn't a horse, but it was something that Charlie Reese would be proud to ride around in.

Rhodes parked behind the new pickup and got out. He hadn't gotten halfway down the walk to the front of the house before the door opened and Charlie swaggered out. Even at home he was decked out in his western garb: boots, jeans, western shirt with pearlized buttons, and a western hat on his head. He wasn't wearing his revolver, which was a bit of a surprise.

"Hey, Sheriff," Charlie said in a mellow baritone. "What're you doing way down here in Thurston?"

"Just dropped by to talk," Rhodes said.

Charlie looked dubious. "A friendly conversation? That doesn't seem too likely to me, if you don't mind my saying so."

It was pretty clear from his tone that Charlie didn't care whether Rhodes minded or not.

"I don't mind," Rhodes told him, "but I think it will be friendly. Just a few questions for you and your wife, and I'll be gone."

Charlie took a couple of steps toward Rhodes. "I was just about to go for a spin in my new truck. Don't know as I have time for questions."

If Charlie thought he was going to push Rhodes around, he had another think coming. Rhodes had to work hard not to grin at his ploy. "You can go for a spin later. Let's go inside, spend a few minutes talking, and get it over with."

Charlie didn't give in that easily. He took another step forward, shoving his bulk toward Rhodes. "Like I said, I don't have time for that stuff."

"Make time," Rhodes said, his tone hardening.

Charlie appeared to be thinking about taking another step, but if he thought of it, he didn't do it. "Well, if you put it that way, I guess I can give you a few minutes."

"Good. I need to speak to your wife, too."

"Let's go in, then. Arlene's doing a little housework, though, and she might not want to be interrupted."

"She won't mind," Rhodes said.

"Maybe not," Charlie said, and he led the way into the house.

They went into a large den with a vaulted ceiling and a big stone fireplace at one end. Next to the fireplace was a gun rack that held a couple of rifles and shotguns. Rhodes thought it was a careless display of firepower, but he didn't comment. He heard a vacuum cleaner roaring in another room.

"I'll go get Arlene," Charlie said. "Be right back. She's not gonna be happy, though."

Rhodes wasn't concerned about Arlene's happiness. He looked around the den, which was about the size of an aircraft hangar and was furnished in Early Cowboy. The couch and chairs had what appeared to be a cowhide covering, with some of the hair still on them. Western paintings hung on the walls, and near the fireplace there was a sculpture of a man on a bucking horse that sat on a small pedestal. Rhodes could tell that someone had been cleaning because he smelled furniture polish.

Charlie came back into the room. He wasn't wearing his hat

anymore. Arlene, a slim woman with a smooth face and big black eyes, was with him. She wasn't wearing western clothes. She had on a plain blue housedress, and her dark hair was done up under a scarf like a housewife in an old magazine.

"Sorry for the interruption," Rhodes told her. "I just have a few questions, and then I'll be out of your way."

"I don't like vacuuming," Arlene said. She didn't look unhappy about the interruption at all. "You have a seat and take as much time as you want to."

Charlie glared at her, but she didn't notice. Rhodes sat in one of the cowhide chairs, and Charlie and Arlene sat on the couch.

"Ask your questions," Charlie said. "I want to get on my way."

Rhodes was tempted to drag things out just to get on Charlie's nerves, but he decided it would be better to get right to the point. "I'm here about the murder at the schoolhouse."

"That was awful," Arlene said. "That poor young man. I read about it online."

"That poor young man was Lawrence Gates. He was at the school to meet somebody about the local controversy about tearing it down."

"Should've been ripped down years ago," Charlie said. "Who's this Gates guy, anyway, sticking his nose into our business. I never heard of him, so he wasn't from around here."

"No, he wasn't," Rhodes said. "That doesn't matter, though. He's dead now, and he died here. I'm going to find out who killed him."

"It wasn't me," Charlie said, "and it wasn't Arlene. You're wasting your time here."

"Maybe, but that's what I'm paid for. Where were you and Arlene last night?"

"Right here. We don't get out much."

"Both of you in the house all the time."

"Damn right."

"No," Arlene said, "that's not right. You went out for a ride on Samson, remember?"

Charlie got red-faced. "So what? That's the same as being right here. I just rode around the property for a while and came back in."

"Well," Arlene said, "you had to take care of Samson before you came in, rub him down and whatever else it is that you do."

Rhodes thought about how long it would take someone to get to the school on horseback. Not long, and there were ways to get there from Charlie's house that wouldn't expose a horseman to any inquiring eyes.

"Are you trying to get me in trouble?" Charlie asked.

"Of course not," Arlene said. "I'm just telling the sheriff what we did last night."

"If I was out of your sight," Charlie said, "you were out of mine. Think about that?"

Arlene just smiled. What Rhodes was thinking about was what interesting times she and Charlie must have when there were no visitors around.

"What about you, Arlene?" Rhodes asked. "Were you in the house all the time?"

"Yes, I was," Arlene said.

"You can't prove it by me," Charlie said, "and you hate that damn school as much as I do. People never treated you well there. Even the teachers didn't like you."

"Some of them did," Arlene said, though she didn't sound confident about it.

"Not a one, and you know it. Maybe it was you that dead fella was going to meet. Maybe you were going to tell him all about how you were treated so bad there."

"I wouldn't kill him, though," Arlene said. "I wouldn't have a reason."

"Neither would I," Charlie said. He looked at Rhodes. "It's stupid for you to be asking us about this. I'm going to complain to the commissioners."

Rhodes stood up. "That's a good idea. I suggest you call Mikey Burns. He's the commissioner for this district, I think. He'd be glad to hear from you."

Charlie stood as well. "Don't get smart with me, Sheriff."

The old school-ground bully was coming out in Charlie. Rhodes didn't mind playing along for a round or two. "Smart? Me? I wouldn't dare."

Arlene giggled, and Charlie turned on her. "You hush up, Arlene."

Arlene just looked at him. It was obvious that she wasn't any more afraid of him than Rhodes was.

"I appreciate your answering my questions," Rhodes said. "I told you it wouldn't take long. I'll just see myself out."

"Come by anytime, Sheriff," Arlene said.

Charlie didn't say anything to that, and Rhodes left them there, looking at each other.

Chapter 15

Once a man named Hod Barrett, who had been none too fond of Rhodes, had owned a small grocery store right in the heart of Thurston, not that the heart was any too big. Hod had passed on, and now the building was owned by a couple whose last name was Kingston. They were from Houston, and Rhodes had no idea how they'd come to own a convenience store and hamburger grill in a tiny Texas hamlet. He'd heard, however, that they made good hamburgers, so that was reason enough to stop in. Not that Ivy didn't make the occasional hamburger, but she liked to make them from ground turkey. Rhodes preferred beef.

The inside of the store smelled like grilled meat, french fries, and onion rings, which Rhodes thought was an encouraging sign. There were a couple of booths on the right-hand side for people who wanted to dine in. The grill was in the back, behind a high counter, and a beverage cooler and groceries lined the left-hand wall. Rhodes was the only customer when he walked in and was greeted by Kingston, whose first name, Rhodes learned when he introduced himself, was Manny.

"Really, it's Manford," Kingston said, "but everybody calls me Manny. Come out here, Gale."

His wife came out from behind the counter that concealed the grill and shook hands with Rhodes. "What brings you to our place, Sheriff?" she asked.

"Hamburgers," Rhodes said. "I hear you make good ones."

"Cheeseburgers are even better," Gale said. "Want to try one?"

"Sounds good," Rhodes said.

"All the way?"

"Cut the tomatoes," Rhodes said. They made a burger too gooshy to suit him.

"How about onion rings or french fries or both?"

"Just the fries," Rhodes said. No need to give in to every temptation.

Rhodes and Manny sat in one of the booths while Gale grilled the burger. After a couple of seconds of conversation about the weather, Rhodes asked Manny what he knew about the school situation.

"Being a new resident here," Manny said, "I don't know a lot. You understand that by *new* I mean anybody who wasn't born here. That's the way the people in town look at it. We moved here because we wanted to get away from the city, and we saw a little business opportunity that we could handle. We're still not thought of as a real part of the community, but we're working on it. Part of that is not taking sides in arguments."

Rhodes heard the sound of meat sizzling on the grill and smelled the french fries. His mouth watered. "Avoiding arguments is generally a good thing, new resident or not, but surely you've heard about the school and the arguments about whether it should be torn down."

"Oh, yes," Manny said. "We've heard about that. People like to talk about it. I try not to listen."

Gale brought out the burger and fries. She set it on the table and asked Rhodes if he'd like something to drink.

"Dr Pepper if you have the kind with real sugar," Rhodes said. "Or water if you don't."

"It'll have to be water, then," Gale told him. "We can't get the kind with real sugar."

"Few people can," Rhodes said. "Water will be fine."

"You go ahead and eat, Sheriff," Manny said. "It's a little early for me."

It was about eleven, which Rhodes didn't think was too early, but then he had to take advantage of the opportunity to eat, no matter what time it was. He picked up the cheeseburger from out of its cardboard boat. The paper that wrapped the burger had a bit of grease on it, another good sign.

Rhodes bit into the burger. It was delicious, and he could tell by the crisp underside of the bun that it had been warmed on the grill, where it had absorbed some of the burger's grease. Rhodes didn't care how that might affect his heart. What he cared about was how good it made the burger taste.

Gale set water in a paper cup on the table and said, "Well?"

Rhodes finished chewing and said, "Great. I'll tell all my friends."

Gale laughed and went to the back of the store. Manny said, "We don't really listen to what people have to say about the school even though they like to talk about it. If you're interested in that kind of thing, we won't be any help."

Rhodes took another bite of his burger and ate a couple of fries, then said, "What about some of the locals who come in here from time to time, then? Do you know Kenny Lambert or Noble Truelove?"

Manny snorted. "Those two. Yeah, I know them. I'll sell a burger or some beer to anybody. I don't have much to say to them or about them, though."

"Would you recognize Kenny's pickup if you saw it?" Rhodes asked.

"That rattletrap?" Manny snorted again. "He parks it out front when he's here. I'm surprised it even runs."

Rhodes drank some water and ate more of his burger and fries. Then he said, "How late do you stay open?"

"In the summer, like now, when the days are long, we stay open until eight-thirty or so. We get a good bit of business in the late afternoon and early evening."

"Kenny come in yesterday?"

"As a matter of fact, he and Noble came in and bought a twelve pack."

So Kenny had been lying about being in Thurston, just as Rhodes had suspected. That made things a bit more interesting.

"What's this all about, Sheriff?" Manny asked. "You haven't mentioned the murder, but I've sure heard about that. Any connection?"

"Don't know," Rhodes said around a mouthful of burger. He finished chewing and added, "It's just something I was wondering about. Did you see any horsemen pass by?"

Manny laughed. "I see one every now and then, but not yesterday. You think there was a cowboy involved in the murder?"

"You never can tell."

Rhodes wadded up the paper that his burger had been wrapped

in and dropped it in the cardboard boat. He drank some water and set the paper cup back on the table.

"Best burger I've had in a long time," he said. "I'll stop by again when I'm in town if I get the chance."

He stood up to go, and Manny stood as well.

"Glad you liked it, Sheriff. You said you'd tell your friends, so don't forget to do that."

"You can count on it," Rhodes said. He picked up his trash.

"We'll try to get you some of that Dr Pepper you like, too."

"You probably can't," Rhodes said, "but I appreciate the thought."

"If I hear anything about that murder," Manny said, "I'll let you know."

"You be sure and do that," Rhodes said, as he tossed his trash into a big round plastic barrel and left the store.

Rhodes thought things over as he drove back to Clearview. He'd learned more than he thought he would from his conversations, but he wasn't sure he was any closer to finding Lawrence's killer.

He was puzzled about what had happened to Lawrence's car, phone, and wallet. It was possible that robbery was the motive for the killing, but somehow Rhodes couldn't convince himself of that. Maybe Seepy Benton had found out something from his examination of Lawrence's computer, and it was possible that Seepy had talked to Roger, who might have thought of some things that would help. If that wasn't the case, Rhodes would talk to Roger himself. Now that Roger had absorbed some of the shock of Lawrence's death, he could have remembered something relevant. Probably not, but it had to be checked out.

Rhodes was about halfway to Clearview when the radio crackled, and Hack came on. "Where are you, Sheriff?"

Rhodes told him, and Hack said, "You're in the right place. Just had a daylight robbery at the Pak-a-Sak."

"Not again," Rhodes said. The Pak-a-Sak was a favorite place for daylight robberies and nighttime robberies.

"Yep, again," Hack said. "Perp is headed your way. Drivin' a white Ford Crown Victoria. Should be easy to spot."

The perp could've turned off on any number of side roads, but if he was trying to get out of the county, he'd still be on the highway.

"Did I mention that it's a woman?" Hack asked.

"No, you didn't mention that," Rhodes said, feeling guilty about his sexist thinking.

"Well, it is. Short but pretty cute, according to Ferris." Ferris was the clerk at the Pak-n-Sak. "How many times now has he been robbed, anyway?"

"Too many," Rhodes said. "Is she armed?"

"Ferris said she had something that looked like a gun. He didn't look too close. You be careful."

"I will," Rhodes said. He looked out his windshield at the road ahead and saw a white Ford barreling down on him. "Here she comes now."

He racked the mic without signing off and didn't hear Hack's reply. As the Crown Vic blew past him, he made a U-turn, using both shoulders, and turned on the Charger's siren and light bars. He wasn't going to have time to think over his conversations, after all. People who thought he worked on one case at a time had no idea of the interruptions he had to deal with and the other tracks he had to take every single day.

The Crown Vic had been speeding, but when the driver spotted

Rhodes, its speed increased. Rhodes wondered if it was the Police Interceptor model. If it was, even the Charger might have trouble keeping up. Those old Crown Vics had a lot of power. Rhodes pushed the accelerator down and the Charger jumped forward.

Rhodes wasn't fond of chasing people in cars. It was too dangerous for all concerned, including innocent motorists or people in the path of the chase. He was especially dubious of chases inside the city limits where the dangers to others were double or triple. That said, he sometimes had to engage in a chase, and this was one of those times. The only good thing about it was that it was taking place on a straight road with few hills and little traffic.

Rhodes had hardly completed the thought before the driver of the Crown Vic made a hard left turn onto the road that led right through the middle of Thurston. Rhodes had no choice but to follow. They zoomed past a cemetery and then into the town. The road was deserted, as it often was in Thurston, and Rhodes was grateful for that.

It took them only seconds to get through the town and into the country again, and they hadn't gone more than a quarter of a mile before the driver of the Crown Vic made another fast left turn, this time onto a graveled county road just to spice things up. While there would be even less traffic, and fewer people along the way, or so Rhodes hoped, the road was a lot more dangerous for anyone driving at high speed, which would include Rhodes and the person he was pursuing.

Unlike the highway, the county road wasn't straight. To say that it was curvy was an understatement. It seemed to have a curve every hundred yards, and the driver of the Crown Vic wasn't afraid to slide around them so fast that she was only a hair from losing control of the car. Too, the road had only one lane, making the possibility of meeting another driver a bit scary at any speed above twenty-five or so, which is what people usually drove on it.

In spite of that, Rhodes followed right along after the Crown Vic, wishing he'd lingered a bit longer over his burger at Manny and Gale's grocery and missed out on the excitement of the chase.

Except that it wasn't exciting to him. Maybe it would've been exciting if he'd been a lot younger, but now it was just nerve-racking. His hands were getting a little sweaty on the steering wheel, and that was something that didn't happen often.

After the fifth or sixth curve, the Crown Vic came to a wooden bridge that crossed Sand Creek. Just at that moment, an old pickup came around the curve ahead of the bridge and kept on coming. The driver had probably driven the road hundreds of times and had never encountered a speeding car at the bridge.

The driver of the Crown Vic wasn't going to turn aside. Rhodes knew that, and the driver of the pickup wasn't going to have time to react when he saw what was going on. Rhodes slowed for the inevitable crash.

He'd misjudged the pickup driver, however. As the robber rumbled across the wooden bridge, the pickup driver came to his senses and whipped his steering wheel to the right just in time to avoid the onrushing car. Unfortunately, there being nowhere else to go, he was steering right down the bank and into the nearly dry creek bed. As Rhodes sped up and crossed the bridge, he saw the pickup driver clutching the wheel, his eyes bugged out, and his mouth open in what must have been a scream. Rhodes hoped he'd be all right, but he was too invested in the chase now to stop and find out.

He wondered if the robber knew where she was going or if she was trying to get away from him, or if she was just enjoying herself.

If it was the latter, her enjoyment ended almost immediately. She came to a sharp curve, slid into it too fast, and overcorrected as the car's tires failed to gain traction. The Crown Vic flipped over three times. It flew over the drainage ditch, smashed through a barbed-wire fence, and stopped upside down in a field of dead grass and weeds.

Rhodes pulled as far to one side of the road as he could, with his right wheels over the edge and into the ditch. He unbuckled his seat belt, took a deep breath, let it out, and got out of the Charger. He didn't see anybody moving in the Crown Vic, but he got his pistol from its ankle holster and walked up to the car.

When he got there, he didn't smell gasoline, which was good. The car wasn't in danger of catching on fire. The roof of the car hadn't caved in, which was also good. Probably reinforced, as in the Interceptor. Grasshoppers jumped and banged against the sides of the car.

Rhodes bent down and looked into the driver's window. A young woman hung upside down, suspended by her seat belt. She didn't seem injured. She grinned at Rhodes.

"That was fun," she said with a wicked grin. "Wanna do it again?"

Chapter 16

▼

It was an old joke, and Rhodes had heard it before. But even if it was a joke, he didn't want to do it again. He wanted to get the robber out of the car, and after a bit of a struggle, he got the door open. She said she couldn't unbuckle the seat belt, so Rhodes stuck his pistol in his waistband, got out his pocketknife, and cut her free. She fell to the roof but was agile enough to twist around and crawl out of the car. Rhodes backed away and let her stand up. Then he cuffed her.

"You didn't need to do that," she said.

"Yes, I did. Now I'm going to pat you down."

"That might be fun."

"Not if I do it right," Rhodes said.

"You have to do it right?"

"Always," Rhodes said, and he did.

He didn't find a weapon, so he relaxed a bit and asked for her name and identification.

"My name's Madison Russell," she said. "My ID is in my purse in the car."

Rhodes looked into the car and saw a leather purse that looked like it had come from Walmart. It lay beneath the steering wheel.

Rhodes figured he had plenty of probable cause to search the car and the purse, but he asked for Madison's permission, anyway.

"Sure, go ahead," she said as if she didn't have a care in the world.

Rhodes told Madison to stay where she was while he retrieved the purse. First he checked for a weapon, but he didn't find one. He did find a handful of crumpled bills, however, probably the loot from her robbery. He moved them aside and found her wallet. Her driver's license was in it, and he looked at it. She hadn't bothered to use an alias when she told him her name, assuming the license wasn't a forgery.

Rhodes returned her license to the purse, closed it, and set it on the ground. Then he placed her under arrest for speeding, reckless driving, and fleeing a police officer.

"I thought we were just having a good time," Madison said.

"Maybe you were," Rhodes said.

She grinned at him. "We could probably both have fun if you wanted to and if you'd take these handcuffs off me."

Rhodes looked at her. She was about twenty-five, with short brown hair and wide brown eyes, a wide mouth and a pug nose that she wrinkled when she grinned.

"I don't think so," Rhodes said. "I have a shirt at home that's older than you are."

Madison continued to grin. "Don't underestimate your abilities, Sheriff."

"I'm not, but I don't fraternize with prisoners."

"That's a fancy word for it."

"I'm a regular thesaurus," Rhodes said. "Did you have a weapon in the car."

Madison laughed. "No. I showed that clerk the handle of a hairbrush."

Ferris wouldn't think that was as funny as she did. Rhodes remembered seeing a hairbrush in the purse, so maybe she was telling the truth. He said, "So you won't have to worry about a weapons charge. We'd better get going. I need to see about the man you ran off the road."

"He got in the way," Madison said.

"Right. You go first. I'll follow you."

Madison started to walk toward the Charger. When she got to the flattened fence, she said, "Don't you want to know why I robbed that place?"

"Nope," Rhodes said. "You did it, and that's what matters."

"What if I had starving children, like that guy who stole a loaf of bread in that movie? I can't remember the name of it. It was in some foreign language. The name, not the movie. It was in English, and Hugh Jackman played the guy."

Rhodes couldn't picture Madison as the mother of starving children, and while he hadn't seen the movie, he knew what she was talking about. It was something he remembered from a long ago English class. He didn't remember the man's name, however, and he didn't care that Hugh Jackman played him in a movie.

"Still wouldn't matter," Rhodes said.

"You're just like that guy who was chasing Hugh Jackman," Madison said. "He had a funny name, too. He never let up. It was just a loaf of bread, but he kept after Hugh Jackman for years."

"You didn't take a loaf of bread," Rhodes said.

"No, but I didn't get much money, either."

"You got some, though, so let's get in the car."

Madison gave in and walked down into the ditch and out onto the road, with Rhodes behind her. He opened the back door of the Charger and got her into the seat. It was a bit awkward with the car being parked at an angle and her being in handcuffs, but he managed it. When it was done, he got into the driver's seat, started the car, and made a U-turn. Then he got Hack on the radio and told him to send a wrecker for the car. "It's upside down."

"Those wrecker guys can deal with that. They're trained professionals. You catch Bonnie Parker?"

"I did. I'm bringing her in."

"No Clyde with her?"

"No, she was a lone wolf," Rhodes said and signed off.

"You really going to see about that guy at the bridge?" Madison asked from behind the mesh screen that separated them.

"I am. It's all part of the job. You should hope that he's doing all right."

Madison wasn't concerned about the man she'd almost crashed into. "That bank's not very steep. He'll be fine."

Rhodes wasn't so sure, but when they got to the bridge, he saw the man standing at the top of the bank and talking on a cell phone. Rhodes parked the Charger and got out. The man put his cell phone in a pocket, and Rhodes asked, "You all right?"

"As all right as I can be, considering what just happened to me. I hope you caught up to that crazy driver."

"I did," Rhodes said. "She wrecked her car, and she's under arrest in the backseat of mine."

"Good," the man said. He wore a sweat-stained baseball cap with a checkerboard logo, a khaki shirt, and blue jeans. "I hope she's insured."

Rhodes laughed. "I wouldn't count on it. Have you called a wrecker?"

"Just got off the phone with one. I'm Ellis Holmes, by the way. I know who you are." He looked down the bank at his pickup that was nosed into the creek bottom. "I sure wish I'd been able to get off the road into a ditch instead of into a creek. Guess it can't be helped now, though."

Rhodes looked at the pickup. "Doesn't look like there's much damage."

"We'll see," Ellis said. "I have insurance, though, so I'm not too worried about that even if that woman isn't insured. I'm just worried about being without my truck. I'll have to rent something."

"Good luck," Rhodes said. "If you're okay, I'll go on to town with my prisoner."

"I'm fine," Ellis said. "You go on ahead. The sooner you get that crazy driver behind bars, the better I'll like it."

"So will I," Rhodes told him.

Almost as soon as they got Madison booked and printed, Seepy Benton came in. He'd spent the morning talking to Roger Prentiss and looking into Lawrence Gates's computer.

"Roger didn't really know much more to tell me that would be helpful," Seepy said. "He couldn't figure out why Lawrence was so interested in the schoolhouse controversy, but that's what's taken up all his time recently."

"We know that," Rhodes said. "He lied to me about why he was doing it. He told me that his grandmother went to school there."

"He was hiding something, then," Seepy said.

"He likely was," Rhodes said, "but what was he hiding? Did anything you saw on the computer give you any clues?"

Seepy looked a little embarrassed. "I checked it out to see if he had any social media accounts under other names. I didn't find any. He didn't have any under his own name, either, naturally."

Rhodes didn't think that was much of an answer. "Did that tell you anything?"

"No," Seepy said.

"So what else did you look for?"

"I looked through all his files. He had a lot on the Thurston school. He'd copied a lot of newspaper articles from various newspaper archives. I looked at all the articles, and they didn't give me any information that we don't have. We already knew that some famous people went to school there, and that was no surprise. There was a lot of military material, too. If you wanted to know about wars, especially twentieth-century wars, Lawrence would've been the one to ask. He had things on all of them, from World War One to the wars in Afghanistan and Iraq. He had more on those last two and Vietnam than anything."

"Still doesn't tell us much," Rhodes said. "Was there anything else?"

Seepy looked at the floor then back up at Rhodes. "I didn't really look at all the files."

"Why not?"

"Some of them are encrypted."

"Encrypted?"

"Converted into code so only the person who knows the key can read them."

"You could break the code," Rhodes said.

"That's right," Seepy said. "Eventually I can. Any code can be broken. It just takes time, and there's some software that can help. I'll get into those files. Don't worry."

"I'll try not to," Rhodes said. "If Lawrence went to that much trouble, he had something to hide."

"It wasn't much trouble for him to encrypt the files," Seepy said. "It's easy enough to do. You're right about him having something to hide, though. He wouldn't have encrypted them otherwise."

"You'll break the code, though."

"Eventually," Seepy said. "You can count on it."

"You know I will," Rhodes said.

After Seepy left, Rhodes called Roger and told him that he wouldn't be by but would talk to him later. Then he went to his office in the courthouse. It was a place where usually nobody would bother him, and he needed some time to think. Jennifer Loam had tracked him down there a time or two, but even if she did it again, which Rhodes didn't expect, he'd be away from Hack and Lawton and wouldn't have to worry about them telling him some endless story about some armadillo assaulting a man.

There were no trials going on that day, so the courthouse was quiet, its hallways almost empty. Although Rhodes could hear people talking in the county offices he passed, he got to his office without being seen. There'd been a time when he'd have stopped by the Dr Pepper machine in the basement, but the new one no longer dispensed the drink in glass bottles, and that took all the pleasure out of buying one. Rhodes could get a can or a plastic bottle just about anywhere, but he wouldn't do that, either, unless he could get one made with real sugar. The good news was that he also wouldn't be buying the orange snack crackers that he liked because they just weren't as good without a Dr Pepper. So he'd avoid a few more calories.

He went straight to his office, slipped inside, and shut the door. When the door was closed, he looked around. The place was as tidy as ever, which it should've been since he hardly ever used it and since the courthouse cleaning crew took good care of it. The chair and desk were much nicer than those in the jail, although Rhodes didn't care about things like that. He was interested in comfort, and the chair was comfortable enough. He sat in it and took a few minutes to organize his thoughts about the interviews he'd had that morning.

It was likely that the people he'd talked to had believed they were giving nothing away, but as was often the case, they'd told Rhodes more than they thought they had, especially the Falkners. It was Leslie who'd given away the most. He'd told Rhodes that he and Faye knew nothing about the firecrackers at the Hunley house, but Rhodes hadn't mentioned firecrackers at all. Con Hunley might've called Leslie to complain, but he hadn't mentioned doing it. So Rhodes figured there was just one way Leslie could've known about them, and that was that he and Faye were guilty of throwing them.

Of course that meant that they'd both been out of the house, although they said they hadn't, and while the Hunleys had said the firecracker incident occurred about three in the morning, Leslie and Faye could've been out much earlier. One or both of them could even have gone to the schoolhouse to meet Lawrence.

Rhodes would talk to them again, if only to make sure they didn't pull any more pranks on the Hunleys, but also to find out about any other lies they'd told.

The Reeses were only a slightly different story. Charlie had tried to get Arlene to lie for him, but she'd told about his leaving the house for a horseback ride, and then Charlie had pointed out that if he hadn't been in the house, maybe she hadn't been, either. So Rhodes had two more suspects in Lawrence's death.

Manny hadn't seen Charlie riding his horse through town, but there was no reason Charlie had to have passed by the store, and he might not even have ridden the horse if he'd gone to the school. His big red truck would have been all too easy to spot, however, so if he'd taken a vehicle, that probably hadn't been the one. He might even have walked to the school.

And then there was Kenny, who'd lied about him and Noble being in Thurston. Kenny was the only one Rhodes knew who had any kind of motive to kill Lawrence, so that put him right atop the suspect list.

Rhodes had plenty of suspects now, and a lot to sort through, but before he could get any further, someone knocked on the door.

Rhodes knew who it had to be. Jennifer Loam had tracked him down yet again. He considered not opening the door, but he knew how persistent she was. If he didn't let her in, she'd stand out in the hallway all day and keep right on knocking. He got up and did what he had to do.

"You're hiding out again," Jennifer said when he opened the door.

"Hack ratted me out, didn't he," Rhodes said.

"I never reveal my sources or my informants," Jennifer said. "Are you going to invite me in?"

"Sure," Rhodes said. What else could he do? "Come on in and have a seat."

Jennifer swept past him and sat in a leather-covered chair near his desk. Rhodes went back to his own chair and resumed his seat.

"Aren't you going to ask me what I'm here for?" Jennifer asked.

"Do I have to ask?"

Jennifer laughed. "No, you don't. I'll tell you. Hack said you had quite a chase and arrest today. I'd like to get the story for my blog."

"There's not much to tell," Rhodes said. "Sounds like you already have your story. I wouldn't want it exaggerated."

"Exaggerate? Moi? You know I wouldn't do that."

"No," Rhodes said, "I know you *would* exaggerate it, probably with some clickbait headline."

Jennifer smiled. "I need Seepy Benton to create those headlines, and now he has another job."

Rhodes thought that the story of the chase would be a good one even without exaggeration, considering the encounter at the bridge and the flipped car, so he gave Jennifer a brief version of it, which she recorded on a small digital device. When he was finished telling her, she put the recorder away and said, "Now I have some information for you. It's about Lawrence Gates."

Rhodes sat up straighter in his chair. "Tell me."

"I talked to Roger Prentiss today about Lawrence Gates for a story I'm doing on the murder. Roger showed me a picture of Lawrence, and I recognized him. He'd called me a few weeks ago and asked to meet and talk. He told me his name was William Smith."

"I've seen some of his movies," Rhodes said. He had fond memories of *Hell Comes to Frogtown*, the kind of bad old movie he liked but which never turned up on TV anymore.

"I didn't know William Smith was a movie star," Jennifer said. "I should've asked for ID when Lawrence and I met, but I didn't. I told him I'd be glad to talk to him but that I didn't think I'd be much help. He said he thought I would, so I agreed. We met at Max's Barbecue for lunch."

She paused, and Rhodes decided that she was yet another one who'd been around Hack and Lawton too long. He thought he might as well play the game. "Was the food good?"

"I had the sliced beef plate. It was great."

"What did Lawrence have?"

Jennifer laughed. "I know what you're doing, but I don't mean to drag this out. While we ate, he asked questions about Thurston and the people who lived there. He was interested in the school, but he was more interested in the people, it seemed to me. He had the sliced beef plate, too, by the way."

"Which people?" Rhodes asked.

"You can probably guess. The three families most involved in the controversy about the school building. He managed to get me interested enough to do a little digging on my own later, and it turns out that Charlie Reese, who seems to own a piece of everything, has a construction company that's going to bid on the new building. I never got to tell Lawrence that."

"One more reason for Charlie to want it torn down," Rhodes said, wondering how that might tie in to the murder or if it did.

"He was interested in the Hunleys, too. It seems he was a big war buff."

"I know that for sure," Rhodes said. "What about the Falkners?"

"I think he had something on them, but he didn't tell me what it was. I gathered that it involved the Hunleys."

Rhodes wondered if Lawrence had heard about the pranks the Falkners had pulled and who might've told him. Maybe he'd heard only about the pranks and figured out who was behind them.

"He knew one thing that's not general knowledge yet," Jennifer said. "Maybe Con Hunley told him."

Rhodes wondered about that. Con had claimed not to have

talked to Lawrence, or John Watson, or anybody about the school. Rhodes asked what Lawrence knew that wasn't public knowledge yet.

"Con's planning a school reunion for the fall, a homecoming, I guess you could call it. Lawrence thought it was more something to glorify Con and Pete than something to benefit the community. A big deal with them at the center of it, lots of talk about what heroes they were and how the school should be saved because of that. Lawrence seemed upset about that for some reason."

Rhodes couldn't think of any reason for Lawrence to be upset. "The Hunleys like publicity," he said, "but there's nothing wrong with that. Some like it and some don't."

"You don't," Jennifer said.

"Let's just say I prefer a low profile."

"You'll be glad for some publicity next year when you're running for office again."

"I might not run," Rhodes said. "I haven't made up my mind."

"You'd be elected by write-in votes if you didn't," Jennifer told him. "You're a popular man around here."

"Thanks to your blog."

"That might have something to do with it, but not much. You do a good job, and you're fair. People know that and appreciate it."

Rhodes didn't like talking about himself or his election prospects. He said, "Con didn't mention the homecoming to me when I talked to him today."

"He's not ready to publicize it, according to Lawrence. It must be just in the planning stages."

Rhodes wondered if the homecoming could be connected to the murder. If Lawrence knew about it that meant he had talked to Con, and that was something worth looking into. Rhodes would need a picture of Lawrence, something he should've thought of sooner. He'd get one from Roger or from Seepy.

"I need to get this story on my blog," Jennifer said, standing up. Rhodes stood, too. "I'll let you know if I find out anything else about Lawrence and the murder."

"You do that," Rhodes said.

Jennifer left, and Rhodes sat back down to filter through his interviews and see what he could come up with. After an hour he hadn't come up with anything, so he went on back to the jail to do some paperwork.

The rest of the afternoon was routine: an arrest for sale of a controlled substance; a couple of calls about thefts; a man on the side of the road waving his arms was brought in for public intoxication. The saddest thing was the arrest of a young woman for the theft of spinach dip from Walmart. Buddy had brought her in, and even he felt sorry for her, which might have been a first. Although the dip cost less than three dollars, the offense was considered a Class B misdemeanor because she had a previous conviction for theft on her record. The punishment in such cases was a sentence of up to a hundred and eighty days in jail or a fine of up to two thousand dollars or both. Rhodes hoped the judge would go easy on her, and so did Buddy, who might've been getting soft after all his years on the job.

Because not much was going on and because it was too late for Rhodes to follow up on any of the thoughts he'd had at the courthouse, it appeared that he would get to go home at a normal time. He called Ivy to let her know.

"Good," she said. "You deserve a break now and then."

"You got that right," Rhodes said.

"We're having Mexican food," Ivy said.

"Sounds great. I plan to spend some time with Speedo and Yancey before I eat. Maybe there'll even be a bad movie on that I want to watch."

"A relaxing evening then."

"Absolutely," Rhodes said.

It didn't work out quite that way, however. That night someone tried to burn the Thurston schoolhouse down.

Chapter 17

The phone call from Wanda Wilkins came just as it was getting dark. Rhodes didn't know how she'd gotten his number, which was concealed in the phone book under Ivy's first initial—I. Rhodes. Ivy always answered the phone and often that was as far as any unauthorized caller got, but not this time.

Rhodes only half-listened to the conversation. So far it had been a relaxing evening even if it hadn't gone quite as planned. He'd given the dogs a romp, but he hadn't found a bad movie to watch, and the Mexican food Ivy promised had turned out to be a veggie enchilada casserole. It wasn't bad, but Rhodes liked his Mexican casseroles with a little meat in them. A lot of meat was even better. Chicken or beef, it didn't matter as long as it was meat. Ivy's casserole had black beans, cauliflower, and sweet potato, among other things. Rhodes wouldn't have thought the sweet potato would work, but it did. He would still have preferred meat, however.

The conversation between Ivy and Wanda ended, and Ivy handed the phone to Rhodes.

"Sheriff?" Wanda said when Rhodes took the phone.

"Yes," Rhodes said. "It's me."

"That wife of yours didn't want to let me talk to you, but I told her how important it was. Did she tell you?"

"No," Rhodes said. "She just told me who was calling, so I knew it was important."

"Good. You need to come down here right now."

"Why?" Rhodes asked.

"There's somebody prowling around in the school. I've been taking a look now and then when there's a commercial on TV, and I saw somebody over there."

Rhodes couldn't figure out what anybody would be doing in the school at night, so he asked Wanda if she was sure. That was a mistake.

"Sure?" she said, almost loud enough to be heard all the way from Thurston without the phone. "Do you think I'm some crazy old woman who doesn't know what she's seeing? When I say there's somebody there, there's somebody there. You ought to know better than to ask, and if there's somebody in the building, then they're up to no good. You can mark my words."

Rhodes hated to ask the next question, but he knew he had to. Wanda's house was across the street, it was almost dark, and she probably didn't have perfect vision. "What did you see to make you so sure?"

"I saw a shadow move in front of a window," Wanda said. "Somebody's in there with a flashlight, and don't tell me I've just made some kind of mistake. When I see a shadow move, then it moved. It looked like the outline of a person, and so that's how I know somebody's in there. You better get down here and take a look or you'll be sorry if something bad happens."

Rhodes sighed but not loudly enough for Wanda to hear. He added, "I'll have to get dressed."

"Well, you better make it snappy. If you don't get here quick enough, I'll go over there myself."

Rhodes knew she meant what she said. "If there's someone in the building, that's too dangerous. You stay put. I'll be there as soon as I can."

"You don't believe me, anyway," Wanda said, "and you can't tell me what to do. I know my rights."

"Just don't do anything until I get there."

"We'll see," Wanda said, and she hung up on him.

"She sounds nice," Ivy said when Rhodes hung up.

"She is," Rhodes said, although he could tell what Ivy really meant. Her tone had made it clear. "She's just overly excited. She thinks someone's messing around in the Thurston schoolhouse."

"That's what she told me," Ivy said. "Do you believe her?"

"I'm not sure, but I'll have to go check it out. I hope she doesn't do anything stupid."

"She just might," Ivy said.

"Durn tootin'," Rhodes said.

The building was already on fire when Rhodes arrived, and the flames appeared to be spreading. A small crowd had gathered, standing a good way away from the building, and Rhodes asked a man if the fire department had been called.

"Sure," the man said. His round face was lit by the fire. "All's we got is a volunteer department, though, and it takes them a little time to get organized. Far as that goes, all's we got is a pump truck since we don't have fire hydrants. A pump truck ain't gonna be much help here."

"They'll call Clearview and other departments," Rhodes said.

"Sure, but they'll just bring pump trucks. That buildin's a goner. Might be a shell of it standin' when it's all over, but that's about all."

A short woman with big eyes tugged at Rhodes's sleeve. "Sheriff?"

Rhodes turned to her and asked what she wanted.

"I got here before anybody else, and I saw Wanda Wilkins running into the schoolhouse. She didn't come out. Somebody needs to get her out of there."

Rhodes looked at the burning building. The fire was mostly on the lower floor, but it would soon spread to the second. He didn't know what he could do, but the woman was right. Somebody needed to get Wanda out of there. Unfortunately there was nobody around but him who appeared even halfway willing or able.

Neither floor was engulfed in flames, so maybe it was still possible to get in and out if he did it fast enough, but finding Wanda quickly might be a problem. If she'd been able to get out on her own, she'd be out already, so something had happened to her, and whatever had happened wouldn't be good.

Hesitating wasn't going to get the job done, and the Thurston fire department still wasn't on the scene. Rhodes asked the woman if she had a handkerchief.

"I have a headscarf," she said. She opened her purse and pulled it out.

"I'll need to borrow it," Rhodes said, taking it from her. "You call the Clearview EMTs and tell them to hurry."

He tied the scarf around his head like a road agent's mask and took off toward the building at as much of a run as he could muster.

It was like running toward a furnace. The closer he got, the hotter it got, but he didn't slow down. He ran up the steps and found that the door was open, so that worry was taken care of. He stopped running when he got inside. It had been a long time since he'd read the Bible, but he remembered the story of Shadrach, Meshach, and Abednego who'd been cast into the fiery furnace. They'd been protected by an angel, but Rhodes had a feeling no angel was going to show up to protect him.

Rhodes didn't have a flashlight, but there was one on his phone. He got the phone out of his pocket and turned on the flashlight. Its beam and the flickering fire gave him enough light to see by, although the smoke was getting thick. The wooden floors in the classrooms were burning, and as the fire got hotter, the heat would quickly lead to stress and cracking of the bricks and masonry. After that, the interior structure of the walls, mostly wood, would start to burn. Rhodes thought he had only a few minutes before that began to happen.

Not that it mattered because the smoke would likely get him first. Inhaling smoke for even a short time had ill effects, and Rhodes's eyes, nose, and throat were already irritated. Things would only get worse, and they'd get worse fast.

Rhodes turned toward the meeting room, hoping he could find Wanda there and get her out quickly. He didn't see her inside, and the floor was already burning. He had no other ideas about where she might be. He went back out into the hallway and called her name, without really expecting an answer, and he didn't get one. His throat was scratchy, and he could hardly yell loud enough to be heard even a short distance away. The fire was making so much noise that even the strongest voice would be drowned out.

Rhodes had no idea about which room to try next. The offices? The auditorium? Another classroom? The auditorium had a lot of wood in it. All the seats were wood, and so was the stage. If someone had spread an accelerant, that would have been the place to start.

Rhodes had to open the door to get inside the auditorium. He pulled the sleeve of his shirt down over his hand to touch the metal handle and flung the door open as fast as he could. He didn't think he'd blistered his hand.

Smoke billowed out and a blast of heat hit Rhodes like a fist. He forced himself inside and saw a little vision of hell. A line from some old song popped into his head, something about fire being the devil's only friend. Many of the auditorium seats were aflame, as was the stage, and Rhodes could easily imagine the devil dancing with delight as the song put it.

The smoke was so thick that Rhodes wasn't sure he'd be able to see Wanda even if she was there. He started down the aisle toward the stage and had gone only a few feet before he tripped over something and fell.

It didn't take Rhodes long to figure out that the something he'd tripped over was a body, probably Wanda's. Now that he'd found her, he had to get her out. That wasn't going to be easy. It wasn't her size or weight that was the problem. It was the smoke.

At one time, Rhodes would have tried to pick Wanda up and use the fireman's carry, but that was no longer considered the best practice, as he'd learned at a short course he'd taken at the Clearview Fire Department. Smoke became worse higher up, so it was better to keep the person down as low as possible, which meant dragging Wanda out by the shoulders. That way Rhodes would have to bend down, putting his own head lower, and dragging would use the strong muscles in Rhodes's upper legs. It was a lot better than trying to put someone over his shoulders, and Rhodes started dragging Wanda up the aisle.

He could no longer see where he was going. He'd lost his phone when he fell, not that it would have done him much good if he'd had it. The aisle was straight, and he was able to follow it without getting burned on the seats. He got to the door well enough. He kicked it open and pulled Wanda into the hall, where the smoke wasn't as bad and the fire wasn't quite as hot.

It wasn't far to the front door now, but Rhodes heard a creaking, tearing noise above him. He didn't look up, but he knew what was about to happen. He tried to move faster, and then the ceiling started to come down. Flaming wood and masonry crashed all around, but only a few cinders landed on Rhodes. They singed him, but they didn't set his clothing on fire. He kept moving.

He got a few feet farther and stumbled and fell. He wondered for a second if he'd be able to get up, but he did. Wanda hadn't moved, and he thought she might be dead. He couldn't leave her even if she was, so he began dragging her again.

He was tired and wasn't sure he could make it outside, but he had to keep trying. He pulled Wanda a few more steps and was on the verge of collapse when someone took him by the shoulders and said, "I've got you. Les will get Wanda. Let's get out of here."

The angel had arrived after all, or two of them had, in the person of two of the Thurston volunteers in their fire-fighting outfits. Rhodes was glad to let them take over, and he allowed the man who was helping him get him outside.

"Wanda might need CPR," Rhodes said, his voice mostly a rasping noise.

"Got it," the man said. "What about you?"

"I'm fine," Rhodes said, and he slumped to the hard ground and lost consciousness.

• • •

When Rhodes came to, he was lying on a gurney with an oxygen mask over his face. The scarf was gone, and he had a feeling the woman he'd taken it from would never get it back. His next thought was it was a good thing the EMTs had arrived. His third thought was about Wanda. He looked around as best he could for someone to ask, but no one was close by. She was lucky that she'd been lying on the floor. Maybe the smoke hadn't gotten to her enough to be life-threatening.

Rhodes decided that he was strong enough to get off the gurney and stand up, which he managed to do with only a little difficulty. He didn't try to remove the mask.

The reason no one was near him was that everyone was focused on the fire, which was by now an inferno. Firemen with hoses affixed to the pump trucks were pouring water on the flames, but it was far too late for the building. All they could do was douse the flames and keep cinders from blowing onto the roofs of houses that were in the vicinity, and that wouldn't be too difficult, as there were no houses behind or on the sides of the school. Wanda's house across the street was the only one in any danger, and the wind wasn't blowing in that direction.

Not too far away from where Rhodes stood, Wanda lay on her own gurney beside the red-and-white EMT ambulance. He hadn't been able to see her when he was lying down, but it was easy enough now that he was standing. She wasn't covered with a sheet, which Rhodes knew was a good sign. An EMT stood beside her. Rhodes took off the oxygen mask and tried breathing without it. He thought he was okay, and he walked over to where Wanda was. She'd been given a breathing tube and wasn't breathing on her own.

"Is she all right?" he asked the EMT.

"No, and you won't be, either, if you don't behave yourself."

"I'm okay," Rhodes said. His voice was stronger, and his throat didn't hurt as much as it had. "I'll put the oxygen mask back on if you'll tell me how she's doing."

"Not well. She might live; she might not. We're about to load her up and take her to the hospital. You, too."

"Not me," Rhodes said. "I have too much to do."

"You won't get it done if you're dead."

"I'll take that chance."

"Then you're just plain crazy, sheriff or not."

Rhodes nodded. "You're probably right."

He went back to his gurney and put the oxygen mask back on. After a few deep breaths he took it off again. He saw Gary Parker, the Clearview fire chief, near one of the pump trucks and started in that direction, only to be accosted by Jennifer Loam. He might've known she'd be one of the first on the scene.

"I was lucky enough to get here in time for some good video of you coming out of the building," she said. "You're going to be a bigger hero than ever by tomorrow morning."

"I'm no hero," Rhodes said.

"Maybe you don't think so, but I know better, and so does everyone else in this county. Sage Barton is a sissy compared to you." She gave Rhodes a thoughtful look. "Did you know that you have an uncanny resemblance to Smokey the Bear? All you need is the little hat."

Rhodes thought of the story of Shadrach, Meshach, and Abednego again. As he recalled it, when they came out of the furnace, their hair wasn't singed, their clothing wasn't scorched, and they didn't even smell of smoke. He had a feeling none of that was true in his case, but what really bothered him was Jennifer's comment about Sage Barton.

"I don't wear hats," he said, "and I wish you wouldn't mention that name."

"What name?" Jennifer looked innocent. "Smokey the Bear?"

"You know what name I meant," Rhodes said.

"Sage Barton?"

"That's the one," Rhodes said.

Sage Barton was a fictional character created by a couple of women named Claudia and Dolly who'd once attended a writing workshop in Blacklin County. They'd used their experience there to help them with their writing, and they'd become quite successful. They'd written a series of best-selling books about a sheriff named Sage Barton, who was everything Rhodes wasn't: dashing, daring, a ladykiller, and a handy man with his Colt .45s. The books sold especially well in Blacklin County, where many people liked to think that Sage Barton was based on Rhodes because of his association with the authors.

Rhodes lived in fear of what might happen after the next book was published, since in preparation for writing it, Claudia and Dolly had dropped by to question him about his sex life. Their publisher had been worried about sales and wanted them to do something to spice up the books. Giving Sage Barton a more vigorous sex life was the answer they'd come up with. Rhodes wasn't sure why anybody would think he could tell them anything about the sex life of a lawman, but since Hack had overheard the conversation, the whole town would know about it. The whole town would also believe that Rhodes's sex life was exactly like Sage Barton's. Rhodes was uncomfortable just thinking about it.

"I'll try to remember not to mention Sage Barton again," Jennifer said. "You're much more heroic than that Sage character anyway, and you're real instead of just a character in a book."

"Sure," Rhodes said. "I'd appreciate it if you didn't put any video on your site until I have time to get home and explain things to my wife. I don't want her to be upset."

"That's easy enough. It won't go up until morning, I promise."

"Thanks," Rhodes said. "I need to talk to Chief Parker now."

"He gave a good interview about you," Jennifer said, "but he thinks you were crazy to go into that burning building."

"I agree with him a hundred percent," Rhodes said.

Chief Parker was a big man, taller and wider than Rhodes, and he was an imposing figure in the light of the fire. Rhodes walked up to him and said, "So you think I'm crazy?"

The chief looked at him. "I sure do, but you saved that woman's life. Maybe it's okay to be a little crazy now and then."

"What about the fire? Any ideas about how it might've started?"

"I don't like to prejudge. Could've been electrical. That old building had wiring from almost a century ago. That's never good."

"I don't like to prejudge, either," Rhodes said, "but the fire sure did spread fast to have been caused by an electrical problem."

The chief grimaced. "I know where you're going with this, and it does look like it might've been an arson fire. I'm not saying it is, though. The state fire marshal will send an investigator; he's the one who'll make the determination."

"That might take a while."

"It will, but we have to go through the process. I've been asked to do a little poking around by the Thurston volunteer chief, but nothing I find will be official."

"You'll let me know, though."

"Sure." Parker looked around. "It's going to be hard to keep people away from here. Just putting some tape up won't do the job. People are too curious, and they can make a real mess of a scene."

"No question about that," Rhodes said. "You call me if you get any ideas about the cause."

Rhodes turned to go to his car and heard the siren of the ambulance as it took Wanda away. He was glad the EMTs had decided not to hunt him down, strap him to the gurney, and take him along, too.

On the other hand, now he had to go home and face Ivy, who wasn't going to be the least bit happy with him.

He might have been better off if he'd turned himself over to the EMTs, but it was too late for that now. Maybe Ivy would let him off easy. He could only hope.

Chapter 18

For once Yancey didn't yip and dance around Rhodes's ankles when he got home. He gave the ankles a couple of quick sniffs and ran off. He sat at a distance and looked at Rhodes with what seemed to be a sad and pitying look. Rhodes couldn't tell if the pity and sadness were for Rhodes's appearance or for the dressing down Rhodes was getting from Ivy.

"Let me be sure I have this right," Ivy said, after Rhodes had explained things. She looked Rhodes up and down. "You ran into a burning building without any kind of protection, and you didn't even know for sure there was anybody inside."

"I had some protection," Rhodes said. "I forgot to mention the scarf I had tied around my face."

"That's about as much protection as a . . . I don't know what," Ivy said, "and you know it."

Rhodes did know it, but he thought the scarf had helped a good deal, not that he was going to say so. He and Ivy were in the little back porch area because Rhodes didn't want to go inside in his sooty clothes. Speedo was outside the screen door, looking in. He didn't appear to be filled with sadness or pity. Rhodes thought he might be laughing, though.

"I was told Wanda Wilkins was in there," Rhodes said. His voice was still a little husky. "I couldn't just leave her to die."

"So you had to be the hero again."

"I didn't do it to be a hero, and I sure don't feel heroic. I feel tired and dirty, and I'm covered with soot and ashes."

"So now you're Cinderella?"

When Ivy said that, Rhodes knew that things were all right.

"I don't feel like Cinderella," he said, "but I could use a fairy godmother to wave her magic wand and say 'Bibbidi-bobbidi-boo.'"

"You want to ride in a pumpkin?"

"No, I want to get out of these clothes and take a shower."

"That's a good idea," Ivy said. "You'd better take your shoes and clothes off out here. Even if you do, you're going to track up the house."

"I'll be as careful as I can," Rhodes said.

Ivy gave him a stern look. "You'd better," she said.

The shower was a mess when Rhodes was finished, but cleaning it could wait. What he wanted to do was go to sleep. He told Ivy good night, got into bed, and was asleep almost as soon as his head touched the pillowcase.

He had bad dreams, most of which he didn't remember the next morning other than that they were all about fire and about being trapped in a burning building with no way out. He was glad when he woke up, but he didn't feel rested. What he did feel was surprise when he looked at the clock. He got up and got dressed as quickly as he could.

"You let me oversleep," he told Ivy as he walked into the kitchen with Yancey dancing around his ankles.

"I thought you needed the rest," she said. "Sit down and I'll fix you some breakfast."

Rhodes was about to say that the kind of rest he'd had wasn't the kind he needed and that he didn't want any breakfast, but he changed his mind on both counts, mainly because he smelled bacon and realized that he did want breakfast, after all. The bacon was turkey bacon, admittedly, but it was better than no bacon at all. Eaten with toast and scrambled eggs, it wasn't terrible.

"I need to call the hospital," Rhodes said. His voice, he was glad to hear, was back to normal. "I want to ask about Wanda Wilkins."

"Go ahead," Ivy said. "Breakfast will be ready by the time you find out how she is."

Rhodes made the call and got some good news. Wanda would be fine, although her complete recovery would take a while. Rhodes had hoped she might be recovered enough by now to talk to him, but that wasn't the case. He'd have to check back that afternoon when she might be recovered enough to talk.

Rhodes called the jail next so he could let Hack know he wouldn't be coming in.

"Figgers," Hack said. "That woman you brought in is giving us trouble. I thought maybe you could calm her down."

"What kind of trouble?"

"Claims the cell is dirty. That made Lawton mad. Said she's a victim of police brutality. Says she never even been to the Pac-a-Sak and it's a case of mistaken identity."

"Tell Ruth to counsel with her," Rhodes said.

"Can she slap her around a little?"

"Wouldn't be prudent at this time," Rhodes said.

"Too bad," Hack said, and hung up.

Rhodes grinned, knowing that Hack was kidding. He told Ivy the news about Wanda and added, "Somebody's going to have to take care of Leroy."

"Who's Leroy?" Ivy asked, setting a plate of eggs and bacon on the table.

Rhodes sat down. "Wanda's cat." He started to eat. Even the bacon tasted good.

Ivy sat down across from him and gave him a direct look. "We both know who's going to take care of the cat, don't we."

"I'll have to do it," Rhodes said. "There's nobody else."

"You do what you have to do. Just don't bring Leroy here. He wouldn't adjust well to our menagerie."

Rhodes knew she was right. He'd see about food and water for Leroy and if he could find someone to take over the job. He already had somebody in mind.

When he'd finished his breakfast, which didn't take long, he told Ivy that he wouldn't have time to give Yancey and Speedo their exercise, so it was up to her.

"I think I'll have time," she said, "but they prefer you."

"Tell them I'll do it tomorrow," Rhodes said. "I have a murder and a near-murder to solve."

"You sound like Sage Barton," Ivy said.

"Please," Rhodes said. "Don't mention that name."

Ivy was still laughing when he left.

Clyde Ballinger was considerably more jovial than he'd been the last time Rhodes had seen him. There were no funerals that day, and Clyde was in his living quarters behind the funeral home. The little two-story brick building had been the home of the servants when the funeral parlor had been a private mansion, and Clyde had taken it over when he'd bought the place. He'd once told Rhodes that it was just right for a single man and that he didn't want to have to take care of anything bigger.

"Nice job at the fire last night," Clyde said when he'd welcomed Rhodes into the downstairs room he used for an office, "but if you're not more careful, you're going to wind up being one of my clients."

"I'm not planning on that," Rhodes said. "Not anytime soon, anyway."

"Well, you be more careful, then," Clyde said. "You want the autopsy report, I guess, since you never make social calls. I have the report for you right here."

He went to his desk and opened the middle drawer. He took out a large envelope and handed it to Rhodes.

"Have a seat while you look it over," Clyde said, and Rhodes did.

He didn't expect to find anything in the report that would help him, and he wasn't surprised when he didn't. What he did find was just what he'd expected. Lawrence Gates had died between the hours of eight and ten from a gunshot wound to the head. A small-caliber bullet had been recovered, but it was impossible to say just what the caliber was. The bullet was too deformed. Dr. White had weighed it, however, and he suggested that Rhodes could compare the weight to that of standard bullets. Maybe that would provide an answer.

Rhodes remembered the .25 caliber pistols that Kenny and Noble had, and he also remembered that Kenny had lied to him about being in Thurston on the night Lawrence was killed. Seeing Kenny was at the top of Rhodes's to-do list for the day.

Rhodes slipped the report back into the envelope and asked Clyde if he had the bullet. Clyde opened the desk drawer again and handed Rhodes a plastic bag.

"Thanks," Rhodes said. "Read any good books lately?"

"I have," Clyde said. "I found an Eighty-Seventh Precinct book I hadn't read. You know that series. I've told you about it before. By a guy named Ed McBain."

"Not his real name," Rhodes said. "I remember."

"Yeah. Anyway, I thought I'd read them all, but I hadn't. It was nice to find the one I skipped somehow. McBain's dead now and won't be writing anymore. I might just start rereading the rest of them. Those boys at the Eight-Seven know how to solve murders. They'd take care of your case in record time."

Rhodes stood up. "If you run into them, send them along. I can use all the help I can get."

"Too bad they aren't real," Clyde said.

"Durn tootin'," Rhodes said.

Curtis Lambert was sitting on his porch and smoking a cigarette when Rhodes arrived at his house. It was almost as if he hadn't moved since the last time Rhodes had been there. Curtis gave a little salute, which Rhodes didn't return. He didn't see Betsy anywhere, so he sat in the Charger and waited. After about a minute, Curtis got up and whistled. Betsy came sprinting up from somewhere in back of the house, and Curtis chained her up. Rhodes got out of the car.

"You sure got back here in a hurry," Curtis said. "You must like me and Betsy a lot."

"Sure," Rhodes said, "but who I really came to see is Kenny."

"Good luck with that," Curtis said. "I ain't got any idea where the devil he is. He came by yesterday after he got sprung from jail and said he was gonna be gone for a few days. I got the idea that he was scared of something, but I don't know what it could be. Maybe it's you, Sheriff."

Rhodes looked at Betsy, who growled at him. "I don't think anybody's scared of me."

"You might be surprised, Sheriff," Curtis said. "Dogs might not be scared of you but some people in this county are."

"Kenny included?"

"Could be."

"But you don't have any idea where he is."

"Not a one. He went off with Noble Truelove, though; I know that much. You might try talking to Noble's mother, see if she knows. If she does, she didn't tell me. But that might be because I didn't ask."

"I'll give her a try," Rhodes said. "Thanks for your help." He started for the Charger, then turned around and said, "Goodbye, Betsy."

Betsy just growled.

Noble's mother lived in a neat little house with a neat little yard, and she was just as neat as they were. She must have liked housecleaning more than Arlene Reese did. She said that she hadn't seen Noble for a while.

"I don't know where he gets off to, Sheriff, I honestly don't. He never tells me anything, never has, not since he got to be a teenager. He's not a bad son, but he does seem to get into trouble a lot. He tells me that it's always a misunderstanding, though, and he hardly ever has to spend any time in jail."

Thanks to lawyers, Rhodes thought. He said, "I'm sure he's a fine son, and I'd like to find him and talk to him."

"He's gone off with that Kenny Lambert," Mrs. Truelove said. "There's just no telling where they are. When those two get together, you just never know. They might even be out of town."

"You have no idea at all?"

"Well, sometimes they go off to an old fishing camp down by Sand Creek."

"Where on the creek?" Rhodes asked.

"I couldn't tell you that. It's just an old shack, or that's what Noble told me once. Whoever owns the land probably doesn't know anybody goes there and might not like it if he did. I tell Noble he shouldn't go, but sometimes he does. He says it's a place where he can get away from it all."

Rhodes thought that all Noble got away from was the people who were after him for one reason or another, and that would include the law as often as not.

"I appreciate your help," Rhodes said.

He left Mrs. Truelove standing on her neat little porch, but he could feel her watching him even as he drove away. He thought she knew Noble was in some kind of trouble and that the feeling was nothing new to her. He wasn't hiding from the law, however, and Rhodes wondered just what had spooked him and Kenny. He'd go looking for them later. Now he had other people to talk to, people who were easier to find. First, though, he had to visit a cat.

Rhodes parked the Charger in front of Wanda Wilkins's house and looked across the street at the school. There wasn't much there. Parts of all four walls still stood, but nothing else was left. Yellow tape on poles driven into the ground ten or fifteen yards from the building was supposed to keep people away, and no one was poking around there at the moment. Rhodes wondered how long that would last.

He got out of the car. There was no smoke or other evidence that the fire might not be out, but Rhodes could smell the burned wood. It was a sad loss in some ways, but the building would most likely have been razed sooner or later. The Reeses and Falkners had won. That was something to think about.

Wanda's house was unlocked, as was to be expected. She wouldn't have bothered to lock up if she was just going across the street to check on the school.

Leroy was none too happy to see Rhodes, or at least Rhodes supposed that was the case. The cat took one look at him and ran into another room. He was clearly puzzled by Wanda's absence and didn't want to have anything to do with anyone else.

Rhodes found an empty cat food dish and a water dish in the kitchen by the stove. The water dish still had water in it, but Rhodes poured out the old water and refilled the bowl. He located the dry cat food in the cabinet under the kitchen sink. As soon as he started pouring some of it into the bowl, Leroy forgot that he didn't want to have anything to do with strangers. He came into the kitchen, looked at Rhodes with disdain, and started to eat.

"Not quite so standoffish now, are you," Rhodes said.

Leroy didn't look up. He just kept eating.

"Don't worry," Rhodes told him. "I'll find somebody to make regular visits until Wanda gets home."

Leroy still didn't look up. Like most cats, he was confident that he'd be taken care of, as was his due. Rhodes left him there and looked around for a house key. He didn't find one, so he'd just have to hope the crime rate in Thurston didn't include burglary of a habitation for the next few days. Leroy had finished eating and was following Rhodes around.

"That's all for this morning," Rhodes told the cat. "If things go well, you'll get fed again this afternoon."

Leroy gave a polite "meow."

"You behave yourself while Wanda's gone," Rhodes said.

"Meow," Leroy said, and Rhodes left to have a look at the schoolhouse.

When he went outside, he saw Gary Parker's car parked up near the yellow tape that surrounded the building. Parker wasn't in sight.

Rhodes walked across the street and ducked under the yellow tape. He wasn't going into what was left of the building. That would be too dangerous, and arson investigation wasn't his job. Parker, however, knew a good bit about it.

"You in there, Gary?" Rhodes called.

"Right here," Gary said. "Barely inside, and don't you come in."

"I don't intend to," Rhodes said. "I'll talk to you when you come out."

"Just a minute and I'll be there," Gary said.

It was longer than a minute, and when he came out, Gary had soot on his face, hands, and clothing. He had a bit of charred wood in his hand.

"Just making sure the fire's out," he said. "It is."

"What's that you're carrying?"

Gary looked down at the piece of wood. "Burned wood."

Everybody in the county was a comedian, Rhodes thought. "I can see that. Why do you have it?"

Gary handed the charred wood to Rhodes. "Take a sniff."

Rhodes took a sniff. The wood smelled like charred wood to him, and he handed it back to Gary.

"You get anything?" Gary asked.

"No," Rhodes said. "Just a burned smell."

"My nose is better trained than yours. I smell coal oil, which would be a good accelerant."

"So you think it was arson."

"Deciding that is the fire marshal's job. I'll reserve judgment."

"What you said sounded like a judgment of arson."

"That was just an observation, but if I were an arsonist, I'd spread the accelerant on the ground floor first, move to the second floor, and get out by the fire escape up there. When I got here it looked like the first floor started burning first."

"Looked that way to me, too," Rhodes said, "and I was here early. Wanda Wilkins was in the building because she thought she saw somebody."

"The fire marshal will figure it out," Gary said. "For now I'm not going to say anything more."

"I'm not either," Rhodes said. "I'll see you around. I have to pay a few visits."

"Have fun," Gary said.

"I plan to," Rhodes told him. "Right now I have to see a man about a cat."

"Sure," Manny said when Rhodes asked him about seeing to Leory. "I don't mind a bit. Gale and I like cats."

Rhodes thanked him and told him where to find the cat food. "This will be a good way for you to build up some goodwill in the community. People appreciate neighbors who help neighbors. Maybe they'll even start to treat you and Gale like natives."

"I don't care about that," Manny said. "I just want to help out." He paused. "Still, if they stopped thinking of me and Gale as outsiders, that would be a nice bonus."

"I'll bet they will when the word gets out," Rhodes said.

"That was some nice work you did last night," Manny said. "I saw it on *A Clear View for Clearview* this morning. Real heroic. I'm glad you're okay. I was worried about you."

Rhodes didn't want to hear about it. "Just doing my job, and I feel fine. I was lucky."

"I'm glad you were. If it weren't for you, somebody would have to take on that cat-feeding job permanently. Any idea how the fire got started?"

"Nope," Rhodes said. "I'm leaving that to the state fire marshal. I'm just a sheriff, and he has the experts to do that kind of job. He'll send one soon enough."

"You think it was arson?"

"I have no idea," Rhodes said, but he did.

Chapter 19

The Falkners didn't appear to be at all happy to see Rhodes again, although Leslie had told him to drop by anytime. Unhappy or not, they invited him in, and Rhodes found himself sitting on the couch in the den again. Faye sat in one of the chairs this time and glared at Rhodes without speaking. Leslie tried to be amiable, although he wasn't very good at it.

"What can we do for you today, Sheriff?" he asked. "You know we're always glad to help."

That was clearly not true, but Rhodes let it pass. He thought the direct approach to telling them how they could help would be the best, so he said, "For starters, you can stop pestering the Hunleys with firecrackers and whatever else you might have in mind."

Faye jumped to her feet. "What do you mean by accusing us of that kind of thing? We'll sue you and the whole county for lying if you spread that story around."

"Calm down, Faye," Leslie said. "I'm sure the sheriff will explain himself. Right, Sheriff?"

"Right," Rhodes said. "I thought I was pretty clear, but I can repeat myself if you want me to."

"Well, I never," Faye said, balling her fists. "You're as much as calling us liars to our faces."

"When it comes to lying," Rhodes said, "you and your husband are the ones who did it. I'm just the messenger."

Faye opened her mouth to say something else, but Rhodes held up a hand to stop her. To his surprise, she shut her mouth.

"Here's how I know," Rhodes said. "The Hunleys have you on video from their surveillance cameras."

"That's impossible," Faye said. "We had on our—" She stopped. She sat back down and looked at the floor.

"Hoodies," Rhodes said. "You were wearing hoodies, but it was you, all right, and I appreciate that you confirmed it. You are on the video, but video's not really how I knew. Leslie mentioned firecrackers the last time I was here. He couldn't have known about them if he hadn't been involved."

Faye looked up from the floor and gave Leslie one of her glares. "Idiot," she said, and Leslie looked sheepish.

Rhodes ignored that little bit of byplay and continued. "So you lied to me about being out of the house. The firecracker incident was at around three in the morning, which is after Lawrence Gates was killed. The question now is, did you lie to me about being out earlier, say about the time of the murder?"

"Look, Sheriff," Leslie said, "I admit that we might have misspoken about being out of the house, and you're right about the firecrackers. We did it. I'm ashamed to admit it, but we did it. Those Hunleys have gotten on our nerves so much that we had to do something. It won't happen again, I promise."

"That wasn't the only thing," Rhodes said.

"We didn't mean them any harm, whatever we did," Leslie said.

"It was just pranks, and it was stupid of us to mess with the Hunleys like we did. As I said, it won't happen again."

"It had better not," Rhodes said.

"It won't. I'm not lying this time. You have my promise."

"Fine. We'll see how that works out. Now how about telling me if you went out earlier than three, and I want the truth."

Faye spoke up. "We were here all through the early evening. I swear it. We'd never kill anybody. That's just crazy."

Rhodes wasn't entirely sure that Faye wasn't capable of doing something crazy, but he said, "I'll accept that for now, but I have some new questions. Where were you yesterday evening about dark?"

"The schoolhouse fire," Leslie said. "Was it arson? You can't possibly think we had anything to do with that."

"Sure I could," Rhodes said, not answering the question about arson. "You wanted it gone, and now it's gone."

Leslie shook his head. "Not because of anything we did."

"Do you have any way of proving you were here at home?"

Leslie looked unhappy about what he was going to say. "No. It was just the two of us again." Leslie paused. "I know what you're thinking, but this time I'm telling the truth."

"He is," Faye said. "You have to believe him."

Rhodes didn't feel obligated to believe anybody, but until he could prove differently, he'd have to take the Falkners' word for where they were. He thought Faye was just unstable enough to burn a building down if she got mad, but for now he'd let her off the hook.

"You've lied before," he said, "but this time maybe you're not. I'll have to keep digging, and you'd better hope I don't find out you've lied to me again."

"You won't," Leslie said.

Faye just nodded. She was more subdued now, almost apathetic. Rhodes didn't like her mood swings. He wondered if Faye were on medication.

"You should talk to the Reeses," Leslie said. "If anybody wanted that school burned, they'd be my top suspects."

Rhodes wasn't surprised to hear that. Leslie was trying to shift suspicion, as was only natural. Rhodes had heard that kind of thing all too many times before.

"I'll talk to them," Rhodes said, "but you and Faye are still right up there with them at the top of my list."

Neither of the Falkners had anything to say to that.

The Reeses were no happier to see Rhodes than the Falkners had been, but Charlie was much more aggressive and open about his displeasure.

"I know why you're here," he said when he came to the door to answer the bell. "You think we had something to do with the fire last night, and we didn't. Case closed. You can leave now."

"I'm not quite ready to leave," Rhodes said. "I'd like to talk to you and Arlene for a minute."

Charlie puffed out his chest. "All right, as long as it's not more than a minute."

"It could be longer," Rhodes said. "That was just an estimate."

"Are you making some kind of joke?" Charlie asked. "If you are, it isn't funny."

Nobody ever thought Rhodes's jokes were funny, much to his disappointment. He said, "Let's go inside. I want to see Arlene. Maybe I can interrupt her housecleaning again."

Charlie looked at Rhodes as if he suspected another attempted joke, but after a couple of seconds he said, "Come in, then, but she's not cleaning today."

They walked into the rustic den, and again Rhodes sat in the cowhide chair. Just as he sat down, Arlene came into the room. She wasn't wearing the cleaning garb this time, but she wasn't wearing western clothing, either, just regular slacks and a blouse. Charlie, of course, had on his western duds.

Rhodes stood up.

"Nice to see you again, Sheriff," Arlene said, and she sounded almost as if she meant it. "You can be seated. To what do we owe the pleasure of your visit?"

"He thinks we burned the schoolhouse down," Charlie said, sitting on the couch. Arlene sat down beside him, and Rhodes sat, too.

"Well, did we?" Arlene asked.

"You're no funnier than he is," Charlie said with a frown. "You know we didn't burn any building, and before you ask, Sheriff, we were both here at home. We didn't leave, not even to gawk at the fire. We don't go chasing after excitement like some people."

Rhodes hadn't seen any of his suspects in the crowd. He thought that was a little strange, but maybe they all had good reasons for staying away, possible guilt being only one of them.

"You were there, though, Sheriff," Arlene said. "I saw you on the internet earlier this morning, and I'm glad you're all right. You looked bad when you came out of the school, but it was wonderful that you were able to save Wanda from the fire."

"Old busybody," Charlie said.

Arlene laid a hand on his arm. "Now, Charlie, don't talk like that."

"She is a busybody, and I'll talk however I please," Charlie said.

Arlene gave Rhodes a look as if to say, *What can I do with him?*

"You have to admit that you'd be the logical suspects if the fire turned out to be arson," Rhodes said.

"Are you accusing us?" Charlie asked, "because if you are—"

"I'm not making any accusations. Just making a remark."

"I don't like your remarks."

"That's a shame," Rhodes said. "Anyway, you wanted the school gone, and now it's gone. You've gotten what you and the Falkners wanted. You won and the Hunleys lost."

"Yeah, but it wasn't because we did anything. If you ask me, the Falkners were the ones who did it."

"No matter who did it, the building's gone."

"That's the way the cookie crumbles," Charlie said.

Rhodes hadn't heard that expression in years, but he didn't mention that to Charlie. He said, "I guess it is. So you didn't go for any horseback rides last night?"

"Damn right, I didn't. I was too upset by your insinuations yesterday to ride. I might not ride today, either."

For such a blustery bully, Charlie was being awfully sensitive. Rhodes said, "That's a shame. I'm sorry I caused you such distress."

"You're joking again," Charlie said. "Or you're being a smartass. One's as bad as the other."

"He's just being kind," Arlene said with a serious look, but Rhodes could tell she was in on the joke or the smartassery, whichever it was.

"She's right," Rhodes lied. He stood up. "Just being kind. I think I'll be going now. I do have one more question for you though, come to think of it. Nothing to do with the fire. Did you ever hear of an old fishing cabin on Sand Creek? Hasn't been used in years, probably."

Charlie thought for a second. "I might know the one you mean. It's down from the wooden bridge across Sand Creek on the county road to the left just outside of town. You know the one I mean?"

Rhodes knew, having so recently had his adventure along that road and by that bridge.

"North or south of the bridge?" he asked.

"South," Reese said. "You planning on going fishing?"

"You could say that," Rhodes told him.

Rhodes couldn't think of any reason the Hunleys would burn the school, so he decided to go looking for Kenny and Noble before talking to them. When he came to the wooden bridge, he noticed that a track had been worn down the bank to the water, which was barely a trickle now. Fishermen must have gone down there a good many times, but there wouldn't be any fishing going on now. He pulled the Charger about halfway into the drainage ditch to get it as far off the road as he could, then got out and made his way down the path. Reese hadn't said how far from the bridge the fishing cabin was. Rhodes hoped it wasn't too far.

As he walked along the creek bank, Rhodes saw a couple of turtles sunning themselves on a big rotten tree branch that had fallen into the creek bed. He was glad to see them. He liked most turtles and terrapins and thought of them as being lucky for him. He wasn't superstitious, or so he told himself. It was just that he associated turtles and terrapins with good things that had happened. Not the alligator snapping turtle, though. There was no luck with that kind of reptile. The snapper he had run across had been guarding a small marijuana field, and that incident had been more scary than anything. Alligator snappers seemed to Rhodes to be some kind of throwback to a prehistoric era. They were like little dinosaurs, although the one he'd encountered hadn't been little except by comparison to those ancient ancestors.

The creek bank made for hard walking, and it was easy to see that nobody had been along there in a while. If Kenny and Noble were at the fishing cabin, they'd found another way to get there, which figured. Rhodes hadn't seen any trace of Kenny's old truck.

Rhodes had walked about half a mile before he turned a bend in the creek and saw a falling-down cabin in a field. Kenny's pickup was parked beside it, covered with white, powdery dust from the county road. The cabin was on the other side of the creek, but that wasn't a problem. While Rhodes wasn't as agile as he'd once been, even he could jump over the dribble of water that remained of Sand Creek.

He jumped across it and walked up the creek bank, stopping at the top to look over the cabin. It sat up on wooden blocks and was in terrible condition. It sat at the bottom of a little hill and appeared to have only a couple of rooms and a porch. The porch had collapsed, and the roof had fallen down at a slant. The only way to get into the cabin through the front door would be to go behind the fallen roof. Rhodes doubted the cabin had a back door.

Rhodes had taken two guns from Kenny lately, and he'd taken one from Noble. But that didn't mean they weren't armed, so Rhodes got his Kel-Tec from the ankle holster just in case Kenny and Noble had acquired more weaponry and didn't want visitors.

The area around the cabin was open, not a tree in sight except at the top of the hill and off to the sides a hundred yards or so. Rhodes thought he might as well announce his presence.

"Hello, the cabin," he called. "Kenny Lambert. Noble Truelove. This is Sheriff Rhodes. If you're in there, show yourselves."

For a full minute there was just quiet from the cabin. Rhodes was patient, though, and finally Kenny poked his head from around the fallen roof.

"What do you want, Sheriff?" he asked. "Can't you leave me and Noble alone?"

"I guess not," Rhodes said. "I could if you'd quit lying to me, but that doesn't seem too likely to happen."

"Everybody lies to the law now and then," Kenny said. "That's just the way it is."

"I'm afraid you're right," Rhodes said, "but I'm going to try to get the truth out of you this time."

Rhodes half expected Kenny to come out with a gun and start shooting, but he didn't. He said, "I guess you won't leave if I ask you to."

"Nope," Rhodes said. "You and Noble come on out and stand in front of the cabin. I want to see your hands."

"Damn," Kenny said. "You don't trust anybody, do you."

"Not very many," Rhodes said. "Get Noble and come on out, hands where I can see them."

Kenny ducked back behind the roof, and Rhodes heard him talking to Noble, though he couldn't make out the words. Noble's voice was raised, and Rhodes figured that whatever he was saying, it wasn't complimentary of Rhodes.

The talking died down, and Kenny stuck his head out again. "We're coming out now, Sheriff. Hands in front. I told Noble you had a pistol, so don't shoot us."

"You don't have to worry about that," Rhodes said.

"Okay. Here we come."

Kenny was about halfway out from behind the door when a board over his head exploded.

Chapter 20

As soon as the board flew apart, Rhodes heard the sound of a rifle shot.

Kenny ducked back behind the door, and Rhodes ran for the cover of the porch roof. Although a rifle bullet might punch right through the boards, an inadequate cover was better than no cover at all. Grasshoppers jumped up from the weeds, thumped into him, and bounced away. He paid them no attention at all.

Rhodes didn't think he could run fast anymore, but he caught up with Kenny and Noble. He found himself pushing Kenny into the house as a bullet slammed into the dirt just under the porch roof.

Kenny, Noble, and Rhodes tumbled into the house and lay on the floor. Rhodes said, "Stay away from the windows."

"You don't have to tell me that twice," Noble said. He looked at the pistol that Rhodes held. "You can't do much with that against a rifle."

Rhodes almost laughed to think that Noble would be giving him that advice after what had happened the previous day between him and Kenny and the Whiteside brothers.

"Pistol is better than nothing," Kenny said, but that wasn't true. The shots had come from the trees, and Rhodes didn't know of anyone who could shoot that far with a pistol and hit anywhere near a target, even if there was a target to shoot at.

"Why would anybody be shooting at you?" Rhodes asked.

"Hell, I don't know," Kenny said. "We never did anything to anybody, but everybody's always picking on us. Well, maybe we bothered the Whitesides a little. Ben and Glen still in the jail?"

"They bonded out just like you did," Rhodes said.

"Well, there you are then," Noble said. "They don't much like us after yesterday. Now they want to kill us."

Rhodes thought that was doubtful, but before he could comment on it, a couple of bullets punched holes in the wall, sending splinters flying.

"Damn," Kenny said, putting his hands over his head, as if he thought hands could ward off bullets. "What're we gonna do?"

"Keep our heads down," Rhodes said. "The shooter will get tired and leave after a while."

Rhodes didn't believe that, and neither did Noble and Kenny.

"He can starve us out if he wants to," Noble said. "We bought some water and jerky, but it's still in the truck."

Two more bullets popped through the wall above them, and Kenny yelled. Rhodes glanced around and saw that a splinter was sticking out of Kenny's right hand.

"You're all right," Rhodes said. "It's just a splinter."

"Get it out," Kenny wailed. "Get it out."

"You're such a wimp," Noble said.

He reached over and pulled out the splinter. Kenny yelled as if he'd been stabbed.

Rhodes ignored him and looked around. There was another room in the house behind the one they were in. That was all.

"What's in the other room?" he asked.

"Nothing," Kenny said, his voice weak with suffering. "This place was cleaned out long ago."

"What about a door?"

"No door."

"Window?"

"Yeah," Noble said. "There's a window."

"Might be a good idea to get out of here, then," Rhodes said, as a couple more bullets punctured the wall. "We can get under the house. He can't get us there."

"Okay with me," Kenny said, and started creeping toward the door to the other room. Rhodes and Noble followed.

The old flooring was rotted in several places, and Rhodes had to avoid a couple of small holes. It might have been easier to break a bigger hole in the floor than to go out the window, but Kenny was already over the sill and dropping down to the ground. Noble was right behind him.

Rhodes had a little more trouble than they did, but that was only natural because they were younger and more limber than he was. When he landed on the ground, they were already out of sight.

They weren't under the house, either. It was dark there, but enough light came in for Rhodes to have seen two men if they'd been there. He crept as fast as he could to the side of the house and looked out just in time to see Noble getting into the pickup on the passenger side. Kenny must have already been inside, having entered the same way, out of sight of the shooter.

Noble closed the door. Rhodes heard the pickup start, and Kenny reversed as fast as he could go. Rhodes heard bullets hitting metal, but Kenny kept on going and before long was over the little hill and gone, trailing a cloud of white dust and sand.

Rhodes relaxed and lay on the cool dirt under the house. The shooter wasn't after him, and for all he knew, Rhodes was in the pickup. It wouldn't take long for the shooter to leave. All Rhodes had to do was wait. He hoped.

As it turned out, he was right. Hardly any time at all went by before Rhodes heard a vehicle start in the woods nearby, and then he heard it drive away. He crawled out from under the house and found he was still holding his pistol. He didn't put it away. He was going to have a look in the woods and see if he could find anything, and he didn't want to be unarmed if he met someone with a gun.

When he got to the trees, it didn't take long to find where the shooter had been set up. He hadn't taken the time to pick up his brass. Maybe he'd been in a hurry because he wanted to catch up with Kenny and Noble. If he did, they were on their own. Rhodes couldn't help them now, not that he'd been much help earlier.

He had no way to secure the crime scene, so he picked up one of the empty shell casings as carefully as he could and looked it over. It was for a thirty-thirty rifle, probably somebody's deer rifle. He put the empty shell in his pocket, then looked around some more and found where the truck had been parked, just on the other side of the trees. The ground was too hard to take tire prints, so the dead weeds crushed into the dust were the only evidence that anyone had parked there.

Rhodes didn't find anything else, so he started the walk back to his county car.

• • •

When he got to the car, Rhodes radioed Hack and told him to send someone to do a crime scene investigation. He gave the location as best he could, and Hack said he'd send Ruth to do the job.

"You gonna tell me what happened?" Hack asked.

"No," Rhodes said. "Over and out."

He hooked the mic and drove to Clearview. His first stop was at the jail to drop off the cartridge shell, and it wasn't easy to get away from Hack's questions without just walking out on him, so Rhodes walked out. He knew Hack's feelings were hurt, but he'd get over it.

His next stop was to get a new cell phone, and after that he went to the Dairy Queen, not for a Blizzard but for lunch. He thought about having a Jalitos Ranch burger, but it turned out to be Bean Day. Bean Day had pretty much died out at Texas Dairy Queens, or so Rhodes had heard, but not in Clearview. One day a week DQ had a big pot of pinto beans cooking, and all the beans and cornbread you could eat were available for one price. As many times as Rhodes had been in the DQ, he'd never tried this treat. He was sorely tempted but went for the Deluxe Cheeseburger Lunch instead. It came with a small sundae, and Rhodes figured that if he didn't eat all the french fries, it would be okay to eat the sundae. Hot fudge was his preference. Julia wasn't working that shift, and nobody asked Rhodes if he wanted "the usual."

On Bean Day, or just about any day, the Dairy Queen had a table or two taken by a group of the town's old-timers who liked to hang out there and tell their stories, often the same ones they'd been telling for years. A couple of the men at one such table waved at Rhodes, and he waved back but didn't join them. He needed to sit alone and think. And to eat his burger. Nobody would think he was rude. They all knew the sheriff wasn't stuck up. They'd understand his reasons for sitting alone.

The cheeseburger was satisfying, and he ate all the fries, after all. And the sundae, too. He'd had a lot of exercise and thought he deserved it.

As he ate, he considered the events of the day so far. He didn't believe for a minute that the Whitesides were shooting at Kenny and Noble, who were just trying to throw Rhodes off the track. Rhodes also wondered if the shooter was a poor shot or if he was sending a warning of some kind.

Catching up to Kenny and Noble again was going to be a tough job, as they'd surely go to ground in a place where no one would look for them. The cabin was too obvious. Rhodes thought about the people who knew he was going to the cabin. Charlie Reese was one, and Mrs. Truelove was the other. Rhodes hadn't mentioned Kenny and Noble to Charlie, so that left Mrs. Truelove. Rhodes would have to go back to Thurston to see her again, and he wanted to talk to the Hunleys. He probably should have done it while he was still there, but he needed a new phone.

He finished his meal and let Hack know where he was going.

"You ain't gonna tell me what happened this mornin'?"

"Maybe later," Rhodes said.

Mrs. Truelove's neat little house hadn't changed a bit. Rhodes knocked on the door, and when she came to see who was there, she said, "I hope you're not here to tell me that Noble's hurt or anything."

"I'm not," Rhodes said. "I saw him at the cabin, and he was just fine."

"That's a relief," Mrs. Truelove said. "How can I help you, then?"

"I wanted to ask if anybody else had been by to question you about where Noble might be."

"No, sir, nobody's been by here since you left. I don't get a lot of visitors. People blame me for Noble, you see, and they don't drop by."

"I'm sorry to hear that," Rhodes said. "You're sure nobody was here?"

"Not a single solitary soul except me."

Rhodes thanked her for her time and left, trying to figure who could have told someone about the cabin. It occurred to him that the person who could was probably Curtis Lambert, who wouldn't have minded one bit lying to Rhodes about not knowing where his son might have been. Rhodes drove to the Lambert house to find out.

What he found when he got there was Betsy lying in the yard with a deep gash in her head. She was breathing but barely conscious. Rhodes left her there and went inside the house. Curtis Lambert was in almost the same condition as Betsy. He sat on the floor of the front room, bruised and beaten. He tried to get up when Rhodes came in, but he couldn't manage it without Rhodes's help.

"Who did this?" Rhodes asked when he'd gotten Curtis into a chair.

"Don't know," Curtis said. "He was wearing a ski mask. Tried to make me tell him where Kenny was. I said I didn't know, but he beat it out of me. I lied to you, Sheriff, and I appreciate you not beating me."

"Not the way I work," Rhodes said. "What kind of vehicle was he in?"

"Don't know that, either. Didn't get a look outside before he hit me. I held out a little while. Guess I shouldn't have. You think Kenny's all right?"

"He was the last time I saw him. Someone found the cabin and took a few shots at us, but nobody was hurt. Kenny and Noble got away. I doubt anybody's going to find them this time."

"Probably not," Curtis said. "What about Betsy? You see her?"

"She's outside, not in good shape. I'll take her to the vet in Clearview. She'll be all right."

"I need to go, too."

"You need a doctor, not a vet. I'll drop you at the hospital. Can you walk to the car?"

"I can walk." Curtis stood up. He was shaky, but he walked to the door ahead of Rhodes, getting sturdier with every step. "Let's go. I want to get Betsy fixed up."

It took both Rhodes and Curtis to lift Betsy into the backseat of the county car. Curtis wasn't much help, but Rhodes wasn't going to tell him not to try. When Betsy was inside, Curtis got in and held her head in his lap.

"She'll make it," he said, more to himself than Rhodes, but Rhodes answered anyway.

"No doubt about it. Dr. Childs will fix her right up."

The parking lot at Dr. Childs's clinic was alive with the sounds of dogs barking and cats yowling inside the building. Rhodes and Curtis took Betsy in, and the receptionist said she'd get Dr. Childs to look at the dog immediately. When she left to get him, Rhodes repeated his offer to take Curtis to the hospital.

"I'm fine now," he said. "I don't need any hospital, and I'm not leaving Betsy. You can go on, Sheriff. I'll find me a ride home, or I might stay in town all night so I can see Betsy in the morning. I sure appreciate your help. If there's ever anything I can do for you—"

"You can tell me where Noble and Kenny are hiding this time," Rhodes said.

"This time I don't know," Curtis said, "and that's the truth."

Rhodes wondered if it was. "Even a guess would help."

"Kenny's mother lives in Obert. We've been divorced for a long time, but I know he goes to see her now and then. That's my best guess."

"What's her name?"

"Karla Vincent, now. She shed my name as quick as she could."

That was a story Rhodes didn't need to hear, and he didn't have to. Dr. Childs came out and took a look at Betsy just then and said he'd have to sew up the cut in her head but that she'd be fine. Curtis seemed relieved, and so was Rhodes for that matter. He left Curtis in the clinic and got on the road again.

Chapter 21

Rhodes called Hack and asked where Karla Vincent lived.

"You ain't been keepin' me in the loop," Hack said. "I don't know what's goin' on, and I can't do my job right if I'm out of the loop."

Rhodes didn't want to get into a discussion of what Hack's job was, so he changed the subject. "Any report from Buddy about that crime scene?"

"You want me to put you in the loop?"

"That's right. Put me in the loop."

"You gonna do the same for me?"

"When I catch up. Now what about Buddy?"

"Found a bunch of empty cartridge shells, tagged 'em and bagged 'em. Didn't find anything else, though."

"Have them checked for prints," Rhodes said.

"You think I don't know what's what? I told Mika to check the one you brought in, too."

"Good work," Rhodes said. "Now what about Karla Vincent?"

"Gimme a minute," Hack said.

It didn't take much longer than that. Hack said, "She lives out on the county road that turns off to the right past what's left of the old school buildin'. It's the third house on the right."

"I love computers," Rhodes said.

"You don't know squat about computers."

"No, but you do. That's all that matters."

"You're just tryin' to butter me up and get on my good side because you won't keep me in the loop."

"Later," Rhodes said, and signed off.

The third house on the right on the county road didn't look like much. It wasn't kept up like the one Mrs. Truelove lived in, but it was in better shape than the one Curtis Lambert had. The lawn was dead, like most lawns at that time of year, and the paint on the house was flaking. A couple of flower beds in front of the house had some plants in them, but the plants were as dead as the lawn.

Rhodes drove up a rutted path and parked the car where it ended near the house. He got out of the car and looked around. He didn't see Kenny's pickup or any sign of where it could be hidden, so he went up onto the little front porch to see if he could rouse Karla Vincent. He didn't have to rouse her, however. She was standing in the doorway, a shadowy figure behind the closed screen, waiting for him.

A cotton ball was attached to the middle of the screen with a bobby pin. Rhodes hadn't seen that for a long time, but for a while when he was growing up, just about every screen door had a cotton ball attached because people believed it would keep flies out of the house when the door was opened. They believed the cotton ball looked like a clutch of spiders' eggs and would fool the flies. Rhodes didn't know if it worked or not.

"Karla Vincent?" Rhodes asked.

"That's me," the woman behind the screen said. "If you're looking for Kenny, he's not here."

"How'd you know I was looking for him?" Rhodes asked.

"I see your car. You're the law, and there's just one person the law would be coming around here to see."

"You're right about me being the law. I'm Sheriff Dan Rhodes. You're right about me looking for Kenny, too."

"What's he done this time?"

"Nothing. I just want to talk to him."

"Like I said, he's not here. He stays with that sorry daddy of his, and he doesn't come by here much anymore."

"I think some bad people might be after him," Rhodes said. "I need to talk to him about that."

"If he was here, you could talk to him, but like I keep telling you, he's not here. I'm not surprised people are after him. He's in and out of trouble all the time. Takes after his daddy that way."

Rhodes could see that this conversation was going nowhere. He said, "I'll be going if he's not here, but if he shows up, you should call the department as soon as he gets here. I really do need to talk to him."

"If I see him, I'll tell him you want to talk to him."

"That won't work," Rhodes said. "It'll just spook him. You call, and don't let him know."

"He won't show up, anyway," Karla said. "He's just about forgot all about me."

"But if he does show up—"

"I'll call you if I can," Karla said.

That was all Rhodes could hope for. He thanked her and left her, a shadowy figure behind a screen door, protected from flies by a cotton ball.

Rhodes had one more visit to make, to the Hunleys, and that meant a drive back to Thurston. The drive gave him time to think about the case, but everything stayed jumbled in his mind. Now and then he thought he'd caught hold of something, but whatever it was, it was too insubstantial to be held on to and always slipped away.

Rhodes didn't think talking to the Hunleys would clear anything up. It was just something else he had to try. It seemed as if that was the way it usually worked. There was no *CSI: Blacklin County*. His methods were old-school ones. He simply kept on talking to people until things cleared up for him or until he caught somebody in a revealing lie.

He thought about the election year coming up. Both Hack and Jennifer Loam had mentioned it, and he'd been honest when he told them that he wasn't sure he'd run for office again. Maybe he was too old-fashioned for the times. Maybe the county deserved somebody who was more up-to-date and who could solve crimes using new methods. Not that he'd failed very often. He thought he had about as good a record as any sheriff in the state, but there was nothing flashy or fancy about what he did, no matter how hard Jennifer worked to make it look like there was on her website. Well, he wasn't going to think about it now. What he had to do now was find out who'd killed Lawrence Gates, and if that meant he had to do more talking, then that's what he'd do.

* * *

The Hunleys were decked out in camo again. Con was in the driveway, washing one of the big Suburbans, although it had been pristine the last time Rhodes had seen it. Pete was there helping him, and Edwina was sweeping out the garage. The table Con had been refinishing was gone, and Rhodes presumed it was now at Pete's house.

Con tossed a big sponge into a bucket of soapy water when Rhodes got out of the county car, and Edwina came out of the garage. Pete stood off to one side, watching.

"Good to see you, Sheriff," Con said, wiping his hands on a towel that had been lying on the hood of the Suburban. He was smiling and his tone was cordial, Rhodes didn't think he sounded as if he meant what he'd said. "I thought you might have come by earlier."

"I've been busy," Rhodes said.

"I'll bet," Edwina said. "That was a wonderful thing you did last night, saving Wanda Wilkins from the fire."

"The fire's what I'm here to talk about," Rhodes said. "I know all of you must be pretty upset at the loss of the building."

"It was just a building," Con said, not showing much concern. "As long as nobody was killed, I don't know that I can complain."

Rhodes was a little surprised to hear that. "As much as you've talked about saving the school, I thought you'd be more upset."

"It was just a building," Pete said, repeating Con's words. "We don't care that much about buildings."

"It was a building you wanted to save," Rhodes said, "and I understand there were plans for a big reunion there later this year."

"Where'd you hear that?" Pete asked.

"I don't reveal my sources," Rhodes said. "Wouldn't be ethical. Is it true about the reunion?"

"It's true," Con said. He tossed the towel back on the Suburban.

"I was hoping to get together a lot of people who'd lived here and who'd gone to the school. I thought I could raise some money to put toward saving the place. Not going to happen now, though."

"You don't sound too disappointed about it," Rhodes said.

Con shrugged. "Nothing I can do about it now. Everything's changed now that there's no building. What would be the point of having a reunion? Time for us to forget about it and move on."

Rhodes thought it was time for him to move on, too, as the conversation had already given him a few things to think about. He told the Hunleys that he was sorry about the school, but they again brushed off the idea that they'd suffered any great loss.

Rhodes got in the Charger and drove back to Clearview. He dreaded facing Hack. It was getting late in the afternoon, and while Hack was sure to demand a full accounting of everything that had happened that day, Rhodes didn't feel up to giving it.

As it turned out, he didn't have to put Hack in the loop since Hack and Lawton had something they'd rather discuss with him, yet another story that they could drag out almost endlessly. It had to do with a certain Mrs. Purcell.

"You know her, don't you?" Hack asked when he told Rhodes that there'd been a problem. "Widow woman lives on a county road just outside of Obert."

"I don't think I've met her," Rhodes said, not sure whether he'd rather hear this story or be forced to tell several of his own.

"She's not a reg'lar customer," Hack said.

"Might be one from now on, though," Lawton said. "She thinks Andy hung the moon."

"I'm the one sent Andy out there," Hack said, "so I'll tell this."

"Just tryin' to set the stage," Lawton said.

"Sure you were," Hack said. "Anyway, Miz Purcell called in about these mysterious things flyin' over her house and stealin' her 'lec-tricity."

Lawton started humming the theme from *The Twilight Zone.*

"You hush up," Hack said.

Lawton stopped humming.

"I figgered Andy'd be the best one to deal with mysterious flyin' things," Hack said, "so I sent him on out there."

"Was birds, is what it was," Lawton said. "The flyin' things, I mean."

"You don't know that," Hack said. "Andy didn't say it was birds."

"That's what it was, though. Had to be birds."

"How can birds steal 'lectricity?"

"They wasn't stealin' anything. You know that."

"I know that, and you know that, but the sheriff don't know that. Now you hush up and let me tell this."

"Just tryin' to help," Lawton said.

Rhodes sagged down in his chair. There was no telling how long this would take, but he'd decided he could stand it better than he could stand telling about his own day.

"You never try to help," Hack told Lawton. "You just mess things up."

"Do not."

"Hold it," Rhodes said, sitting up straighter. "You're losing the thread here."

"Not my fault," Hack said. "Where was I?"

"Mysterious flying things," Rhodes said.

"Birds," Lawton said.

"Dagnabbit, Lawton," Hack said.

"That's enough," Rhodes said. "Get on with it, Hack."

"Well, what Miz Purcell said was that these mysterious flyin' things was stealin' her 'lectricity. Andy didn't put much stock in that, but he went out to see what he could do, and sure enough, he found out what was wrong."

"Wasn't anything mysterious about it," Lawton said.

Hack didn't bother to notice Lawton this time, other than heaving a sigh. He said, "Andy asked about how Miz Purcell knew the 'lectricity was bein' stolen, and she said that it went on and off. Andy asked her if she'd called the power company, and she said she had. They said there was nothin' wrong with her 'lectricity, and she kinda let on to Andy that they didn't think too much about her idea that mysterious flyin' things was stealin' it."

"Easy to see why," Lawton said, but Hack ignored him again.

"Andy didn't agree or disagree with her about the flyin' things," Hack went on. "He just asked her where her circuit breaker box was. House was so old, it didn't have circuit breakers. Had a fuse box."

Rhodes thought he knew where the story was going now, but he let Hack finish it.

"Fuse box was in a little pantry in back of the kitchen," Hack said, "so Andy took a look. Sure enough, one of the fuses was loose. He screwed it in tight, and ever'thing was jim dandy."

"What about the mysterious flying things?" Rhodes asked, although he hated himself for doing it.

"She figgered they'd got in the house somehow and loosened the fuse. Andy told her he didn't think that was likely but that she ought to get a 'lectrician out there to check that fuse box. She said she didn't know anybody to call, so Andy called Willie Seward. Willie'll check it out and fix her up."

"Oughta put in a breaker box, is what she oughta do," Lawton said. "That fuse box's downright dangerous."

"Maybe she'll replace it," Hack said, "if she can afford it."

"Wirin' in the house is probably eighty years old," Lawton said. "Firetrap, that's what the place is."

Rhodes didn't want to talk about firetraps. He said, "I hope nobody was robbing the bank while Andy was working on the fuse box."

"We gotta do a little community service now and then," Hack said. "Keep the public happy, what with an election year comin' up and all."

Rhodes didn't want to talk about the election year, either, so he changed the subject. "Did Mika find any fingerprints on those shells?"

"She didn't come in today," Hack said. "She'll be here tomorrow."

Rhodes could wait. He didn't think she'd find any fingerprints, anyway. The shooter would never have left the shells if there'd been fingerprints. No solid clues to anything in the case existed, but Rhodes was beginning to have a better idea of how things might have happened, not that he could prove any of it.

"Have you heard anything from Seepy Benton today?" Rhodes asked Hack.

"Not a peep," Hack said. "He's probably off somewhere tryin' on trench coats."

"Take more'n that to make him look like Alan Ladd or Bogie," Lawton said.

"I think he's perfectly happy to look just the way he does," Rhodes said.

"Could be," Hack said. "Takes all kinds."

"He's a rare bird," Lawton said.

"That's the truth," Hack agreed.

Rhodes couldn't remember a time when Hack had agreed so quickly with Lawton, so he decided to get away before anything else was said. First, though, he called the hospital and was told that Wanda would be able to talk to him, but not for long. Rhodes hoped she'd have some information that he could use.

"Woman nearly burned up," Hack said when Rhodes told him where he was going. "She won't remember a thing."

"You never can tell," Rhodes said. "She might break this case wide open."

"Yeah, and I might sprout wings and lay eggs for tomorrow's breakfast."

Lawton cackled like a chicken.

"Sounds right natural," Hack said. "Oughtn't you to be a rooster, though?"

"Never could cock-a-doodle-do that good," Lawton said.

"I'm not su'prised," Hack said.

Rhodes got up and got out the door before they could get started on each other again.

Chapter 22

Wanda lay in the hospital bed, hooked up to a couple of IVs. She looked pale and weak, and her voice hadn't recovered the way Rhodes's had.

"First thing, Sheriff, I want to thank you," she said. "They told me you carried me out of the schoolhouse."

"Glad to do it," Rhodes said. "All part of the job."

"Part of the job or not, I appreciate it. I know I shouldn't've been there."

Rhodes couldn't disagree with her.

"I went because I saw somebody," Wanda said, "and I knew you couldn't get there in time to stop him."

"Did you see who it was?" Rhodes asked.

"No. He was wearing one of those masks you pull down over your head."

"A ski mask," Rhodes said, thinking of Curtis Lambert.

"I guess so. He was up on the stage, splashing something all over, and I tried to run down the aisle to stop him. I fell down. That's all I remember until I woke up here in the hospital. I'm sorry I can't be any more help."

Rhodes was a bit disappointed, although he hadn't really expected anything more. He told Wanda not to worry about it and that he'd find whoever was in the building sooner or later.

"I believe you will," Wanda said. She looked away, then back. "I hate to ask a favor, but there's one thing that I do worry about, and that's Leroy."

"You don't have to worry about him," Rhodes said. "Manny Kingston'll be going by to see about him every day. He'll take care of everything."

"I don't know him very well," Wanda said. "I've just been to his store once or twice."

"He's okay," Rhodes said. "I had a long talk with him. You can be sure Leroy will be well taken care of. That reminds me, though, that I couldn't lock your house. Do you have a key?"

"There's one in my purse. It's in the bedroom in the top drawer of the dresser."

"I'll have Manny get the key and be sure the house is locked," Rhodes said.

"You think we can trust him?"

"I'm sure of it," Rhodes said.

"You better be," Wanda told him.

That evening after Rhodes came in from romping with Yancey and Speedo, Ivy served up a dish she described as zucchini-stuffed lasagna. Rhodes wasn't sure it was possible to have lasagna without the wide, flat noodles, but he didn't mention that fact, and the dish turned out to be pretty good even without them. It even smelled like lasagna, although Rhodes was pretty sure the meat was ground turkey instead of ground beef. At any rate, the Italian seasoning made the kind of meat a moot point. Also, Rhodes had allowed himself to have one of the Dr Peppers made with real sugar that he kept in the refrigerator. That made up for any shortcomings in the meal.

Yancey sat on one side of the kitchen, flattened out on the floor, his ears perked and alert and his eyes watching every bite Rhodes and Ivy took in the hopes that something would fall on the floor. Nothing did, so when Rhodes was helping to clean the table, Yancey got up, shook himself, and went off to bed. The cats, as usual, slept or woke at intervals and stayed right where they were. They weren't much interested in anything the humans or the dogs did.

After the things were cleared away and the dishes were washed, Rhodes and Ivy sat at the table. Rhodes wanted to talk the case over with Ivy because she often had good ideas about things that he might have overlooked. He filled her in on everything.

"I don't like it when you get shot at," Ivy said after he was finished.

"Nobody was shooting at me."

"I'll let that pass for now," Ivy said, "but you were there in the line of fire."

"Not really," Rhodes said.

"Really," Ivy said, "but I'm letting it pass, remember?"

"I remember."

"Good. Let's look at your suspects. Roger Prentiss could've killed Lawrence. What if they'd ridden together to the school? Roger could have killed him and driven the car back home."

"I can't come up with a motive for Roger," Rhodes said, "and there's no sign of the car at Roger's house. I'm sure someone got into the building from the second floor so he wouldn't be seen, and Roger wouldn't have done that."

"That would rule out Kenny, too, then," Ivy said.

"Not necessarily. Noble could have let him out in the back, then driven off in the pickup. Kenny could have killed Lawrence and stolen the car."

"Then where is the car?"

"Kenny could have driven it to Houston, sold it, and gotten back to Thurston all in one evening easily enough."

"What are Kenny and Noble hiding from, then?" Ivy wanted to know. "And who's trying to kill them?"

"Good question," Rhodes said. "I have no idea." He paused. "Or I have one, but it's not a great one."

"Any idea is better than none," Ivy said. "Let's hear it."

"I'm not sure anybody was trying to kill them," Rhodes said. "I think it was more like a warning."

"That's your idea?"

"No. My idea is that Kenny and Noble were driving around Thurston on the night Lawrence was killed, and they saw something. Or somebody. Whoever it was isn't happy about it and wants them to keep quiet."

Ivy sat and looked down at the table for a few seconds. Then she looked up and asked, "How dumb are those two?"

"Not dumb," Rhodes said, "but not exactly the kind to be voted most likely to succeed."

Ivy grinned. "What if they *were* trying to succeed? What if they tried to blackmail whoever they saw, if they saw anybody. That's the kind of thing that could make somebody very unhappy."

"I wish I'd thought of that," Rhodes said, remembering how

quickly Noble had tried to make him believe that the Whiteside boys were the ones doing the shooting. "It's a possibility."

"What about the shooter? Why not just kill them?"

"Maybe he wanted to, but if he did, he was a terrible shot."

"Any good shooters in the suspect group?"

"Charlie Reese is a hunter and likes guns," Rhodes said. "He has some on display in his den." Rhodes thought about the rifles he'd seen. "One of them is even the right caliber, but just about everybody in the county has a thirty-thirty."

"What about the others?"

"I don't know about the Falkners. I didn't see any guns, and I haven't heard that either of them liked to hunt. That doesn't mean they don't have guns, though. This is Texas, after all. Guns are a way of life."

"And the Hunleys?"

"Con and Pete Hunley were in the army and probably both of them have marksman medals. Just about everybody gets one of those, though."

"They have every other medal," Ivy said. "They like to talk about them, too, or at least the son does. Pete. He's made his father proud."

"Every son wants to," Rhodes said.

"His war was a lot different from his father's. Desert instead of jungle. How much do you remember about the First Gulf War, anyway?"

"Not much," Rhodes said. "Shock and awe. Operation Desert Storm. A quick win."

"You're already mixed up," Ivy said. "Shock and awe is from the Iraq war, which wasn't a quick win."

"Then I know even less than I thought I did. How quick a win was the first Gulf War?"

"Really quick. In fact, the ground war didn't last long at all, maybe a month. I don't remember much more than that. The shock and awe went on longer. You'd have to ask an expert."

"Lawrence Gates was an expert. Not just on that war but on all wars, or that's what it seemed like, according to Roger. I can't ask him, though."

"Lawrence wasn't in any wars," Ivy said.

"Not as far as we know," Rhodes said. "His expertise is all intellectual, based on reading books and information from the internet."

"Then we'd better move on. You say that all of your suspects are alibiing each other and that any of them could have been in town when Roger was killed."

"That's right, except for Kenny and Noble. The Reeses and the Falkners lied to me about that. So did Kenny and Noble, but we've covered them already."

"We haven't figured out where they are."

Rhodes shrugged his shoulders. "No, and I wish we could. I told Kenny's mother to call me if they showed up at her house, but I don't think she will. I'm at a dead end with those two."

"What do you think about Faye Falkner?" Ivy asked.

Rhodes considered his answer for a second. "She's a little excitable."

Ivy laughed. "Is that what you call it? I'll bet you a dollar she's the one who thought of those 'pranks' to play on the Hunleys. It sounds like something she'd do."

"It's possible," Rhodes said, "but if she came up with the ideas, Leslie's the one who worked them out. Faye's more spontaneous. She kind of erupts without thinking. If she killed Lawrence, it would have had to be a spur-of-the-moment thing, and I'm sure she doesn't carry a pistol. The killing took some planning, too, and that's not her strong point."

"What about her husband?" Ivy asked.

"Leslie? He might've done it. She might even have asked him to do it, but I can't figure out why the two of them would be at the school when Lawrence was."

"You're not much help," Ivy said. "Every time I make a suggestion about who might have done it, you shoot it down. So to speak."

"That's what I'm here for," Rhodes said.

"Right. So what about the Reeses? Charlie was out on the horse, so he could've gone to the school."

"If he had," Rhodes said, "he would've been noticed. Thurston might be a small town, but there aren't a lot of people out riding horses any time of day."

"He's a bully, he likes guns, and he likes to kill feral hogs," Ivy said.

"I wish more people liked to kill feral hogs," Rhodes said. "If things go on the way they are, the hogs will have taken over in a few hundred years. It's going to be like *Planet of the Apes*, but with hogs."

Ivy laughed again. "I think we've drifted off the subject here. You spend too much time around Hack and Lawton."

"Worst fears realized," Rhodes said. "Let me get back on track. Charlie is a bully, all right, but like most bullies, he's all hat and no cattle. It doesn't take much to back him down, and there's a big difference between shooting a feral hog and a human being. As for the guns, lots of people like guns. Nothing wrong with that, as long as you use them the right way."

"What about the man who beat up Curtis Lambert?" Ivy asked. "Could that have been Reese?"

Rhodes gave the idea some thought. "Like I said, he's a bully, but he's easy to back down. That might not apply in Curtis's case. He didn't fight back, as far as I know. Here's another thing. The man who beat him was wearing a mask. Sometimes it's easier for someone to act when his identity is hidden. So, yes, Reese could have done it."

"Something to consider, then," Ivy said. "What do you think about his wife?"

"Arlene? She seems normal enough. She seems more likely to use a vacuum cleaner than a gun, but doesn't care for housework."

"Who does?" Ivy asked.

Rhodes knew better than to get into that discussion.

"She and Charlie seem to have some issues," he said, "but nothing serious."

"About housework?"

"Among other things."

"I'm glad we don't have issues," Ivy said.

Rhodes thought about all the healthy meals he'd eaten in the last few years, which was sort of an issue, but he thought this would be a bad time to mention it. So he didn't.

I'm glad, too," he said. "Peace and harmony, that's us."

"Don't make it sound so icky," Ivy said.

"I didn't mean to. Does this mean we have issues?"

"I don't think so," Ivy said, "but you'd better watch your step."

"Count on it," Rhodes said, "but aren't we getting away from the subject again?"

"I blame Hack and Lawton," Ivy said. "Where were we?"

"Charlie and Arlene Reese."

"I hate to write them and the Falkners off. They all wanted to get rid of the old school building, and now it's gone."

"That might account for the fire," Rhodes said. "It doesn't account for Lawrence, though, and I'm not writing anybody off for either of those things."

"So you think the murder and the fire might not be connected?"

"That's right. There's no reason why they should be."

"It just seems like they would be," Ivy said.

"Seems that way to me, too, but I haven't come up with the connection yet."

"Maybe you just need to sleep on it, or if that's not what you need, we could go outside and clear our heads."

"Going outside sounds like a good idea to me," Rhodes said, and they got up from the table and went into the backyard.

It was cooler now than it had been during the day, but not a lot. It would be midnight before the temperature started to drop much, and even then it wouldn't go below the low seventies. The night air made it seem a little cooler than it was, though, and Speedo emerged from his Styrofoam igloo and ambled over to them, wagging his tail. Rhodes rubbed his head and told him he was a good boy but that they weren't going to play.

"We're just here to look at the sky," Rhodes said.

As if he understood, Speedo sat back on his haunches and looked up. Rhodes wondered what he was seeing. Could dogs see the stars? Rhodes had no idea.

In spite of its name, Clearview didn't provide an entirely clear view of the stars. A bit of light pollution had crept in, even though the nearest city of any size was nearly forty miles away. Even Clearview provided some of the light that dimmed the stars a little.

Rhodes could remember going out into his backyard on summer nights when he was small. It was darker then. He'd lived in the country, of course, which made the nights even darker. There had been no light pollution at all. Lightning bugs flickered all around, and the sky was blistered with stars. The Milky Way was like a wide highway across the darkness. Rhodes could even identify some of the constellations then, although the only ones he could remember with any certainty now were the Big Dipper and the Little Dipper. He could see the man in the moon in those days, but now he wasn't so sure. It didn't matter at the moment since the moon was in the first quarter and not showing much of a face.

Ivy stood close to him and he put his arm around her. "Think we'll ever send anybody else to the moon?" he asked.

"Not in our lifetimes," Ivy said. "We lost sight of that goal somewhere along the way."

"Too bad," Rhodes said. "Or maybe not. We might not belong up there, anyway."

"You're feeling philosophical tonight," Ivy said.

"That's a bad sign," Rhodes said. "Time to go in and go to sleep. You, too, Speedo."

Speedo went back to his igloo, and Rhodes and Ivy went inside.

Sleep would have been a good idea if it had been restful, but Rhodes didn't sleep well, and he got very little rest. He got up at the usual time, sat on the edge of the bed, and rubbed his face with both hands. His head had been full of dreams all night. Or nightmares, which were becoming a bad habit, although he could hardly remember any of them in the morning. Most of them involved fire, as best he could recall, but some of them had to do with being shot at while pinned down in an old house. He was pretty sure there was one about him walking on the moon. That one hadn't been too bad.

Rhodes knew that there were people who believed that dreams

were a way in which a person's unconscious was trying to communicate something to the sleeper, but he couldn't think of a thing that had been communicated to him. He needed something more clearly stated, like having somebody in the dream hold up a sign that said "The Killer Is . . ." Or "The Arsonist Is . . ." That would clarify things if the blanks were filled in, and it would make his job a lot easier. Or it would if dreams could be trusted to tell the truth.

Could you really trust something you recalled from a dream? Some people might believe that. Seepy Benton, for example. Seepy had once told Rhodes that he was a "lucid dreamer," which meant that he had control of his dreams, at least to some extent, and could even manipulate them.

"I never have to worry about nightmares," Seepy had said. "If bad things happen in a dream, I can either change them to good things or wake myself up. Usually bad things don't happen, though, since I'm pretty much in charge."

Rhodes never knew whether to take Seepy at his word, but he'd sounded perfectly serious when talking about the lucid dreaming. Rhodes wondered if Seepy could also interpret dreams. Even if he could, he wouldn't be of any use to Rhodes, since Rhodes couldn't remember his dreams. Even Seepy, with that brain he was so proud of, wouldn't be able to interpret the fragments and phantoms that Rhodes could recall.

Maybe not being able to recall his dreams was a good thing. Except for the one about walking on the moon. He'd like to remember that one. He was still thinking about it when the phone rang. Ivy answered and called him.

"It's Seepy Benton," she said.

Seepy never called Rhodes at home, although he had the number, so Rhodes knew the call was important. He got up and went to the phone.

"This is the sheriff," he said.

"Great," Seepy said. "I have good news for you."

"I could use some," Rhodes said. "What is it?"

"I've cracked the case," Seepy said.

Chapter 23

Rhodes wasn't sure Seepy knew what it meant to crack a case, but he figured it would be a good idea to find out.

"Tell me about it," he said.

"I'll meet you at Roger Prentiss's house in half an hour," Seepy said. "I'll tell you then. I don't want to go into it over the phone. I've already called him, and he'll be ready for us when we get there. Don't eat breakfast. He says he'll pick up some doughnuts."

The doughnuts sounded good. Rhodes hoped Prentiss would pick up some buttermilk doughnuts. They were Rhodes's favorites, and it had been so long since he'd had one that he couldn't remember when it was.

"I'll be there," Rhodes said.

He hung up the phone and went to get dressed. Once again he had to turn the morning romp with the dogs over to Ivy.

"I can handle that," she said. "I think they're starting to have more fun with me than they do with you."

"You trying to make me jealous?" Rhodes asked.

"Not in the least," Ivy said. "Where are you off to in such a rush?"

"To see Roger Prentiss and Seepy. Seepy says he's cracked the case."

"I'll believe that when I see it," Ivy said. "Are you going to let Hack know where you'll be?"

"I'll do that right now," Rhodes said, going to the phone.

"You gonna put me in the loop?" Hack asked when Rhodes told him that he'd be late getting in.

"As soon as I see you again," Rhodes said. "Right now even I don't know any more than that Seepy Benton says he's cracked the case."

"Fat chance," Hack said. "Now let me put you in the loop on something."

Uh-oh, Rhodes thought. "Go ahead."

"You remember that woman robber you brought in yesterday?"

"How could I forget?" Rhodes asked.

"Well, she bonded out right after you left yesterday."

"I'm not surprised," Rhodes said. "It happens all the time."

"Yeah, but not ever'body does what she did when they leave."

Rhodes knew he'd have to ask if he wanted to know what Madison had done. Hack would never tell him without spending ten minutes building up to it. "What did she do?"

"She stopped right in front of me and said, 'I'll be back.'"

"Was it a friendly 'I'll be back' or a Terminator 'I'll be back'?" Rhodes asked.

"Terminator," Hack said. "You think we need to put some steel doors on the front of the jail?"

"Probably too late for that," Rhodes said, "although considering the way she drives, it might not be a bad idea. You might want to move your desk into the cellblock just in case."

"You ain't near as funny as you think you are, you know that?"

"I should. People keep telling me."

"Well, they're right about it," Hack said.

"I'll try to do better."

"Don't do that. Just stop tryin' to make jokes."

"I'll think about it."

"You do that," Hack said.

Rhodes hung up and told Ivy that he wouldn't have time for breakfast. He didn't mention the doughnuts.

"I have to get right on over to Roger's house," he said. "I don't want Seepy to get impatient."

"I don't think he's the impatient type," Ivy said. "I think he's at one with the universe."

"Now who's getting philosophical?" Rhodes asked.

"Not me," Ivy said. "Speaking of being at one with the universe, where's Yancey?"

"Still asleep," Rhodes said. "He rests better than I do."

"Then wake him up. Time for him and me to have some fun."

Rhodes whistled, and Yancey came into the kitchen, his claws clicking on the floor. He danced around Rhodes's ankles until Rhodes told him that Ivy was going outside with him.

Ivy went to the back door, and Yancey ran over to her, not looking back at Rhodes.

Maybe Ivy was right about Yancey and Speedo having more fun with her than with him. He had to admit, but only to himself, that it did make him a little jealous. He thought he'd get over it, though, especially if Roger had a buttermilk doughnut. Or two.

Clearview in the early morning was not a bustling hive of activity, but Rhodes did see a few people out on their lawns. One man was drinking coffee, and he raised his cup to Rhodes as the sheriff drove by. Another was smoking a cigarette, and a third was looking for something in his pickup. A mother urged a couple of teenagers into a car. In a little while they'd be going off to work or school without much of a thought for Lawrence Gates or the old schoolhouse in Thurston or Madison Russell or any of the other crimes and misdemeanors of Blacklin County.

Most people were likely to be unaware of the crime that went on all around them other than the sensationalized stories that Jennifer Loam put on her news blog. Most of them never considered all the things happening most of the day and night, like driving under the influence or while distracted by texting, or doing something else on a phone. The people he saw in their yards knew that Rhodes and the Charger represented the law, and they no doubt had some respect for the law, depending on their experience or their lack of experience with it, but few of them understood what was involved in policing even a sparsely populated county like the one they lived in. They had their own lives to live, going to work, taking the kids to school, paying the bills, and all the ordinary living involved.

Rhodes wondered if it mattered that people didn't know any more than they did about the criminal underbelly, such as it was, of the county. If he ran for reelection, he'd have to remind them of all the things his department did to keep the county safe. Some of them might be appreciative, but others might be scared to think that they lived in a place where such things happened. Whoever ran against him, and there would inevitably be somebody who thought he or she could do the job better than Rhodes, would try to scare people a lot more than anything Rhodes said would scare them.

Everything either of them said would get plenty of publicity from Jennifer Loam. The stories she'd done about Rhodes in the past might even be brought up again, not by his opponent but by Jennifer, who was a good newsperson but who couldn't resist a bit of exaggeration when it came to getting clicks on her blog. The publicity might help Rhodes's campaign if he ran again, but he didn't like the idea of having that kind of thing mentioned over and over. He liked to do his job and keep a low profile.

Running for office wasn't anything he had to worry about at the moment, though, and he put it out of his mind. Right now what concerned him was finding out who killed Lawrence and who burned the schoolhouse. Not to mention whether Roger had picked up any buttermilk doughnuts.

Seepy Benton was already at Roger's house when Rhodes arrived. He was going up the sidewalk to the door, but when Rhodes pulled to the curb, Seepy stopped to wait for him. Rhodes got out of the Charger and joined him.

"So you've cracked the case," Rhodes said.

Seepy kicked at a crack in the sidewalk. "I might have overstated things a little."

"I was afraid of that. How much is a little?"

"Let's go inside, and I'll tell you. Roger might want to hear it, too, and he's my client, after all. Plus he said he'd have doughnuts."

They went up the walk, and Rhodes knocked on the door. Roger opened it and invited them inside.

"Let's go in the kitchen," he said. "I bought some doughnuts at Freshie's Doughnut Hole, and I have coffee ready."

"What kind of doughnuts?" Seepy asked.

"All kinds," Roger said. "I got an assortment."

That sounded promising to Rhodes.

The kitchen was old-fashioned, with white Formica countertops, a white porcelain sink, and cabinets that had a couple of sagging doors. Three chairs sat at a small maple table with foldout sides. A white box with a dozen doughnuts sat open in the middle of the table, and Rhodes was happy to see that two of them were buttermilk. Cake plates sat on the table in front of each chair, with a paper napkin, fork, and teaspoon beside each one.

"Have a seat," Roger said. "Coffee?"

"None for me," Rhodes said. "It smells good, but I'll take water."

"I'll have a cup," Seepy said. "Black with sugar."

"Help yourselves to the doughnuts," Roger said.

Rhodes didn't hesitate. He took his fork and nailed a buttermilk doughnut. Seepy went for a plain glazed one.

Roger set a cup of coffee on a saucer in front of Seepy and put a dish with sugar packets beside it.

"I'll let you sweeten your own," he said to Seepy while placing a glass of water beside Rhodes's plate.

Seepy paused his doughnut eating and opened a packet of sugar. He poured the contents into his coffee and stirred.

Roger sat down with his own coffee, took a chocolate-filled doughnut from the box, and said to Seepy, "You told me that you'd solved the case. I'm ready to hear about it. Did it have to do with the encrypted files?"

"Yes," Seepy said. He took a sip of coffee and another bite of his doughnut, moves that Rhodes recognized as classic stalling techniques.

"Well?" Roger said.

"Let me ask you something first," Seepy said. "You never did tell us why Lawrence moved here."

"Sure I did," Roger said. "College buddies, remember? Reconnected on Facebook, and so on."

"That's not a reason," Seepy said. "Not a real one, anyway. He came here for something. He must have. He started the blog, or if he didn't, it was his idea. He was obsessed with the Thurston school."

"I don't see that it matters," Roger said. "We were friends. That was good enough for me."

Seepy stirred his coffee again. "Maybe it doesn't matter, but I think it does. It couldn't have been just friendship. He was collecting information on people in Thurston, mainly the Reeses, the Falkners, and the Hunleys."

"My suspects," Rhodes said. "Did he have anything on Kenny Lambert?"

"Nothing," Seepy said. "He had plenty on the others, though."

"For example?" Rhodes said.

"Let's start with the Reeses, or Charlie Reese," Seepy said. "You know him?"

"I've talked to him and his wife a few times lately," Rhodes said, not giving anything away.

"You know how he made his money?"

"Yes," Rhodes said. "Wheeling and dealing, a fine old Texas tradition."

"That's one way to put it," Seepy said. "Lawrence had dug into some of the dealing. His conclusion was that it wasn't all on the up-and-up."

"Did he have specifics?"

"Not in every instance."

Rhodes resisted a sigh. "Name one."

"It happened in another county. Some man named Ross Ellisor bought some land from Reese. Reese carried the loan himself and naturally charged interest. Not an unfair amount. Ellisor was injured in a car accident a few years later and couldn't keep up the payments. Reese took back the land after Ellisor missed one payment. Ellisor and his wife were both upset by the way it was handled. Ellisor's argument was that he could've continued the payments after he got back on his feet. He needed a little time, but he'd pay eventually. Reese didn't care. The loan agreement Ellisor signed said that he'd lose the land if he missed a payment. Reese didn't care about being paid eventually. He kept the land and later sold it again for a good bit more money."

"I can see the article on the blog now," Roger said. "That was the kind of thing Lawrence loved."

"Except he didn't publish it," Seepy said. "There are a couple of similar incidents that as far as I know were never on the blog, either. Not that I was a regular reader."

Rhodes snorted.

"Well, maybe I was," Seepy said. "That's beside the point. He had the information and didn't use it. Why not?"

"I have no idea," Roger said.

"What about the Falkners?" Rhodes asked.

"That's a good one," Seepy said. "You know how they got their money?"

"The old-fashioned way," Rhodes said. "They inherited it."

"That's right," Seepy said, "but do you know where the money came from?"

"Some rich relative who started a fast-food chain out in California," Rhodes said, "or that's the story I've heard. I don't think anybody knows for sure."

"Lawrence knew," Seepy said. He looked at his plate, which had nothing on it but crumbs. "I think I'll have another doughnut."

Roger stood up. "I'll get you some more coffee."

Rhodes took advantage of the opportunity to spear the second and last buttermilk doughnut.

Roger came back to the table with a carafe of coffee and poured some in Seepy's cup. He put the carafe back in the coffeemaker and sat down.

"Are you going to tell us what Lawrence knew," Rhodes asked, "or are you just going to let us guess?"

"The money didn't come from a fast-food franchise," Seepy said. He took a bite of doughnut.

Rhodes thought Seepy was looking more and more like Lawton every day. "So tell us where it did come from."

"Marijuana," Seepy said. "Or cannabis as I prefer to call it."

"They were dope dealers?" Roger said.

"Not them. The rich relative. He wasn't a dealer, exactly. He was a medical cannabis grower. Perfectly legal in California. Not so legal in Texas, although it should be."

"That doesn't sound like such a big deal," Roger said.

"It is, though," Seepy said. "Think about how it would look on your blog with a clickbait headline. Besides, as I said, this isn't California. In Texas the idea of cannabis use of any kind is considered sinful and worse. The Falkners would be ostracized by most of the population of the county."

"You might be underestimating the people around here," Rhodes said.

"I could be," Seepy said, "but I don't think I am."

It was an argument that Rhodes didn't want to get into, and Seepy was right about how Lawrence could have approached the story. He could have made things seem much worse than they were.

"I'll concede the point," Rhodes said. "What else did you find out?"

"That's all about the Falkners."

"So that leaves the Hunleys."

"Right," Seepy said. "That's kind of tricky."

More stalling. "How tricky?"

"It's not easy to get military records, but that's what Lawrence was trying to do. I guess he couldn't dig up anything on Con or Pete in recent years, so he was going back to their military careers."

"It's hard even for law enforcement to get military records," Rhodes said. "It can be done, but it's a long, slow process."

"Lawrence was pretty closemouthed about what he was doing," Roger put in. "I didn't know about any of this stuff. He did let one thing slip, though."

"What would that be?" Rhodes asked.

"He had an uncle who served in the first Gulf War," Roger said. "That's all I know."

"Who was the uncle?"

"He didn't tell me that. It was just a passing remark when I asked him what he was working on. I don't know much about his family."

"You know his mother and father," Rhodes said. "You got in touch with them about Lawrence's murder."

"Yes," Roger said.

"If you could get the name of the uncle for me, I'd like to ask him if he knew what Lawrence was working on."

"I'll call," Roger said. "I don't even know if his uncle is still alive. He could've been killed over there for all I know."

"It would be good if you could call right now," Rhodes said.

"Sure," Roger said. He stood up. "My phone's in the other room. I'll be right back."

"Do you think the uncle will be any help?" Seepy asked as Roger left the kitchen.

Rhodes shrugged. "Who knows?"

"I guess I didn't really crack the case," Seepy said, "but I did give you some information that you can use when you question your suspects again."

"I'll give you credit for that," Rhodes said. "You should learn not to exaggerate, though."

"I got carried away," Seepy said. "What do you think about the Falkners and the Reeses now?"

"I think they're good suspects for murder, but then I always did. I've been interviewing them for a couple of days. They've always been suspects."

"Not the Hunleys?"

"Them, too, but I can't find a motive for them. Maybe the uncle will give us one."

"Because he was in the Gulf War?"

"Pretty chancy," Rhodes said, "but right now it's all we have."

"It doesn't seem like much," Seepy said.

"That's because it's not."

Roger came back into the room. "I called Lawrence's parents. The uncle's name is Henry Gates. I wrote down his number."

He handed Rhodes a piece of paper. Rhodes folded it and stuck it in his pocket.

"I'll give him a call from the jail," Rhodes said. He stood up. "I'd better get on over there and find out what's going on around the county."

"If you can get Hack and Lawton to tell you," Seepy said.

"They always tell me," Rhodes said, "but very slowly."

Roger pushed the doughnut box in Rhodes's direction. "Better take one for the road."

Rhodes looked into the box. No more buttermilk doughnuts, but there was one with chocolate frosting that tempted him.

"I'll get you a fresh napkin to wrap it in," Roger said, getting up from the table.

That was all Rhodes needed to hear to give in to the temptation. He took the doughnut and wrapped it in the napkin that Roger handed him.

"You're going to tell me what the uncle said, aren't you?" Seepy asked.

"I'll keep you in the loop," Rhodes said.

Chapter 24

Amazingly enough, Hack and Lawton didn't have any stories to tell other than the one about Madison Russell, and Hack had already given that one away.

"Why would she say somethin' like that?" Hack asked Rhodes when Rhodes had gotten seated at his desk. "She doesn't look like an incorrigible."

"What does an incorrigible look like?" Rhodes asked.

"Like that Kenny Lambert with the snake tattooed on his neck. You can bet he'll be back, and more than once."

"If somebody doesn't shoot him first," Lawton said.

Rhodes thought it would make his job a lot easier if he could identify criminals by their appearance, but he'd never been able to do that. All his suspects in the murder of Lawrence Gates looked like fine, upstanding citizens. Maybe they were. Maybe he was on the wrong track and had been all along, although he didn't think so.

He stood up. "I'm going over to the courthouse. Don't tell Jennifer Loam if she comes asking."

"We don't have to tell her," Hack said. "She knows where to find you if you're in town. You need a new hideout."

"That's a good idea," Rhodes said. "Any suggestions?"

"You could go home," Lawton said. "Nobody there during the day."

"I think I'll stick with the courthouse," Rhodes said. "I'll be back later."

As soon as he left the jail, Rhodes drove straight home. Yancey was glad to see him, if a little puzzled as to why Rhodes had shown up at such an unusual time. Rhodes went into the kitchen with Yancey yipping along behind him. The cats looked him over, then closed their eyes. They didn't care when he came home.

Rhodes set his wrapped doughnut on the kitchen table and went to the refrigerator, where he got out a Dr Pepper. He popped the can open and set it on the table by the doughnut. Three doughnuts and a Dr Pepper with real sugar. Life was good.

"You're not going to tell Ivy, are you?" he asked Yancey.

Yancey yipped. Rhodes knew he wasn't a squealer, but he wasn't so sure about the cats. They could be watching even when they didn't appear to be. Cats were sneaky that way. Rhodes didn't care. He sat down, unwrapped the doughnut, took a bite, and savored it. He followed with a swallow of Dr Pepper.

"I know it's not good for me," Rhodes told Yancey, "but I can quit any time I want to."

That was true. He'd quit Dr Pepper before, and his boycott had lasted for at least a couple of years. He was glad he'd given the boycott up, though.

After a couple of bites of the doughnut and a couple of swallows of his drink, Rhodes started to think about the case of Lawrence Gates. He'd been adding little things up almost since the beginning, and he had a list of them now. He wanted to talk to Henry Gates before seeing how they all added up, so he made the call, using his new cell phone.

Henry Gates had a strong baritone voice. He was a bit surprised to be getting a call from a small-town sheriff in Texas.

"You say this has to do with Lawrence's murder?" he asked.

"It does," Rhodes said, "but I'm not sure how. Lawrence was working on an article about the first Gulf War, and I know you were a veteran of that one. I think there's a connection between you and that article. I also think there's a connection between that article and his murder. Maybe he talked to you about it."

"He talked to me about it, all right," Henry said. "The truth is, I feel a little guilty about his death. I'm afraid I'm the one who caused him to go to Texas in the first place."

It was Rhodes's turn to be surprised. "How did that happen?"

"You know he was living with his friend Roger Prentiss in your county?"

"I know," Rhodes said.

"They'd reconnected on Facebook," Henry said, "and I mentioned to Lawrence that I knew somebody who lived in Blacklin County. His name is Pete Hunley. Lawrence asked me how I knew him, and I told him that we served together in Operation Desert Storm. Lawrence looked him up, and learned that he was a big war hero. I told Lawrence that I'd read something about that, which is how I knew where he lived."

"I know all about the stories," Rhodes said. "It was a big deal here when he came home from the war, and it's been brought up every now and then since then."

“Yeah,” Henry said, “but there’s a catch.”

Rhodes wondered if the Hack-Lawton disease had spread all over the country.

“What’s the catch?” he asked, to get things moving.

“It never happened,” Henry said. “Pete being a hero, I mean. He was the biggest goldbrick in the outfit. He did see a little combat, but when there was shooting, he was as far from it as he could get. All that stuff about him being a hero is baloney.”

“Stolen valor,” Rhodes said.

“You got it. That’s what interested Lawrence, and he didn’t like the idea of somebody getting away with that kind of scam. I’d never pursued it, but Lawrence was apparently more interested than I was.”

“That’s a big help,” Rhodes said. “Do you have a name and number for somebody who could corroborate your story? It’s not that I don’t trust you, but you know the old saying about trusting and verifying. The more evidence of what Pete did that I can get, the better.”

“I know what you mean,” Henry said, “and I know how hard it is to get into the army’s records to get the kind of information you need. I have one friend from those days, Woody Winters. Hang on just a second while I look up his number.”

Rhodes waited, and then Henry came back on and gave him the number.

“Thanks,” Rhodes said. “I appreciate your taking the time to talk to me.”

“You think Pete killed Lawrence?”

“It’s starting to look that way,” Rhodes said.

“You get him and lock his ass up,” Henry said. “Throw away the key.”

“I’ll do what I can,” Rhodes said.

He thanked Henry again for his help and ended the call. Then he punched in the number Henry had given him for Woody Winters. Winters was even more surprised than Henry had been to be getting a call from a sheriff in East Texas, but when Rhodes had mentioned Henry's name and explained the reason for the call, Woody said, "Sure, I knew Pete Hunley when we were over there in the sand pile. What do you want to know about him?"

"He's something of a legend around here," Rhodes said, "because of his heroic actions over there during the war."

Woody gave a sharp laugh. "Heroic actions? You must have the wrong man, Sheriff. Pete Hunley was about the least heroic man in the outfit. He wasn't exactly a coward, I'm not saying that, but he could find more ways to avoid getting shot at than anybody I ever knew. If there was an ailment he didn't develop to get out of duty, I don't know what it was."

"Too bad," Rhodes said. "Those stories I've heard about his heroism must not be true."

"Damn right, they're not," Woody said. "You can believe me on that."

"I do," Rhodes said.

"If you'd like a few more names of people who knew Pete in Iraq, I can give them to you."

"I'd appreciate that," Rhodes said.

It took Woody a few minutes to get the information, but when he did, Rhodes wrote it all down. He didn't need to call anyone on the list, which had four names on it, at least not now. He thought he had more than enough information already to get an arrest warrant.

"I hope that helps," Woody said.

"It does," Rhodes told him. He thanked Woody, cut off the call, and set the cell phone down on the table. The Hunleys had always been suspects, but Rhodes hadn't been able to come up with a motive for any of them. Now he had one. It wasn't at all hard to believe that someone like Pete would kill to keep the truth about his stolen valor from coming out. Pete would be laughed out of the county if people had found out. Lawrence might have had trouble getting the army records, but when he'd told his story about Pete's stolen valor, he'd have gotten them sooner or later. Pete couldn't let that happen.

Pete might have avoided battles in Iraq and Kuwait, but it didn't take a lot of courage to shoot a man in the back of the head when the man was distracted. Lawrence must have called Pete about meeting and talking things over. Pete had seen his chance and suggested that they meet at the school building, well away from his home. Then he'd tricked Lawrence into writing something on the board and eliminated the threat of the exposure of his secret.

Lawrence's phone records would be coming in soon, and there'd be a call to Pete on them, but that might not help Rhodes's case. Lawrence had called all the suspects, maybe more than once. On the other hand, if Pete had been the one to arrange the meeting, the incoming call would be another bit of evidence, circumstantial but suggestive.

Rhodes didn't know what Pete had done with Lawrence's car, but the old rock pit in back of the Hunley houses was a good bet to be its final resting place. Checking on that could come later.

Rhodes finished the doughnut and the Dr Pepper and disposed of the can and napkin. He looked around for Yancey and saw him at the back door. Ivy came home every day at noon and let Yancey out for a little time in the yard, but Yancey wasn't above taking advantage of Rhodes and getting out early.

Rhodes went to the door and opened it and the screen. Yancey plunged through the doorway and out into the yard, probably with the intention of bedeviling Speedo, who was lying in the shade of a pecan tree. Yancey charged over to him and started yipping. Speedo got up, and Yancey took off with Speedo in hot pursuit.

Once he saw that Yancey and Speedo were having a good time, Rhodes went back to the table to sit down and go over his little mental list of other things he'd been adding together. They hadn't seemed like much, but now they were more significant.

First there was the way the killer had entered the school building. He'd have to know the building pretty well to get in through the second-floor window by using the fire escape, and while the Reeses and Falkners had gone to school there when they were young, the Hunleys were the ones who were more familiar with the building now because of their interest in its preservation. Rhodes didn't doubt that Pete could walk there without being seen.

If the Hunleys were so interested in saving the building, however, why had Pete burned it, as Rhodes was now pretty sure he had. The reason had to be related to the reunion that Con had planned. Pete must have been afraid that someone in a large group might do a little background checking or maybe a Gulf War veteran who knew too much would be in the crowd of people attending.

Maybe Pete wasn't the arsonist, but he did know someone who had some kerosene that he could use for an accelerant. Rhodes had smelled it in Con's garage, where Con had been using it as a paint stripper. Pete could easily have taken it from there.

The final thing that had stuck with Rhodes was the washing of the black Suburban. It had been spotless the previous time when Rhodes saw it, and while there were a number of ways it could have gotten covered in dirt and dust, driving the unpaved county roads and going off onto someone's land on a sandy road would be one sure way to do it. Why Con might've been washing Pete's vehicle was another question, but Pete was there helping, so maybe keeping vehicles clean was a family thing.

Rhodes picked up his new cell phone again and called Judge Casey to ask for the arrest warrant.

"So you think Pete Hunley killed this Lawrence Gates," Casey said after Rhodes had explained the situation. "What if you're wrong?"

"I think I'm right, and I have the evidence to back it up," Rhodes said.

"You don't have any real evidence," Casey said. "Mostly you have just speculation. If you're wrong, it would be a real black eye for you and the county. The Hunleys are held in high regard around here."

"I know that," Rhodes said, "but maybe that high regard should be lowered. The stolen valor is real."

"Maybe," Casey said. "You have only the word of two men."

"I believe them. I can call four more men who were in Pete's outfit and see what they have to say if you think it's necessary. We'll get the army records and prove it later on if Pete doesn't confess. Or maybe you'd rather give me a search warrant for that rock pit in back of the Hunley homes. I think Lawrence's car is in there."

"More speculation," Rogers said.

Things weren't going as smoothly as Rhodes had thought they would. He hadn't counted on one simple fact, something that he should have thought of, a friendship between the Hunleys and Casey. Rhodes wasn't going to mention that possibility, though. He knew it would only make things worse if he did.

"I have witnesses who saw Pete going into the school building around the time Lawrence was killed," Rhodes said, stretching the truth as far as it would go.

"Where are they?" Casey asked.

"I don't have them right here," Rhodes said, "but I can put my hand on them when I need them."

"Are they reliable?"

Rhodes thought about Kenny and Noble. He remembered what Hack had said about Kenny and how Kenny would look on the witness stand. The jury would be impressed with the snake tattoo, but not in the right way.

"They're reliable," Rhodes said, stretching the truth again, "but they might not look good in front of a jury."

"They aren't much help, then."

"Look," Rhodes said, "I have enough evidence to have probable cause for Pete's arrest without a warrant. I just wanted it to be more official so there wouldn't be any problems down the line. If you don't want to issue a warrant, I'm going to have to act on my own."

"But the consequences . . ."

"I know what the consequences might be. I'm willing to take the responsibility."

"Next year's an election year," Casey said.

"I know that," Rhodes said. "I might decide not to run."

Casey laughed. "You've been sheriff for too long not to run. Everybody expects it."

"Sometimes you have to do the unexpected," Rhodes said. "What about that warrant?"

"I'll get it ready for you," Casey said, "but if there's any fallout it's going to fall right on you."

"I can take it," Rhodes said. "I'll have one of the deputies pick up the warrant right away."

"I'll have it ready," Casey said. "Good luck. You're going to need it."

"I don't doubt it for a minute," Rhodes said.

He hung up and called Hack at the jail. "Who's on patrol around town?"

"Buddy," Hack said. "Why?"

"I want him to run by the courthouse and pick up an arrest warrant from Judge Casey."

"I thought you were at the courthouse," Hack said.

"Well, I'm not. Have Buddy drop the warrant off at my house."

"I get the feelin' I'm out of the loop again," Hack said.

"You'll be back in it soon enough. Who's working the south part of the county?"

"Ruth."

Rhodes looked at his watch. "Have her meet me at Manny Kingston's grocery store in an hour," he said.

"I hear he has good hamburgers," Hack said.

"You hear right."

"You and Ruth gonna eat one?"

"I'll put you in the loop on that later," Rhodes said.

"You could bring me and Lawton one. Might make up for keepin' us out of the loop."

"I'll see what I can do," Rhodes said.

Buddy brought the warrant by and asked Rhodes if he needed backup when serving it.

"Ruth's already in Thurston," Rhodes said. "She'll be the backup."

Buddy patted his sidearm. "I'm ready if you need me."

"I hope it'll all be peaceful," Rhodes said.

"That's the trouble with this county," Buddy said. "Too peaceful."

"Except for murders and fires and such."

"Yeah, well, except for that kind of thing. I never seem to get in on any of the fun."

Rhodes grinned. "You've been in on your share."

Buddy grinned, too. "I guess I have at that, but if you need any more help, you be sure to put out a call."

"You know I will," Rhodes said.

"Yep," Buddy said, "but I want you to call me specifically."

"We'll see," Rhodes said.

Chapter 25

Ruth was waiting at Kingston's store when Rhodes got there. She was in a booth, and she and Manny were talking when Rhodes walked in. Manny said, "Your ears burning, Sheriff?"

"Not so I can tell it," Rhodes said, taking in the odor of french fries and grilled meat. "Should they be?"

"Mr. Kingston was telling me about Ms. Wilkins's cat and how you arranged for his care," Ruth said, "and I was telling him about how many animals you've taken in."

"Not so many," Rhodes said. "Only four."

"Not counting the one you palmed off on Seepy," Ruth said.

Rhodes had arranged for Seepy to become the owner of a fine dog named Bruce.

"I'd have taken him, myself," Rhodes said, "but he might have scooped Yancey up and eaten him in one bite."

"Bruce is a sweetheart," Ruth said. "He and Yancey would get along just fine."

"Maybe," Rhodes said, "but Yancey can be irritating now and then."

"Leroy's a sweetheart, too," Manny said. "He and I are pals already. Do you know when Wanda will be coming home?"

Rhodes felt a little guilty that he hadn't checked with the hospital that day, but he'd had a lot on his mind. He said, "I don't know, but I expect it will be another day or two."

"That's okay with me," Manny said. "I like visiting Leroy."

"That reminds me," Rhodes said. "Wanda told me that the house key is in her purse in the top drawer of her dresser. You might want to get it and lock the door when you're there next."

"I'll do that," Manny said. "We don't have a lot of break-ins around here, but it pays to be careful. Do you two want burgers?"

"Maybe later," Rhodes said. "We have a little business to do first. If you could give us a minute, I need to talk things over with my deputy."

"No problem," Manny said. "I'll leave you two alone to talk."

Manny drifted to the back of the store to wait for a customer to come in, and Rhodes explained to Ruth what they were there for.

"Do you think there'll be trouble?" Ruth asked when Rhodes was finished.

"Probably not. He'll be surprised to see us. We'll just serve the warrant, arrest him, and that will be that."

"Sounds easy," Ruth said, "but a lot of things sound easier when you're just talking about them."

"Two of us, one of him," Rhodes said. "What could possibly go wrong?"

"I wish you hadn't asked that," Ruth said.

• • •

The two Chargers came to a stop in front of Pete Hunley's house. Rhodes and Ruth got out of the cars, and Rhodes reached down to remove the Kel-Tec pistol from his ankle holster. Keeping in mind the Boy Scout motto, he stuck the pistol in his belt at the back of his pants.

Ruth walked over to him and said, "How do we play this?"

"We go to the door. If Pete comes to let us in, I serve him with the warrant. If it's his wife, we ask to see Pete. His wife's name is Linda, by the way. I don't think I mentioned that."

"You didn't," Ruth said, "but I doubt that we'll have time to bond or anything."

"You're right," Rhodes said, "and she won't like us much when we do what we came to do."

"Speaking of that," Ruth said, "let's do it."

They walked to the front door, and Ruth rang the bell. In a few seconds, Linda opened the door. She was dressed much as she'd been before, shirt, jeans, and running shoes, but this time the shirt was white. She looked from Rhodes to Ruth and back at Rhodes.

"Can I help you, Sheriff?" she asked.

"We'd like to talk to Pete," Rhodes said.

"Come right in, then," Linda said, moving aside.

Rhodes and Ruth went past her into the house. She closed the door and said, "I'll get Pete. You can wait in the den."

She led the way to the den, a large room with a lot of light thanks to a back wall that had a sliding glass door that opened onto a patio.

"Have a seat," Linda said. "I'll be right back."

Rhodes and Ruth didn't have a seat. They stood in the middle of the room by a couch. Ruth said in a low voice, "You think she's on to us?"

"Could be," Rhodes answered, keeping his voice down as well. "The two of us showing up might have worried her."

Pete came into the room then. He was wearing his camo outfit. Or maybe it was a different one. "What's up, Sheriff?"

Rhodes didn't think there was anything to gain by mincing words. He said, "I'm here to arrest you for the murder of Lawrence Gates."

"Damn," Pete said. "I didn't kill anybody, so I don't think you can arrest me."

"I have the warrant right here," Rhodes said, reaching into his pocket.

"Here, Pete," Linda said from behind her husband. She tossed something to him.

Rhodes knew immediately what it was from just a glimpse. It was not good news. It was a semiautomatic rifle.

Pete caught the rifle and pointed it at Ruth and Rhodes, neither of whom had had time to draw a sidearm.

"I think you two had better leave now," Pete said. "I told you that you couldn't arrest me, and I meant it. I told you I didn't kill anybody. I meant that, too."

Rhodes didn't care what Pete meant, but he didn't like the rifle being pointed at him. He said, "Put the rifle down and we can talk about it."

"You must think I'm stupid, Sheriff," Pete said. "If I put down my rifle, you'll arrest me, right? Tell the truth now."

Rhodes didn't say anything, which Pete took as a *yes*.

"I thought so," Pete said. "Linda, get their sidearms. Be careful. They're tricky."

Rhodes wondered how Pete knew that. He was right, but he was probably just guessing.

Linda circled around from behind her husband and approached

Ruth. As soon as she got close enough, Ruth proved Pete's point by jumping for Linda, grabbing her shirt, and pulling her to the floor.

As soon as Ruth moved, Rhodes moved as well, falling to the floor and clawing behind his back for his pistol.

Pete didn't wait around to see what would happen to his wife. He turned to the right and fired three quick bursts from his rifle while running toward the sliding door. The glass in the door shattered and fell in shards, and Pete ran through and out onto the patio.

Rhodes stood up, pistol in hand, just in time to see Ruth give Linda a healthy clout to the jaw. Linda's eyes rolled up in her head and Ruth pushed herself to her feet with one hand on the couch and drew her sidearm. She ran after Pete, and Rhodes was right behind her.

He wasn't right behind her for long, however. It had been a good number of years since Rhodes had been known briefly as Will-o'-the-Wisp Dan Rhodes, a nickname he got because he'd made a long kickoff return for a touchdown when he'd played for the Clearview Catamounts. He could still run, but he was no match for a younger person like Ruth. She was already across the patio when Rhodes came through the opening where the door had been. Pete wasn't exactly young, but he was fit, and he was nearing the water-filled rock pit. He skirted the edge and ran into the woods behind it.

Ruth didn't slow down, so Rhodes yelled at her. "Stop at the trees. He knows where he's going, and we don't."

Ruth stopped, but even at a distance Rhodes could tell she wasn't happy about it. When he reached her, trying his best not to pant and succeeding about as well as could be expected, she said, "He has on camo, so he'll be invisible, right?"

"Your jokes are as bad as mine," Rhodes told her.

Ruth smiled. "I wouldn't say that. What do we do?"

Rhodes wasn't sure what to tell her. "We have to think about what Pete can do. He can try to circle back and get away in his Suburban. He can go on running. He can stop and give himself up. Or he can hope that we'll come in after him and he'll try to get rid of us. The rock pit would be a good place to dispose of a couple of bodies. I think there's likely to be a car in there already."

"You don't have much faith in most any of those, do you?" Ruth asked.

"No," Rhodes said. "I don't. Which do you think is the one he'll pick?"

"If I were him, I'd wait in there and try to pick us off." She looked at the rock pit. "I don't think there's room for two more cars in there, though. Just bodies."

"Good point," Rhodes said. "He'd find somewhere else for the cars, though. I wonder how far these woods go."

"Could be a long way," Ruth said. "He might have changed direction once he got in there, too. Are you a good tracker?"

"I'm okay. How about you?"

"Why don't we find out?"

"Might as well," Rhodes said. "We have to do something, and going after him is as good a choice as any. Let's not waste any more time."

They went into the trees, which were thick with underbrush. It was hot outside the woods, and the shade of the trees didn't make things any better. For some reason Rhodes thought of a poem he'd had to study in high school, something about a woods that was lovely and dark. That woods was seen in a winter snowfall, much different weather from what Rhodes was experiencing. The Hunley woods weren't dark, as shafts of light from the sun got through everywhere. They were lovely in their way, thick with dead leaves on the ground and stuck in the underbrush, but they were hot and airless because there was no breeze to give the slightest motion to the leaves still on the trees.

It was quiet in the woods, and Rhodes thought it had probably been quiet in the woods in the poem. The man in the poem didn't have to go into them after someone with a semiautomatic rifle. That made a difference.

Pete wasn't hard to track. Broken twigs and mangled underbrush made it clear which way he'd gone. Rhodes wasn't sure that was a good thing. He stopped and whispered, "He wants us to follow him."

"I think so, too," Ruth said. "It would be a good idea for us not to be too close together."

Rhodes had been going to say the same thing, but he'd been a little slower than Ruth, who was ahead of him in both running and thinking, which made him wonder again about running for reelection. The county didn't need somebody who was getting slow in any way at all.

"Somebody has to stay with the trail," Rhodes said. "I'll do that. You move over a few yards."

"Are you just sticking with the trail because I'm a woman?" Ruth asked.

"No," Rhodes told her. "I'm doing it because I'm the sheriff and it's my job to take the lead."

"Okay," Ruth said. "I was just checking."

She moved away from Rhodes, who started along the path Pete had made for him, wondering just what Pete had planned. Was there someplace in the woods where he could hole up or was there a spot that would be ideal for an ambush? Pete would know. Rhodes would just have to hope he could figure something out as he went along.

One thing Rhodes had learned in his law enforcement career was that you couldn't just keep your eyes on the ground when you were chasing someone in the woods. You had to look up, because trees made convenient hiding places.

Every now and then Rhodes stopped to listen. The woods were still quiet. The birds and squirrels had all moved on somewhere else when the humans had entered, or if they hadn't, they weren't making any noise. Neither was Pete, and that had Rhodes a little worried. He knew that he and Ruth were making noise. Why wasn't Pete?

The logical answer was that he'd stopped somewhere. But where? Rhodes saw some mashed vines just ahead, so Pete had passed that way. Could he have turned back to the house?

Rhodes walked a little farther into the woods, and through the trees ahead of him he saw a deadfall. The long trunk was banked with dead limbs that had green, thorn-covered vines growing over and through and around them. The thick roots were partially covered in hardened dirt that had come up with them when the tree had fallen in some storm. The track led right to it.

Rhodes didn't know what was on the other side of the deadfall, but he suspected that Pete might very well be back there with his rifle, waiting for Ruth and Rhodes to come along.

Ruth was on Rhodes's left. He indicated for her to go around the fallen tree in that direction. He'd take the right end where the roots were. Ruth nodded that she understood and moved out. So did Rhodes.

Neither of them got very far because Pete popped up and started shooting.

Rhodes heard a bullet buzz by him just before he hit the ground. A couple of small limbs fell on him, and he rolled to his right, coming up ready to shoot, but Pete had disappeared behind the deadfall after firing a few more shots. Buddy would be sorry he'd missed this.

Ruth sat with her back to the trunk of a tree, well protected from Pete's bullets. She asked Rhodes if he was all right.

"Sure," Rhodes said. "I don't think Pete had any spare clips, do you?"

"Probably not," Ruth said, "but he had thirty rounds or so to start with."

"I think he's fired ten or fifteen," Rhodes said. "Half, maybe."

"Or maybe not. You think he'll try to slip away?"

Rhodes wasn't going to let that happen. He bent to a crouch and scuttled toward the deadfall. When he got there, he sat and listened. He thought he could hear an occasional sound from the other side.

"You back there, Pete?" he asked.

If Pete was there, he didn't answer. Rhodes could have looked, but he didn't think that would be wise. Instead, he waved to Ruth, indicating that he wanted her to go on around to the left end of the log.

Ruth nodded to show that she understood, and Rhodes waited until she'd gotten there before he went to the roots and looked around them.

Pete stared him right in the face from about two feet away with the rifle pointed at Rhodes's belly.

Rhodes fired his pistol, shooting over Pete's head, and Pete's rifle flew upward as he fell and triggered off shot after shot.

Rhodes didn't know why Pete had fallen, because he knew he hadn't been hit unless Rhodes's aim was badly off.

Rhodes looked down at Pete, who wasn't moving. Ruth was walking toward them from the other end of the deadfall.

Rhodes motioned for her to stop. He wanted to know what trick

Pete was trying to pull. Keeping his pistol trained on the prone gunman, Rhodes took a couple of steps forward and kicked Pete's foot. Pete didn't move. His eyes were closed.

Moving as cautiously as he could, Rhodes reached down for the rifle and removed it from Pete's hand.

"Is he dead?" Ruth asked, moving toward them.

"No," Rhodes said. "He's not dead. I think he fainted."

"You're kidding me."

"No, this isn't one of my bad jokes. Here, take the rifle."

Ruth reached out and took the rifle. Rhodes stuck his pistol in his belt at the back of his pants and pulled Pete into a sitting position, propping him against the log.

"We'll give him a couple of minutes," Rhodes said, standing up. "He'll be okay when he comes to."

Ruth holstered her sidearm and ejected the clip from the rifle.

"Kel-Tec Sub-2000," she said, looking at the rifle. "Very nice. Lightweight. He wasn't very good with it, though. Funny that a combat hero wouldn't be good with a rifle. Even funnier that he'd faint when shot at."

"He was no hero," Rhodes said. "That was all fake news. His father was the real hero in the family."

Ruth looked over Rhodes's shoulder. "Speak of the Devil."

Rhodes looked around and saw Con Hunley, who was holding a rifle very much like the one his son had used. Probably the same model. It was pointed in Rhodes's general direction, but it could be fired at Ruth, too. Rhodes figured she regretted ejecting the clip from Pete's rifle. Rhodes regretted it, too.

"I'm not the Devil," Con said, "but I guess I'm close enough."

"What are you doing here, Con?" Rhodes asked.

"Linda called me and told me you were going to arrest Pete. I went over to their house and heard shooting from the woods. So here I am. Did you kill my son?"

"I didn't even hurt him," Rhodes said. "He just passed out. You can put down the rifle."

"I don't think so," Con said. "I need to see about Pete and then get him out of here."

"I'm taking him to jail," Rhodes said.

"Nope," Con said. "I can't let you do that. Wouldn't be prudent at this time."

Everybody's a comedian, Rhodes thought.

"I have to do it," Rhodes said. "I have a warrant for his arrest for murder."

"Warrant doesn't mean much out here in the woods," Hunley said. "I have to take care of my son. Deputy, you drop that rifle and then take your sidearm out of the holster and lay it on the ground. Use two fingers."

"Sheriff?" Ruth said.

"Better do it," Rhodes said. "He looks like a man who'd shoot, and I think his aim would be better than Pete's."

"It is if I want it to be. You heard him, Deputy. Do it."

Ruth did as he said.

"Now kick the rifle and sidearm away from you," Hunley told her.

Ruth did that, too.

"What about you, Sheriff?" Hunley asked. "Where's your sidearm?"

"Would you believe I don't have one?"

"Not for a second. Let's see it, and be real careful."

Rhodes reached behind his back for his pistol.

"Two fingers," Con said.

"Right," Rhodes said.

He held the Kel-Tec with two fingers and brought it from behind his back.

"Now lay it on the ground."

Rhodes didn't follow orders. Instead he started to bend, then flicked the pistol at Con.

Con flinched only a fraction of a second, but it was enough of a fraction for Rhodes to charge him, head down. He hit Con in the stomach as hard as he could from such a short distance, and it was a bit like hitting a brick wall. Con was an old man. How could he be in such good shape? He must have worked out a lot.

Rhodes wrapped his arms around Con, planted his feet, and pushed. Con bent backward but didn't fall. He hit Rhodes in the shoulder with the rifle, but Rhodes held on and kept pushing.

Rhodes heard a noise behind him and knew Ruth would be coming to help him. Or she would have been if Pete hadn't tackled her. Rhodes couldn't see it happening, but he guessed from the noise that's what it was. Pete had come to just in time, or maybe he'd been playing possum for a while, waiting to see how things turned out. He had size and weight on his side, but Ruth was tough. She might still help Rhodes if he could hang on long enough, which seemed doubtful.

He needed to get the rifle out of Con's hand. He had an idea about how to go about it, but it wouldn't be easy. Con was now hitting him in the side of the head with his left fist. Rhodes couldn't take much of that, so he gave one more big push, up and back, and he and Con fell to the ground. Rhodes was on top. He used his advantage to grab Con's right wrist. There was no way he could break Con's grip with only his strength, so he resorted to trickery and unfair tactics, if any tactics could be called unfair in a fight. He bit Con on the back of the hand, not hard enough to make his teeth meet through the skin, although it was close enough to draw blood.

Con yelled and relaxed his grip on the rifle, which Rhodes pushed away. Then he turned as quickly as he could and head-butted Con on the nose. The nose crumpled satisfactorily, but Con didn't even seem to notice. He threw Rhodes off and jumped to his feet.

Rhodes saw a combat boot headed toward his own nose. He grabbed it and twisted, bringing Con down again. Con didn't even lose his breath when he hit. He reached for the rifle but didn't quite make it.

Rhodes did but couldn't get a grip on it. He pushed it further away, and Con hit him in the side of the head again. Rhodes wondered if there was a concussion protocol for sheriffs, but he didn't have time to wonder long because Con was getting back on his feet once more.

It wasn't easy, but Rhodes got to his feet, too. The two men faced each other. Rhodes was panting a little. Con wasn't. Blood dripped from his nose and the back of his hand, but he wasn't winded.

Con took a boxing stance. "I'm sorry to have to do this, Sheriff, but you made it necessary."

He advanced on Rhodes giving a couple of experimental jabs as he came.

Rhodes wasn't a boxer, but he put up his hands and backed away. He didn't dare even risk a glance at Ruth to see if she'd subdued Pete. If he took his eyes off Con for even an instant, he'd get creamed immediately. He'd probably get creamed, anyway.

Con advanced on him and struck as fast as a rattler, his right fist opening up a cut on Rhodes's cheekbone. Rhodes dipped and dodged and wondered how he could avoid getting cut to pieces.

Con's hands flicked out and cut Rhodes's face twice more. Rhodes was feeling dizzy. He knew he couldn't last much longer, and Ruth wasn't going to be able to help him. He had to do something, but he didn't know what.

He almost tripped over Con's rifle, though he had no chance of picking it up. Con was moving in for the kill.

And then he wasn't. He stopped, and a shiver ran through his body. He put his hands to his head, shook it from side to side, and fell down at Rhodes's feet without making a sound, and didn't move.

Chapter 26

The first thing that Rhodes did was to check on Ruth, who was doing just fine. She had Pete in handcuffs and had dragged him back up against the fallen tree. Rhodes knew he should've put Pete in handcuffs to begin with. A rookie mistake that made him wonder once again if he should run for office one more time. He bent down and checked Con's pulse. It was strong and steady.

"What happened to Con?" Ruth asked.

Rhodes didn't know, and Pete didn't have anything to say. He had a dazed look in his eyes. The side of his head was bloody, and Rhodes wondered what Ruth had done to him, not that Rhodes was going to ask.

"I'd like to say it was my lightning-fast fists," Rhodes told her, "but it wasn't. He just fell down."

"Better cuff him," Ruth said.

She tossed Rhodes a pair of cuffs, and he put them on Con's wrists. Con was a big man, and Rhodes needed Ruth's help to prop him next to Pete.

"How will we get them out of these woods?" Ruth asked.

"If they can't walk, we can get help," Rhodes said.

He looked at the two men side by side, and something flipped in his brain. He realized that he'd had a piece of his puzzle in the wrong place, had forced it to fit when it really didn't. It had seemed to fit, but it hadn't quite done so. He thought he had the right piece in place now, but he couldn't find out until Pete and Con were able to talk.

"Pete's fine," Ruth said. "I managed to get my hands on my pistol, and I hit him with it."

"Good work," Rhodes said. "Keep it handy. You might need it again. I'd better gather up the rest of the guns."

He got his own pistol and strapped it back in the ankle holster. He put the two rifles well out of the reach of Pete and Con.

Pete stirred, jerked as if suddenly awakened from a bad dream, and tried to stand up. Rhodes put a hand on his shoulder to hold him in place, and Pete noticed Con beside him.

"What did you do to my dad?" Pete asked.

"Nothing," Rhodes said. "He fell down. You have any idea why?"

"I don't have anything to say to you. You want to arrest me, go ahead. Just leave my dad alone."

"We need to get him to a hospital," Rhodes said.

"He'll be okay. He has these spells now and then. Give him a few minutes."

Rhodes wasn't sure Pete knew what he was talking about, but Con started to move around, and then his eyes popped open. He looked around but didn't say anything.

"Can you walk?" Rhodes asked him.

"In a minute," Con said. "It takes me a little while." He looked at Pete. "Are you all right, son?"

"I'm okay," Pete said.

Con turned back to Rhodes. "I was just about to get you, Sheriff. You got lucky."

"I admit it," Rhodes said, "but if you'd gotten me, my deputy would've shot you."

Con looked at Ruth and then at Pete. "I believe she would have. Is she the one who hit Pete in the head?"

"She's the one," Rhodes said. "You don't want to mess with her."

"I wasn't planning to. I don't think I could mess with a sick kitten right now."

"Can you walk?"

"Like I said, give me a minute. I'll be okay."

Rhodes wasn't sure he believed him, but giving him a minute wouldn't hurt.

"You got it all figured out, Sheriff?" Con asked.

"Pretty much, I think," Rhodes said. "I had it wrong for a while, but now things are a little more clear to me. You want to tell me about it?"

"Not right this instant. I can stand up now. Give me a hand."

Rhodes slipped a hand under Con's right armpit and helped him to his feet. Ruth did the same for Pete, who said, "Don't tell him anything. He doesn't know squat."

"He's not stupid, Pete," Con said. "He knows a lot more than you think he does. Right, Sheriff?"

"We'll have to find out," Rhodes said. "Are you steady enough to walk now?"

"I think so," Con said. "Where are we going?"

"Jail," Rhodes said.

• • •

There was a bit of a problem with Linda when they got back to the house, but it involved only shouting. No guns. She said that she was going to call a lawyer, and Rhodes told her that was fine. When she ran into the house, Rhodes and Ruth put Pete and Con in the Chargers and drove to town.

After the prisoners were booked, Rhodes asked if they wanted to talk to him before their lawyer got there or if they preferred to wait. Pete didn't answer. Con said he'd be glad to talk. He didn't want a lawyer.

"You understand your rights?" Rhodes asked.

"The part about how anything I say can and will be used against me?" Con asked. "It doesn't matter. There's not a lot you can do to me. I'll be dead in a few months, anyway."

Pete looked away, and Rhodes thought he might cry.

"The family knows," Con said. "They know all about everything. Where can we talk?"

"I'll show you," Rhodes said, and led Con to the interview room.

Con looked around. "Nice place."

"We like for people to be comfortable," Rhodes said. "Have a seat."

Con sat at the scarred table, and Rhodes sat across from him. In the middle of the table was a digital voice recorder. Rhodes indicated it. "You know what that is?"

"Recording device," Con said. "I expected you'd have one."

Rhodes turned the recorder on, said who he was and who he was interviewing. Then he said, "Ready?"

"Where do you want to start?" Con asked.

"The beginning is usually a good place," Rhodes told him, "but this time let's start at the end. What's this about dying?"

Con shrugged. "Brain tumor. Inoperable. Gives me terrible headaches, but that's the first time one has knocked me out. Not that much different from what a certain senator had. Maybe both of us got a little too much Agent Orange."

"I'm sorry," Rhodes said.

"Don't be. I've lived a long time, even if I don't think it's been long enough. I've had a pretty good life, too. Healthy as a horse until they found this thing a few months ago. Nobody knows about it but my family and the doctors."

"What about treatment?"

"Chemo and radiation? Wind up a husk of a man and die anyway? No thanks. 'Nuff said."

Rhodes couldn't say that he blamed him for the choice. "Then let's go back to the beginning. How long have you known about Pete?"

"All his life," Con said. "Or maybe not quite that long, but ever since the time I took him deer hunting. He was about twelve. Couldn't pull the trigger. Almost cried. After that, I knew he'd never be a soldier."

"He was, though," Rhodes said.

Con shrugged. "I guess you could call it that. Not a real one, though."

"Why'd he do it?"

"My fault," Con said. "All his life he looked up to me. I was a real hero, he thought, and so did a lot of other people. His grandfather was a hero, too, a real one. What I did wasn't heroic, though. I was scared to death the whole time. Even when I was doing things that people thought of as brave, I was scared. I was just trying to stay alive and keep my friends alive at the same time. Nothing heroic about it. Necessity, maybe. That's all."

"You didn't mind being thought of as a hero around here," Rhodes said.

"You know why? Because when we came home, a lot of people didn't think we were heroes. They thought we were baby killers or worse. So I didn't mind taking on a little glory if people were willing to give it to me. I thought it might help somebody else along the line. It was a mistake, though."

"Why?" Rhodes asked.

"Because of Pete. He looked up to me, thought I was something special. I tried to tell him what I just told you. It didn't sink in. Nothing would do but that he be a soldier like me. When he couldn't be, he lied about it. Took the things some of his platoon did and claimed them for his own. At first it didn't matter, or I thought it didn't. Nobody around here bothered to look into it, and small-town papers like ours didn't get much outside readership. Lately, though, the internet started to worry me, and then, sure enough, somebody got suspicious. I've also realized that what Pete did was terrible. He stole something from real heroes and lied about it being his. I should've known that from the start, but since I didn't, I had to do something to protect him."

"Like killing Lawrence Gates."

"That's him."

"Why kill him?"

"I couldn't bribe him," Con said. "I tried. He wouldn't listen. So I had to protect my son. There was just one way, and I took it. Drove his car to my place and ran it in the rock pit."

"Burning the school, though? I thought you loved that place."

"Had to do it. Too much chance somebody coming to a reunion might get too curious. The reunion wasn't my idea, anyway. That was purely Edwina and Pete. They thought I'd enjoy it. They were wrong."

"So you killed a man, nearly killed a woman, and burned a historic building to protect your son. You even tried to kill witnesses."

"Witnesses? I didn't try to kill them. I just wanted to scare them. They tried to blackmail me."

So Ivy had been right about that. Rhodes hoped he could find Kenny and Noble now that Con was in custody and get them to talk.

"You scared them, all right," Rhodes said, "but you killed Lawrence and nearly killed Wanda Wilkins."

"Why not?" Con asked. "I'm a dead man, anyway, and something had to be done. A man owes his son something, and I blame myself for what he did."

"It's all going to come out, anyway," Rhodes said.

"Yeah," Con said. "That's the only thing I regret."

Somehow Rhodes didn't believe him.

Seepy Benton had never visited Rhodes at home, but late that afternoon when Rhodes was sitting on the back steps watching Speedo and Yancey romp around the yard, Seepy called and asked if he could drop by.

Since Ivy was the one who answered the phone, and since Ivy was much more gracious than Rhodes was, she invited Seepy to join them for supper. After the conversation was over, she came outside and told Rhodes.

"We're having vegetarian meatballs," she said, sitting on the steps beside Rhodes. "Seepy said he loves vegetarian meatballs."

"He would," Rhodes said, "but I have a question. How can they be meatballs if they're vegetarian?"

Ivy poked him in the upper arm. "Don't be so literal."

"Seepy's not bringing Bruce, is he?" Rhodes asked.

"Not as far as I know. He didn't mention it."

That didn't mean a thing, but Rhodes knew when to keep quiet.

"Sometimes I wish I could be a dog," Rhodes said. "Or at least one of our dogs. Nice place to live, plenty of food, not a lot of work."

"There are cats, though," Ivy said.

"They don't get outside, so Speedo doesn't know about them, and Yancey doesn't mind." Rhodes paused. "Much."

"You're not a dog, though," Ivy said. "You're the sheriff."

"Maybe not for long," Rhodes said. "I might not run again."

"Don't joke with me, Dan Rhodes," Ivy said.

"I'm not joking."

"You might not think so, but I know better. Now let's go in and get cleaned up. Seepy will be here soon."

"I can hardly wait," Rhodes said.

Rhodes had to admit that the so-called meatballs weren't terrible. Seepy, of course, went on and on about how they were the tastiest things he'd ever put into his mouth. Ivy smiled and acted as if she believed him. Maybe she did.

After the dishes were cleared away, everyone sat around the table while Rhodes told them about Con Hunley's confession.

"I knew it was him all along," Seepy said.

"I don't believe that," Rhodes said.

"You're going to hurt my feelings again."

"I'll try to do better," Rhodes said.

Ivy laughed. "He says that all the time."

"You're supposed to defend me," Rhodes told her. He thought about Con Hunley's defense of his son, and the puzzle pieces shifted again. Rhodes had thought he had everything in place, but now it didn't seem that way at all.

He stood up. "I'm going to the jail. I need to talk to Con Hunley some more."

"I'll go with you," Seepy said. "It's my case, too, you know."

"I'll stay here and watch TV," Ivy said. It's not my case at all."

"You can tag along," Rhodes told Seepy, "but you can't come into the interview room."

"I'll let Hack and Lawton entertain me," Seepy said.

"Better you than me," Rhodes said.

When Rhodes walked into the jail, Hack had something else for him.

"Karla Vincent just called," Hack said. "She says Kenny and Noble are there. They don't know she called."

Rhodes hadn't thought Karla would get back to him, but he was glad she had. "I'll go out there right now. You and Lawton can entertain Seepy for me."

"Seepy?" Hack said. "I don't see him."

The door opened and Seepy came in.

"Speak of the Devil," Hack said.

Seepy looked around. "Where is he?"

"Never mind," Rhodes said. "You sit tight. I have a visit to make."

Kenny's old Chevy pickup was parked beside Karla's house, and Rhodes parked behind it. He got out of the county car and went to the door. Karla answered his knock.

"Kenny and Noble are eating in the kitchen," she told Rhodes. "I fixed hamburgers for them. I didn't tell them you were coming."

Rhodes thanked her and went into the kitchen. Kenny and Noble almost strangled on their burgers when they saw him.

"I thought you could trust your own mother," Noble said, glaring at Kenny.

"So did I," Kenny said.

"You two don't have a thing to worry about," Rhodes said. "I have the Hunleys in jail, and they'll be there for a while. Karla just wanted to let you boys get on the good side of the law for a change."

"How're we gonna do that?" Kenny asked.

"You're going to tell me what you saw at the Thurston school the night Lawrence Gates was killed," Rhodes said.

"Damn," Kenny said. "That's already got us nearly killed once."

"It won't happen again," Rhodes said. "I can promise you that."

"What you think, Noble?" Kenny asked.

"Hell, we might's well tell him. We've run out of places to hide, anyway."

"Okay, then," Kenny said. "You tell him. You got a better memory than I do, and you'd drunk less beers."

So Noble told Rhodes the whole thing. It didn't take long, and it was what Rhodes had expected.

"I appreciate the help. You finish your burgers now and thank Karla for phoning me. She did you both a favor."

"Sure she did," Kenny said.

"Don't be a dumbass, Kenny," Noble said. "She really did."

"You think?"

"I do."

"Okay, then," Kenny said.

Rhodes had Con brought to the interview room. When Con was seated, Rhodes said, "You lied to me, Con."

Con didn't change expression. "No, Sheriff. I told you the truth."

"You told me what you wanted me to believe, and I believed it because I thought everything fit. I was wrong, though."

Con sat silently, just looking at Rhodes.

"You said you'd do anything to protect your son," Rhodes said, "and since you're dying, why not take the blame for him. It was him all along. Well, mostly."

Con still didn't have anything to say.

"You're a real soldier, a man who believes in certain rules," Rhodes continued. "You wouldn't have shot Lawrence Gates while his back was turned. If you did, tell me how you got him to face the blackboard."

"I asked him to write down his evidence," Con said. "I wanted to see it."

"You didn't do that. Pete did. He couldn't face a man he was going to kill. I'm a little surprised he could pull the trigger even then."

"He didn't," Con said.

"He did, and here's another thing. You're not the kind of person who'd leave an old woman to die in a fire. You'd have gotten Wanda Wilkins out of that building even if it meant being arrested. Not Pete, though. He's no hero."

"So you say."

"I do believe you did two things," Rhodes said, ignoring Con. "I believe you beat up Curtis Lambert and his dog, and you took those shots at Kenny and Noble. You didn't want to kill them, just scare them, and you did a fine job of it. Now that you're in jail, though, they didn't mind talking to me. Or maybe it's three things because I believe you told me the truth about most everything else, except those were Pete's motives and not yours."

"You don't know what you're talking about," Con said, "and those witnesses of yours are just cheap hoods and druggies. Nobody will believe whatever they told you."

"They saw Pete coming out of the school the night Lawrence was killed. He came down the fire escape and went around to the front and got in Lawrence's car. Even Kenny and Noble could figure that one out when they heard about the murder."

"Like I said, nobody will believe them."

"Maybe not, but they'll believe Pete. I talked with him before getting you in here. He's admitted what he did."

Con's face crumpled. "You're lying."

"No, I'm not lying," Rhodes said. "Pete wasn't able to hold up very well when I told him about the witnesses. He confessed to everything."

"Damn you to hell," Con said. "Why couldn't you leave things alone? You had a confession. You could have let me go to jail and die there. You didn't have to do any more."

"Yes I did," Rhodes said. "I couldn't let a killer off the hook for what he'd done."

"Pete's no killer. He just made a mistake."

"Lots of mistakes were made," Rhodes said. "All along the line. I almost made one, myself."

"Damn you," Con said. "Damn you, damn you, damn you."

Rhodes went to the door and called for Lawton to take Con back to his cell.

The next day Rhodes went by the hospital, where he found Wanda Wilkins in fine fettle.

"They say I can go home today," she told Rhodes. "I'll be happy to see Leroy, and he'll be happy to see me, you bet. Somebody told me you caught the man who burned the school and did the killing. Good for you. I'll vote for you next time. I always vote for you, anyway, but next time I'll feel different about it."

"I appreciate it," Rhodes said, "but I might not run."

"You have to," Wanda said. "How can I vote for you if you don't?"

"Write-in," Rhodes said.

"Not the same. I like to see a name on the ballot. You better run."

"I'll think it over," Rhodes said.

That afternoon Curtis Lambert called the jail and asked to speak with Rhodes.

"I wanted to thank you for what you did," Curtis said. "For me and Betsy, I mean. Kenny wouldn't ever thank you, but you did right by him, too."

"He should've come forward," Rhodes said, "and he shouldn't have tried to blackmail Pete Hunley."

"He knows that now. It was dumb, but then Kenny does a lot of dumb things. Look at that snake on his neck."

"I've looked," Rhodes said.

"The drugs, too," Curtis said. "I've had a talk with him about that. Maybe it'll help."

"You never can tell," Rhodes said, but he didn't think Kenny would have listened to that kind of talk for long.

"Betsy's going to be fine," Curtis said. "Kenny, too. It'll all work out."

Rhodes thought that optimism was a good thing, so he said, "I hope so."

Before Rhodes left that afternoon, Hack wanted to talk about the election year that was coming up.

"I think you need to start planning now," Hack said. "Get yourself an organization. Won't need much of one, but it'd be a start."

"I haven't decided if I'm going to run," Rhodes said.

"You gotta do it. County needs you. Crime would explode without you to keep it in check."

Rhodes laughed. "You know better than that."

"You just wait and see what happens if you don't run. I'll be the first one to say I told you so."

"If Lawton doesn't beat you to it," Rhodes said.

"He better not," Hack said. "Anyway, you're gonna run."

Rhodes smiled. "I'll give it some thought," he said.

THE END

Acknowledgments

I would never have had a writing career without the encouragement of my late wife, Judy, and I would never have been able to continue it without her unfailing support. She was my first reader, my toughest critic, and a super copy reader. Everything I've achieved in my career was thanks to her. I told her that often, and I'm glad I did.

My daughter and son, Angela and Allen, had to put up with a father who often sat behind closed doors in the evening instead of watching TV or playing board games with the family. They never complained. Maybe they were just glad to get rid of me for a while, but I like to think they understood what I was doing and forgave my absence.

The late Ruth Cavin was the editor who bought the first Sheriff Dan Rhodes novel and edited many after that. I've been lucky to have a number of fine editors over the years, and I've appreciated each of them. They've helped me shape the series and continue writing it for over thirty years now. It's been a pleasure.

And it's been a pleasure to work with my agents, first Ray and Barbara Puechner and now Kim Lionetti. Without them, the Sheriff Rhodes books would have languished long ago.

Any errors in the books have been mine alone, or at least I'm willing to take the blame for them. The buck stops here.

Writing about the sheriff and my many other characters has been a great experience all along the line, and I hope the sheriff decides to run again and then gets reelected. We'll see.